The warrior's target bolted for the house

Before the Executioner could aim and fire, a squad of guerrillas closed in on his flank, the frantic voice of their commander urging them on.

A bullet whispered past Bolan's ear, and he veered hard right, seeking temporary cover in the shadows of the smoldering cocaine lab. Loping past the warehouse, he sprung a pair of thermite bombs, yanked the pins and lobbed the grenades through the frosted windows.

He half expected his pursuers to give up before they reached the forest, but they took him by surprise. Ten minutes later they were still behind him, their noisy progress putting startled birds to flight.

The warrior's survival lay in speed, and there the jungle joined in a conspiracy against him, reaching out with ferns and creepers in a bid to snare him, to bring him down.

Grim and determined, Bolan led his enemy south toward the river, toward his only chance of getting out alive....

MACK BOLAN®

The Executioner

DON PENDLETON's EXECUTIONER

MACK BOLAN.

Line of Fire

A GOLD EAGLE BOOK FROM

WORLDWIDE.

TORONTO • NEW YORK • LONDON • PARIS
AMSTERDAM • STOCKHOLM • HAMBURG
ATHENS • MILAN • TOKYO • SYDNEY

First edition November 1988

ISBN 0-373-61119-6

Special thanks and acknowledgment to
Mike Newton for his contribution to this work.

Justice is like a train that's nearly always late.
—Yevgeny Yevtushenko, 1963

It's perfectly obvious that somebody's responsible and somebody's innocent. Otherwise it makes no sense at all.
—Ugo Betti, 1936

I recognize the men responsible for bringing poison to our streets, our schools. The justice train may be a little late in catching up with them, but when it does, they'll be riding to the end of the line.
—Mack Bolan

To the 426 American police officers who gave their lives in performance of their duty, 1985–1987. Rest in peace.

PROLOGUE

The village slept. Another day of toil with small reward was coming, but as dawn's first light began to break behind the Cordillera peaks, there seemed to be no urgency, no call for haste. Another hour—or two—would do as well.

A sentry had been posted on the outskirts of the village, keeping watch, but he hadn't been faithful. Wrapped in a serape, with his ancient Mauser rifle propped beside him, he had dozed by two o'clock, surrendering to dreams of love and wealth that he would never know in life.

And so the village slept, its people unaware of sudden death approaching from the west. The helicopters carried six men each, not counting pilots or the dark man in command of the attack force. All of them were wide awake and ready to perform on cue.

In retrospect, the young man thanked his bladder for the fact that he was still alive. He'd been roused from sleep by nature's call, resisting it at first, surrendering when it became apparent that he faced a choice of sink or swim. With any luck, he thought, he might be able to recapture his situation in the dream before Teresa lost the mood.

Outside, the forest floor was lost in curling mist. It was too cool for snakes to be about and active, but the young man watched his step regardless, moving downslope toward the trench that served as a communal lavatory. He could find it in the dark, by smell, but a degree of caution was required. The odor sometimes lured forest preda-tors—though God alone knew why—and there were other, smaller risks. Last week a boy of seven years had over-stepped his bounds and plunged headfirst into the trench. The three-foot drop had caused no injury, but he was still required to play upwind of his companions, taking meals outside the family hut.

The sound of rotors, muffled by the forest, reached his ears as he was buttoning his cotton trousers. Turning from the slit trench, moving toward the village proper, he was still concealed within the tree line when the helicopters thundered overhead. They made a circuit of the village, prehistoric dragonflies in search of easy prey; then they settled in the square.

No more than fifty yards from home, the young man heeded instinct, which told him to remain in place, con-cealed from hostile eyes. He settled down to watch and wait.

The troops unloaded swiftly, some of them dressed in military green, the others wearing ragtag uniforms of leather, denim and brightly colored shirts. He counted thirteen men—twelve armed with automatic weapons, and a dark man, empty-handed, who appeared to give the or-ders.

The arrival of the helicopters had aroused the village sentry from his slumber and brought him lurching to his feet, his antique rifle in his hands. Before he recognized the nature of his peril, he had triggered off a shot by acci-dent, its sharp report alerting the attackers to his pres-ence. He was grappling with the Mauser's rusty bolt and getting nowhere when converging streams of fire de-scended, blowing him away before he had a chance to clear the chamber.

Everyone in the village was awake by then, the combi-nation of helicopter engines and gunfire jarring them to varying degrees of consciousness. A few were cautiously emerging as the dark man issued orders to his men, deploying them around the square. They broke off into teams of two and three, immediately moving from house to house. The occupants were herded toward a prearranged collection point behind the southern line of huts, within plain sight of the latrine.

The young man saw his widowed mother and his sister join the rest, subconsciously aware of what was coming though his mind rebelled at the suggestion. He could reach the fallen sentry, take his rifle and—

He gave up the notion before it had a chance to run its course. He had no skill with weapons, and the Mauser was already jammed. He would accomplish nothing in the face of men with automatic rifles, other than to sacrifice his life in vain. Ashamed, he wept hot tears of rage and concentrated on the dark man's face, committing it to memory.

He didn't need to count the villagers to know there were forty-two collected in a circle, ringed by guns. Five men had gone to San Vicente del Caguán the day before, and with the lookout dead, himself in hiding, everybody was accounted for. The raiders had achieved complete surprise.

The dark man took a moment to address his hostages, words audible across the distance only when he raised his voice. He spoke of treachery, ingratitude, betrayal. Treason was a serious offense. The punishment must fit the crime.

Some of the girls were weeping openly now, young mothers clinging to their children. Nothing moved the dark man as he swept his eyes along the firing line, arm raised to give the signal.

When it fell, the dozen guns went off together. The young man hid his face, arms clasped around his head to muffle the sound of men and women dying, bullets slapping into helpless flesh. He bit his tongue to lock a rising scream inside, aware that any sound would mean his death, committed to survival now with a vengeance.

It took some time to murder forty people, even with machine guns. When the initial work was done, survivors had to be weeded out, administered coups de grace to guarantee that there would be no witnesses. An old man here, a squalling infant there; all were silenced in the end.

The young man didn't raise his eyes until the scattered pistol shots had died away and the voices of the killers faded as they retreated toward the square. Before him, on the grassy slope, limp bodies lay like cast-off rag dolls in the pearly light of dawn. The crimson of their blood was bright in contrast with the earth.

He couldn't see his mother or his sister, but he knew they would be there. He hadn't helped them when the opportunity was in his hands, and now he could do nothing more than see them safely buried.

If he lived that long.

A wisp of smoke curled upward from the nearest hut, immediately followed by a leaping tongue of flame. Within a moment, other huts were burning, wind contributing to the destruction as it fanned the fire. He caught a glimpse of men with torches, moving in between the hovels, pausing here and there to grace the walls and eaves with vivid, leaping color.

Half an hour passed before the helicopters lifted off and circled once above the ruins of the village, finally disappearing to the west. The young man waited half an hour more to satisfy himself that it wasn't a trick, that no gunners had been left behind to lie in wait for stray survivors.

He had time. His family and neighbors weren't going anywhere.

Before he focused on the dead, he made a tour of the burned-out village. Huts and sheds had been reduced to ash, with glowing coals still bright amid the residue. He found the ruins of a small communal toolshed, used a stick to probe the ashes, looking for a spade. Its wooden handle had been burned away, but it would serve his purpose, once it cooled enough for him to hold it.

The daylight hours would be spent doing nothing but digging graves, but the work couldn't be postponed. Already vultures were circling, alighting in the trees, and dusk would bring the forest scavengers in search of meat. He couldn't stand them off alone, and he would have no help until the men returned the next day—if they came on time. The digging must be finished before dark.

The young man started by burying his mother, dug a small grave for his sister next, progressing to the bodies of his neighbors in their turn. He worked mechanically, breaking now and then for rest, his mind consumed with images of vengeance and a single face.

The dark man.

It didn't occur to him to notify the police of what had happened. Several of the killers had worn military uniforms, and there was reason to believe the dark man had others on his payroll. An official charge would simply warn the enemy of a surviving witness to the massacre, another target to be hunted down and slain before he had a chance to testify.

If there was any justice, it wouldn't be found in courts where judges wore expensive suits beneath their solemn robes. It wouldn't be obtained from officers who closed their eyes to crime and palmed their weekly bribes without a second thought.

If justice still existed, he would have to seek it for himself—alone, or in the company of others who had given up their civilized illusions. In a land where law meant nothing, he would be a law unto himself.

And if he found there was no justice, he would settle for revenge against the dark man. He would never rest until the debt of blood had been repaid in full.

Four graves were still unfinished when the shadows overtook him and the scavengers arrived.

1

Inevitably Mack Bolan's first glimpse of the Blue Ridge Mountains from the air took him by surprise. Though he'd seen them hundreds of times before, the peaks, wreathed in early-morning mist, still had the power to take his breath away.

It wasn't simply memory, he decided, as the helicopter's pilot brought them down to treetop level. There were old, familiar ghosts close by, but they couldn't account for Bolan's unfailing gut reaction on the flight to Stony Man Farm.

There was a primal power in the mountain range itself, he thought, which made a lowly human being stand in awe. Man had the power to destroy this place, if he so desired, but he could never build it back again or raise another like it on the face of Mother Earth. The mountains were a constant testimony to the fact that life goes on, reminding man that he was not, in fact, the god—or the monster—he sometimes tried to be.

No matter what your vantage point, even from a helicopter, you couldn't see the mountains all at once, nor could you predict what you'd find if you strayed off the highway, left the network of established trails, to poke among the canyons and the ridges. In Blue Ridge country hikers still got lost frequently—some of them forever. There were predators at large there, invisible from above beneath the cover of the treetops, and their presence put a lethal edge on Eden, adding mystery and danger to the beauty of it all.

"Five minutes, sir."

The pilot's warning brought Bolan back to here and now, reality encroaching on illusion. They were nearing Stony Man, and in a few moments he would know the reason for Brognola's urgent summons.

Bolan frowned, thinking he knew the gist of it already. He was merely lacking details, the essential odds and ends of who, and where, and why.

Brognola met him on the helipad, his hair whipped into spiky chaos by the rotor wash. The big Fed's handshake was a vise, as firm and strong as ever. He didn't speak until they cleared the pad and had a chance to hear each other short of screaming.

"Flight okay?"

"The usual. No problems."

"Good. I'm sorry I had to rush you in from L.A. like this."

"Forget it."

Los Angeles had been a pit stop on the road back from Macao. Bolan had been following a trail of opium and blood that had led him to a stronghold of the Triads—Chinese rivals of the Mafia—and he had spent a grim three days settling some overdue accounts. He could have used some R & R, but urgent calls from Brognola, these days, weren't so frequent that he felt inclined to turn one down.

"You want some lunch?" the big Fed asked. "We've got a brand-new chef, and he has a way with enchiladas."

"Maybe later."

"Yeah, I guess we'd better not keep Aaron waiting. He gets testy."

Aaron Kurtzman, alias "The Bear," was waiting for them in the underground briefing room. Wounded in the raid that once nearly closed the Stony Man facility, Kurtzman now spent his days in a wheelchair, but though he was paralyzed below the waist, nothing slowed him down. His involvement in the Farm's day-to-day routine kept things in motion, from collecting intelligence on an international scale to the mundane scheduling of staff. With Aaron at the terminal of his computer, nothing seemed irrevocably out of reach.

When he saw Bolan, Kurtzman raised a hand. "What's happening?"

"You're asking me? I thought you were the answer man."

The Bear put on a rueful grin. "You must have me confused with Mr. Wizard. I just come up with the questions."

Bolan found a seat and settled in, with Brognola across the table. Downrange, the giant viewing screen was in position, Aaron sitting ready at the video controls.

"Let's play a word association game," Brognola said. "Colombia."

The soldier frowned. "Cocaine."

"We have a lucky winner."

"This is news?"

"Unfortunately, no. The news is, we've been asked—hell, *I've* been *told*—to take a stab at changing history."

"I'm listening."

"Okay. What do you *really* know about the coke trade?"

"Basics," Bolan answered. "If you plan on asking for a chemical analysis, I'll have to pass."

"Not necessary. The analysis I need from you will be logistical."

"Still listening."

Brognola's nod to Aaron dimmed the lights. Bolan focused on a large map of Colombia that filled the viewing screen.

"You're looking at the source for eighty-five percent of our domestic coke," Brognola said. "The DEA informs me that our sterling citizens shelled out eight *billion* dollars for their favorite blow last year, and we have reason to believe the figure is conservative."

"Free enterprise."

"Not quite. According to the latest information, you've got maybe twenty gangs involved in distribution, but the ultimate control is traceable to four or five specific individuals."

"That leaves a healthy profit margin."

"Healthy's not the word," the Bear put in. "These guys started out as *contrabandistas*—smugglers—in the early 1960s, running everything from cigarettes and Scotch to radio transistors. Anything there was a market for in the United States. They've all got rap sheets stateside—mostly customs violations, moving stolen property, a sprinkling of assault and battery—but they were still your basic small potatoes."

"Flower power changed all that. Doc Leary, Woodstock, Charlie Manson—hell, you know the history as well as I do. Overnight, our *contrabandistas* saw there was money to be made on marijuana, even more on heroin and sweet cocaine. I gather Prohibition must have been about the same: a seller's market, rough-and-ready youngbloods moving in to skim the cream. Before you know it, you've got one-time border runners sitting on plantations, lighting their cigars with hundred-dollar bills."

"And four or five effectively control the industry?"

Another nod from Brognola, and Bolan watched as the map on the screen dissolved to something like a close-up, focused on the Andes and the major population centers of Colombia.

"You're looking at an area the DEA is calling the Cocaine Triangle," the Fed explained. "Its corners lie in Bogotá, Cali and Medellín. The most important of the three is Medellín. According to our information, it's the seat of the cartel."

Another close-up, this time of a street map blown up to giant size.

"The second largest city in Colombia," Brognola said, sounding like a tour guide. "It's big on industry and slums, with roughly one and a half million people. It's also big on street crime. The police in Medellín have logged two thousand murders in the past eight years, and most of them are linked directly to the traffic in cocaine."

"Somebody's weeding out the competition."

"With a vengeance," Brognola agreed. "Of course, for every independent operator killed, another half dozen take his place, but that's no problem. When it comes to weeding people out, Colombia has lots of gardeners."

A nod. Colombia dissolved into a map of southern Florida. The Bear took over as narrator.

"Between early 1979 and mid-'82, South Florida recorded 250 drug-related homicides. That's 250 we *know* about. God knows how many others fertilized the Everglades, but I've heard DEA men draw connections with the recent glut of well-fed alligators, and I couldn't swear that they were joking."

"What went down in '82?"

"The killing dwindled back to normal levels," Kurtzman replied. "Sure, you still find half a dozen Florida communities on any given top-ten chart for yearly homicides, but now at least they get some competition from Detroit, New York, Los Angeles. The cocaine wars are over, and any violence now is more like cleaning house."

"Or weeding?"

"Bingo. Competition is discouraged energetically—and permanently. Rolling into peacetime, we were looking at a more or less complete monopoly on the supply side. Sure, the Mob sells off its stock to so-called independents, and it lets them take the risk on transportation when the loads are small enough to be expendable, but if you're selling coke in the United States, the odds are four to one that it originated with the Medellín cartel. In 1982 their product was so plentiful they had to cut the kilo price in half—from fifty thousand dollars down to twenty-five—and that included stock of greater purity than the DEA had ever seen before."

The map of Florida gave way to a series of photographs as the narration shifted back to Brognola.

"Two tons of blow were confiscated at Miami International in 1982. Last year, in West Palm Beach, a single raid pulled in three and a half tons. The Feds and locals have been making major scores in Vegas, Southern California, New York City, but they're fighting cancer with a Band-Aid."

Scenes of crates and burlap bags piled up on streets and runways were replaced by combat photographs, complete with troops in action, torching what appeared to be a giant warehouse complex.

"Tranquilandia," Brognola announced. "It was the largest cocaine laboratory complex in Colombia, maintained by members of the Medellín cartel on what they thought was neutral ground. For once, the government disagreed with them. Military forces staged a raid in 1984 and burned up fourteen *tons* of flake. You could hear the big boys screaming all the way to Tallahassee."

"Instant shortage?"

"Let's just say the price was radically adjusted. What the cartel really wanted was revenge."

A smiling face flashed on the screen, replaced immediately by a picture of the same man crumpled on a sidewalk, profile haloed by a pool of blood.

"They put out a contract on the minister of justice, one Rodrigo Bonilla—you've probably heard about that. It was stupid, but nobody ever said these guys were tied for honors in the Einstein sweepstakes, right? Bonilla's murder brought down so much heat that cartel leaders had to take some hasty R & R in Panama."

"You'll love this," Kurtzman interrupted. "Even with the heat on, these slugs were confident enough to try and cut a deal. They wanted amnesty—on the Bonilla beef, on everything—and in return for same, they promised to retire from smuggling completely. Better yet, they came up with a plan to help Colombia discover 'agricultural alternatives' and get her addicts off the street. The cocky bastards used a former president to sell the plan in Bogotá.''

"Except it didn't sell."

"Damn right it didn't sell. By this time, the establishment was suffering from an attack of virtue. No one really counted on the heat to last, but it was interesting for a while. In the meantime, the cartel had to cut a deal with Nicaragua, and Ortega's boys were happy to oblige.''

"How much of that is still in progress?" Bolan asked.

"The Nicaraguan end of things is mostly second-string," Brognola replied. "A fallback option. The cartel had no intention of abandoning Colombia. When Bogotá announced its plan to extradite selected dealers stateside, members of the syndicate responded with a threat to murder five Americans for every man sent out of the country.''

The scene shifted. Another sidewalk, strewed with rubble, and the headless body of a woman sprawled at center screen.

"Within a week of the cartel's announcement, 'persons unknown' set off a car bomb outside the U.S. Embassy in Bogotá. No casualties among the staff, but a pedestrian was killed by flying glass. She was Colombian, of course, with no connection to the embassy or to the justice system. What the hell, she just picked the wrong street for a stroll.''

Brognola's voice was tight, and Kurtzman took the ball as more shots of mutilated, bullet-riddled bodies filled the screen.

"Things started heating up in '85, when it became apparent that the government intended to pursue its course of extraditions. This is Justice Tulio Gil, of the superior court in Bogotá. He didn't take the hint when he was warned to drop the investigation of Bonilla's murder. Thirteen bullets did the trick.''

"Persons unknown?"

"Who else?"

The next corpse wore a bloody uniform. "Meet the warden of La Picota Prison in Bogotá," Kurtzman said. "He found out that a couple of the *narcotraficantes* in his lockup had an unscheduled vacation in mind, and he scotched it. Wouldn't take the bribes they offered, which is damned unusual in Colombia. Two gunners on a motorcycle took him down outside his home a few days later."

Another change, and Bolan was looking at a stately building, wreathed in smoke, with antiterrorist commandos scrambling across the roof. A car burned at the curb.

"November 1985," Brognola told him. "Rebels from the M-19 guerrilla movement hit the Palace of Justice in Bogotá. They held out for twenty-eight hours, left ninety-five dead. Eleven of those were supreme court justices, believed to be the primary targets of the raid. We have substantial evidence that members of the Medellín cartel arranged the strike and covered all expenses, with a bounty paid to M-19 for every judge they put away."

"I didn't know the link with M-19 was documented."

"Well, there's nothing they can take to court in Bogotá, but DEA is satisfied, and frankly, so am I. Informants have delivered names and dates, the context of a dozen meetings held before the raid went down. It's sure as sure can be, without confessions from the men on top."

Another face filled the screen.

"This joker is a triggerman imported from Honduras to eliminate a DEA official. We got lucky, and the bastard was convicted, but he didn't stick around the prison long. The day he walked—through seven different doors—it was discovered that he spent two million dollars setting up the stunt. They tell me ten or fifteen guards are set for life on that one."

"And the shooter's whereabouts?"

"The usual. Unknown."

Another street scene, this one blurred with snow, and Bolan knew he wasn't looking at Colombia. A prostrate body stained the snowy sidewalk with a slick of blood.

"The cartel has a long arm and a longer memory," the Bear informed him. "January 1987, Bogotá dispatched a former justice minister to Budapest as their ambassador. They thought a post behind the iron curtain would protect him from the dealers who were on his case. Hungarian officials still can't say who tracked him down and shot him in the middle of a raging blizzard. Things like that don't happen in the East—at least, they didn't in the past."

"I get the drift."

"Not quite," Brognola said. "In three years' time, the Medellín cartel has knocked off fifty judges, better than a dozen journalists, a cabinet minister, well over five hundred policemen and informants. The Colombian security police—the rough equivalent of our own FBI—have seventy percent of their two thousand agents assigned as bodyguards for government officials. Investigative work is virtually at a standstill."

"And the smuggling goes on as usual."

"In spades. The weird part is that all this killing in the trade is just a sideshow. You're familiar with *la violencia*?"

"I've heard the term."

The big Fed frowned. "From 1948 to 1962, Colombia had about two hundred thousand homicides ascribed to politics, committed by guerrillas of the right, the left, you name it. Ancient history, okay? Except that now *la violencia* is making one hell of a comeback."

Scenes of death began to march across the viewing screen in swift succession. Each of them was new to Bolan, but he recognized the style. Knee-cappings. Executions. Bodies broken, hacked or burned. He gave up counting, concentrated on Brognola's voice, a link to sanity.

"In 1986 Colombia had eleven thousand murders overall, five times our per capita rate in the States. A lot of those were drug related, but the politics is also heating up. There were twelve hundred political murders in the first ten months of 1987, and a single party—the Patriotic Union— has had five hundred members killed in the past eighteen months. Throw in your outlaw gangs, and now you're looking at a crazy free-for-all. They recently logged sixteen murders in a single afternoon, allegedly committed by the members of two rival emerald-smuggling gangs."

The Executioner could think of no response that wouldn't trivialize the violence. He sat in silence, listening as Kurtzman took the lead again.

"On top of the cartel, Colombian officials have released a list of paramilitary groups now active in the country-side—138 in all. And those are just the ones with nerve enough to give themselves a name. The biggies on the left are M-19 and the Colombian Revolutionary Armed Forces, the FARC, Most of the right wing factions fall in line, one way or another, with the Colombian Anti-Communist Association. Then you've got your crazy independents, vigilantes, crackpots with an ax to grind. They run around with names like Love for Medellín, the Clean-Up Squad of Cali, Rambo and the Terminator. Anyway, we know they like the movies."

"And their targets?"

"Anyone and everyone, it seems. Between them, they take credit for assassinating homosexuals, transvestites, petty criminals and social undesirables. A few have even taken shots at the cartel, but it's a losing proposition. Those who manage to survive are quick to see the writing on the wall. First chance, they climb on board the gravy train and take on odd assignments for the big boys, when they're not too busy killing off each other."

"It's a goddamned circus!" Brognola exploded. "And everyone agrees the Medellín cartel is basically responsible—if nothing else, for undermining law and order with their payoffs, greasing everyone in sight until the grass roots population has no trust in anyone.''

A scowling face with lifeless eyes filled the screen. Dark hair curled low around the collar of a denim shirt. The squarish jaw had gone too long without a shave.

"Meet Carlos Lehder, kingpin of the Medellín cartel. Perhaps I should say former kingpin, since his extradition to the States may finally close the guy's case."

"One down."

"And three to go."

Another face on screen, this one a trifle older, softer, with a pencil-thin mustache, a frame of curly hair shot through with gray.

"Miguel Aguirre. Least impressive of the other three big fish, in terms of troops and nerve. If there's a weak link in the chain, you're looking at it—which is not to say this bird's a pushover, by any means. We reckon he's good for thirty homicides on U.S. soil, at least."

"A choirboy."

"Sure, if you compare him to the scum he hangs around with."

Number three. A meaty face, made memorable by a jagged scar across one flabby cheek.

"That's Julio Navarro. Bigger than Aguirre in the scheme of things, he's also more inclined to issue contracts on the competition. There's a rumor that his second cousin pulled the trigger on Bonilla, back in '84, but so far Bogotá's got nothing firm enough for an indictment. On the side, this scumbag goes for little boys—and we're not talking Boy Scouts of America."

The final snapshot was a candid photograph of three men walking down a street, presumably in Bogotá or Medellín. Aguirre and Navarro were immediately recognizable, but the tall man in the center was a stranger.

"And last, but certainly not least, meet Hector Gustavo Pedilla. Street talk has him ranked as number one in the cartel, since Lehder went away. The others may not like it, but they're taking it—so far. Pedilla's got connections in the civil government, the military, the police. You name it, and he either owns it or he's working on a payment plan. We estimate his standing hard force at around five hundred guns."

"I take it none of these were hampered by the expeditionary force."

Brognola scowled at mention of the 1986 U.S. attempt to back Colombia's official war on drugs with loans of military personnel. "What, hampered? Christ, they saw our people coming from *Miami*. Every move by DEA appears to be an open book before they get it out of hypotheticals. We're stymied, Striker, and that's the godforsaken bottom line."

"Which brings us to new business."

"Right." Brognola cleared his throat and raised his eyes to meet the soldier's gaze. "The Man believes his problem with the expeditionary force was numbers. Too damned many people knew the plan, itinerary, everything from top to bottom. There was no way in the world to keep that kind of secret."

"So?"

"Okay—as if you didn't know. He thinks one man might have a better chance to do the job. Not all of it—hell, no one seriously thinks the traffic can be stopped. But if these three should suffer accidents, let's say, and lose their inventory in the process . . . well, I'll let you do the math. Subtracting eighty-five percent of the available cocaine from circulation, even if it's only for a day or two, has got to make some changes, give the troops some breathing room."

"All right."

Brognola did a jerky double take, as if he'd expected something in the nature of an argument. "How's that?"

Mack Bolan smiled. "I said, when do I leave?"

2

The roseate light of dawn roused Bolan from a dream of death and brought him instantly awake. Before his eyes were fully open he remembered where he was and took stock of his position. He made no sudden move to throw himself off balance. The forest floor lay thirty feet below him, and the first step was a killer.

Bolan's back and legs were stiff, his buttocks cramped where he had wedged himself into the tree fork. Wrapped around his waist, the narrow nylon safety line was chafing, and his bladder made its own discomfort known as he shifted, working on the knots that held him fast.

The tree had been an impulse, after six nights of sleeping on the ground—when he had slept at all. Secure from any major predators, including man, the Executioner had passed his night in relative security.

But he couldn't escape the dreams.

His fingers worked the first knot free, attacked the second as his stomach started grumbling for food. Another moment and he had it, reeling in the line and coiling it around his arm, securing it to his webbing with a Velcro strap.

Before descending, Bolan spent a moment studying the forest, starting with the ancient tree in which he perched and worked downward, toward the ground. Experience had taught him that the jungle wasn't hostile; it was merely neutral in the game of life and death, and therefore every bit as dangerous. The jungle simply didn't care.

He scanned the limbs within arm's reach, leaned out to study those below him, finally satisfied no hunting cats or vipers were in residence. His survey of the forest floor took longer; he studied the undergrowth, comparing what he saw to images he had previously logged in memory. Alert to any sign of human trespass, any indication of a lurking ambush, Bolan spent the better part of fifteen minutes on his search, dismissing hunger and the pressure in his groin while the routines of raw survival took priority.

When he was confident his perch hadn't been found and staked out in the night, the soldier started his descent, hand over hand, entrusting all his weight to branches only when they had been tested, proved reliable. When he was halfway down, a fat tarantula attached itself to his pant leg. He slapped the spider into free-fall. It struck the bed of leaves below, then righted itself and wobbled out of sight.

On touchdown Bolan swung the Colt Commando automatic rifle forward on its sling, allowing easy access as he spent a moment pacing off the stiffness in his legs. Despite the latitude there was a chill of early morning in the air, exaggerated on the forest floor, which seldom felt the sun. He knew, though, that by the time of the usual midafternoon rainfall, the jungle would be steaming.

He cracked a can of rations, ate them cold and used his Ka-bar fighting knife to dig a small grave for the can. There was no point in leaving traces to be found by any government patrols or private hunters who might be on his track.

In the seven days since Jack Grimaldi dropped him north of Tres Esquinas in Colombia's Caquetá Province, Bolan had traveled light and swiftly, steering clear of contact with the native population. At the moment he was two hundred miles due south of Bogotá; the nearest major city was Florencia, the provincial capital, located seventy-five miles due east of his position in the foothills of the Cordillera

Oriental. So far, to his knowledge, he had been observed by no one who had survived to tell the tale.

His targets had been preselected, accessibility balanced against maximum effect. Up to now, the strike had gone like clockwork, leaving one objective—the most formidable of the lot—to be destroyed. He had deliberately saved the worst for last.

Miguel Aguirre's coca ranch had been the first and easiest of Bolan's marks, defended by a ragtag force of amateurs who proved to be both overconfident and undertrained. Eliminating them had been like dropping cutout targets in a shooting gallery, and Bolan had drawn no satisfaction from the game. He had been pleased, however, to see the coca warehouse burning, fueled by thermite and exploding drums of ether, lethal clouds of smoke enveloping the sentries as they tried to organize a fire brigade. In the confusion frightened sentries hadn't noticed Aguirre was missing, but Bolan supposed they must have found his corpse by now... if anything of substance had been left behind by forest predators.

Julio Navarro had been number two. His operation, rated fourth in the production of Colombian cocaine for export, was both more substantial than Aguirre's and more ably defended. Navarro was a major target of the DEA and Justice in the United States, but his high-placed friends in Bogotá had stalled American attempts at extradition, leaving him at liberty in deference to the contributions Navarro lavished on their favorite charities. Effectively above the law, Navarro did fear rash competitors who might be envious of his success, and he employed a private army to defend his empire. Where Aguirre's soldiers had been brash and careless, those recruited by Navarro were professionals, including former military officers, retired policemen and the cream of Bogotá's substantial underworld. The *narcotraficante* was supposed to have at least a hundred guns on salary, and Bolan estimated half of them were in attendance when he hit Navarro's compound in Caquetá Province on the fifth night of his mission in Colombia.

It might have been a massacre, with Bolan caught on the receiving end, except for the advantage of surprise. Aguirre's ruin, three nights earlier, had been explained away as the result of violent competition in the drug trade—some blamed disaffection on the part of his own troops—and so Navarro had taken no extraordinary measures to protect himself against attack. His *ordinary* measures were substantial, granted, but the sentries around his forest compound were trained to be on guard against roving Indians and raiding parties organized by brash competitors. On rare occasions the police might pay a visit, calling well ahead and granting Julio the time required to put his house in order.

No one in Navarro's camp had weighed the possibility of an audacious strike conducted by a single man. They hadn't reckoned with the Executioner.

In fact, the move against Navarro had been easier than Bolan had dared anticipate. The laboratory and assorted storage houses had been wired for doomsday when a sentry looking for a place to snooze had stumbled over Bolan unexpectedly. The firefight that followed had been hairy—and Navarro had escaped in the confusion—but his inventory was in ashes and he would be weeks rebuilding, losing income all the while.

Which brought the soldier down to number three, his final strike before the scheduled rendezvous and lift-off four days hence. Hector Pedilla was worse than the other two. By all accounts he was an octopus in human form whose tentacles extended from the courts of Bogotá and Medellín to outposts in Miami, New York City and Montreal. His name was known in Europe, and respected there by the "celebrities" who got their kicks from drugs and danger once removed.

Except that with Pedilla, danger was a day-to-day reality, an ever-present risk. His deals had a habit of collecting overdue accounts at knife point, and he kept a hard corps of enforcers on the payroll as a hedge against those "special cases" that arose from time to time. Police informants were a fact of life for coke suppliers, and Pedilla handled every snitch the same way. His soldiers were adept at rough interrogation; a suspect who was proved guilty of betrayal was invariably treated to a "Colombian necktie"—his throat slashed ear to ear, with the offending tongue pulled out and downward through the open wound.

A wag at DEA once mailed Pedilla an anonymous congratulation on his contributions to the world of fashion, and the street talk had it that Pedilla kept the letter framed, between his all-time favorite photographs: a color snapshot of his parents and a black-and-white of Adolf Hitler in the good old days.

The guy had sentiment, if nothing else.

He also had totalitarian control over an empire valued in the billions, moving coke—with smaller quantities of heroin and marijuana on the side—to every major nation in the Western world. His party favors were renowned in Hollywood and Aspen, Cannes and Soho, anywhere the sunbleached beauties of the jet set tried to fly without a plane. The money poured in daily, a deluge of never-ending dollars, francs and pounds that swelled Pedilla's coffers, keeping the machine in operation.

But the roots were here, and Bolan meant to blight them if he could.

He had sufficient hardware for the job—twenty pounds of C-4 plastique, with assorted timers, impact fuses and incendiary charges to complete the task he had in mind, as well as the Colt Commando and his side arms, ammunition all around, with half a dozen frag grenades remaining from his earlier engagements. Not enough to stop an army perhaps, but the Executioner's strength lay in surprise and mobility, skills derived from jungle combat on a hundred different killing grounds.

He was expecting solid opposition from Pedilla, but with luck the opposition wouldn't be expecting *him*. The world of major coke suppliers was a paranoid milieu of dog-eat-jackal, and the men with the most to fear were those who had the most to lose. Aguirre's death might have been dismissed as simple business run amok. Navarro's late misfortune, however, was bound to have sent out shock waves, and with Julio still alive his competition might expect reprisals on the strength of his mere suspicion. War was brewing in an atmosphere where violence came as easily as summer rain, and Bolan counted on the general chaos to provide him with an edge.

He had another thirty kilometers to cover yet before he reached the Yarí River and began to travel north. If he met no obstacles, he should be on Pedilla's ground by nightfall, ready to begin his final recon in the morning. Meanwhile all he had to do was cover ground and stay away from patrolling federal troops, Pedilla's scouts or any of the several paramilitary bands that roamed Caquetá Province.

Simple.

Bolan felt at home within the forest, but he recognized its dangers all the same. The land was unforgiving, quick to seize upon mistakes; men who let themselves grow overconfident were sometimes swallowed up alive. The jungles of Colombia bore small resemblance to those of Vietnam, but they were similar in all the ways that mattered. Both knew how to test a man, and how to break him if he failed.

The Executioner had come of age in Asia's jungles. He still remembered all the lessons taught by unforgiving nature, by an enemy who had worn the forest like a second skin. He'd become adept at living off the land—and killing on the land, when worthy targets were presented. Later, in the urban jungles of America, he had discovered that the war was everywhere, that the game of life and death was universal.

Touring the jungles of Colombia now seemed like a visit home: his first campaign as Colonel Phoenix, in search of other savages, had delivered Bolan to the borderland between Colombia and Panama. But he was conscious of the fact that visits home were seldom what they seemed. Digression to nostalgia now could get him killed, and there was no escape hatch, no convenient troop of cavalry on standby, poised to save the day if he fumbled.

Bolan was on his own. Again.

All things considered, he wouldn't have had it any other way.

The empty ration can disposed of, Bolan slipped on his pack, shouldered the Commando and struck off eastbound along a narrow game trail. Toward the Yarí.

Toward Pedilla.

Following the game trail was a calculated risk. Those highways through the jungle were employed by men as well as animals in search of food or water. *Narcotraficantes* used them in the transport of their wares, and antigovernment guerrillas took advantage of the interlocking network, making up for lack of numbers with mobility and speed. If federal troops were in the area, they might decide to lay an ambush, hoping to surprise a band of revolutionaries, coca mules—whatever.

The surprise would be theirs if they encountered Bolan, but the Executioner was counting on his combat instincts to alert him in advance of any trap. If there was danger up ahead—or following behind—he had no choice except to play the cards as they were dealt. His mission took priority, and it demanded that he travel east with all deliberate speed.

The unofficial ruler of Caquetá Province had a date with Bolan. It was a rendezvous that Bolan meant to keep at any cost, and God help anyone who tried to stop him.

The Executioner was on a roll, and he was playing for his life.

3

By dawn the dark man had disposed of breakfast, spent almost forty minutes working out with weights in his gymnasium, showered and dressed. The hour was unusually early—he usually rose at precisely nine o'clock—but in troubled times a man was often forced to change his schedule.

The jeep was waiting for Pedilla when he left the house, his driver and the shotgun rider looking sullen in the first pale light of day. He had no interest in their moods as long as they performed on cue and obeyed his instructions to the letter. They weren't required to love him or to understand his motives. They were paid—and handsomely at that—to make themselves available upon command, and thus far they had never failed him. If and when they did, Pedilla would dispose of them and find more willing hands to take their place.

His tours of the property had been sporadic in the past four years. The ritual of personal appearance for the benefit of the peasants was one Pedilla practiced sparingly, refusing to become familiar with the drones who worked his fields and manned his laboratories. But for the past six days he had made rounds each morning and again in early afternoon to reassure his people and let them know their *patróne* was standing watch.

In troubled times a leader had to let himself be seen in order to maintain the confidence and trust of his subordinates. Unlike some military officers and politicians he could have named, Pedilla believed a leader had some minimal responsibility to those who served him. At the very least a general could let his soldiers know he stood behind them in their time of trial.

And trials were coming. He no longer had the slightest doubt of that.

The murder of Aguirre hadn't moved him; it had just sparked his curiosity. Such a move against a member of the Medellín cartel was audacious, but then Aguirre had undeniably been the weak link in their chain. Less ruthless than his comrades, less aggressive, frankly less intelligent, he was enough to make Pedilla wonder, sometimes, how Aguirre had survived so long as a dealer in cocaine. At one time he must have demonstrated qualities of leadership, for if he'd been so weak from the beginning, he would never have survived his first transaction in the trade. With time and money, though, Aguirre had grown soft. His removal by force had come as no surprise.

The rash destruction of Aguirre's inventory, though, that *was* surprising. Even granting that Aguirre's troops had been able to withstand the first assault—a rash assumption in the face of his reported casualties—it stood to reason that after the assassination Aguirre's killer would have presented some ultimatum to the other members of the cartel, laying claim to stock on hand or arguing in favor of joining the group.

Of course such a ransom would have been irrelevant if Aguirre's killer came from inside the association—someone acting in the interests of group security, perhaps, who recognized Aguirre's weakness and could see down the road to some point where the dealer might be "turned" by drug enforcement agents, sucked into a situation where his only options might be testimony or life imprisonment. Viewed in this light, taking out Aguirre made sense as preventive medicine.

But once again the destruction of his inventory was the stumbling block to reason. If Navarro—even Lehder—had decided to eliminate Aguirre as a matter of security, his stock on hand would certainly have been preserved. Pedilla's figures weren't totally reliable, as yet, but he believed something close to seven million dollars had gone up in smoke when the Aguirre warehouse complex burned six nights ago.

And *that*, the sheer illogic of it, had concerned him. He had instituted tours of the ranch next day as a precaution. But he hadn't started to worry. The effort to assassinate Julio Navarro three nights later changed his mind.

Until he received his first reports of that attack, Hector Pedilla had considered Julio to be the likeliest suspect in the murder of Aguirre. Someday, he had supposed, they would discuss the matter over cocktails and he would discern Navarro's motive for destroying so much inventory in the process of the killing. But the raid against Navarro's property changed Pedilla's mind. He wouldn't have put it past the wily bastard to have arranged a fake attempt upon his life, but he was confident Navarro wouldn't have wasted an ounce of coca—let alone six hundred kilos of refined cocaine—to make his alibi more credible. Above all else, Navarro was a pig for money, and destruction of his stock, along with the facility itself, would have been unthinkable for him.

With his most likely suspect cleared, at least in theory, Hector had been forced to search for other workable hypotheses. The government could be ruled out. His contacts would have tipped him in advance of any raid, and even if some faction of the state security police had managed to maintain their secret, in defiance of all odds, by now they would have been boasting about their coup, proclaiming one more triumph in their so-called war against cocaine.

That left competitors or paramilitaries. Pedilla racked his brain without eliciting the name of any single suspect who possessed the requisite intelligence and nerve to challenge the cartel in open war. Navarro, hiding out in Medellín, was no help. Despite the fact that he'd murdered several hundred men in his career, despite the recent placement of his name on a list of *narcotraficantes* slated for potential extradition to America on charges of conspiracy, the idiot insisted on proclaiming that he had no enemies on earth. Believing himself beloved by all, Navarro couldn't understand why anyone would wish him harm or seek to terminate his humble enterprise.

Competitors were numerous of course, in both Colombia and the United States. They multiplied like roaches, swarming over one another in their hunger for a small taste of the megadollars earned each day by leaders of the Medellín cartel. Some came with hats in hand to plead for backing and support, a helping hand to set them on their way. How many others schemed in secret, dreaming of the day when they would scale the pinnacles of power, Pedilla couldn't begin to estimate. There must be hundreds, at the very least, and thousands didn't strain his credibility. Would any peasant, suddenly confronted with the possibility of fame and fortune, turn his back without at least a second thought?

It was that second thought that narrowed down Pedilla's field of suspects, for the Medellín cartel had built a reputation on its ruthless handling of rivals. Tales of sudden death or lingering dissection were a staple of the local folklore, grim enough to weed out all but the most confident competitors. A few of those would be selected for induction to the firm, at lower levels, where their cunning might be channeled and controlled. The majority were simply killed, their bodies dumped in alleyways and gutters as a lesson to their peers.

As for guerrillas, Hector felt no apprehension on that score. The revolutionary left had made its peace with members of the Medellín cartel in 1985, before the massacre in

Bogotá, and contributions to the cause kept leaders of the
syndicate on friendly terms with M-19, the FARC and assorted others. On the right, a number of guerrilla "armies"
had declared themselves opposed to traffic in narcotics, but
they also needed money, arms and ammunition for the
prosecution of their war on homosexuals and Communists.
Completely apolitical, Pedilla realized that paying off both
sides was good for business, and with his numbered bank
accounts accruing interest at the rate of half a million dollars every *hour*, seven days a week, he could afford to share
the wealth.

A fleeting thought of Carlos Lehder crossed Hector's
mind. He smiled. He wouldn't put it past their leader—their
former leader—to betray old comrades in the interest of his
own security. With Lehder facing trial and probable imprisonment in the United States, aware of profits rolling in
while he was locked away, such tactics would make a twisted
kind of sense; if Lehder couldn't walk the streets in liberty
to share in the bonanza, why should his associates be fa-
vored? If he had no hope of walking free again, why should
his greedy "friends" be left to carve up his portion of the
empire among themselves?

Despite his extradition and incarceration, Carlos Lehder
still had strength and influence enough to pull it off. Pedilla could recite the names of men who owed their life-
styles—or their lives—to Carlos from the old days, men who
would repay their debts with blood if called upon to do so.
Still ...

It was a theory, but it didn't *feel* correct. If Lehder had
gone sour, Hector thought he would have sensed his former
comrade's treachery, despite the miles that lay between
them. Somehow Hector would have known, just as he could
tell when Julio Navarro lied about his sex life, talking up his
nonexistent conquests with a string of debutantes and ac-
tresses. Pedilla would have known, because the members of

the Medellín cartel, for good or ill, were bound in mind and spirit, as they were by common greed.

The mystery might have unnerved another man, but Hector viewed it as a curiosity to be examined and resolved. He recognized the danger to himself, made no attempt to minimize his risk, but neither would he live his life in fear, locked up inside his country home like some demented recluse. He had business to administer, a reputation to uphold, and when the showdown came, he would be equal to the challenge of his enemies.

Pedilla had become a murderer at age thirteen, his skill with knives applied more energetically than necessary in a street fight over food. It had troubled him at first, the notion of arrest, imprisonment, potential execution or a life behind gray walls. His hand-to-mouth existence in the slums of Bogotá was nothing to be cherished, though, and on reflection, Hector had decided prison couldn't be much worse. Inside, at least the men were regularly fed, without resort to robbing garbage cans or begging on the streets. If he was caught and caged, the state would pay his room and board, while he relaxed and studied methods of eventual escape.

Pedilla learned his error three years later, serving out eleven months on smuggling charges. They had captured him with cigarettes—a portion of the shipment he moved for others, men too old and rich to take risks for themselves. While no one believed that Hector stole the smokes or created the smuggling ring himself, his stubborn silence left the court no choice. A smuggler in hand was worth a hundred still at large, and Hector had a lesson coming to him about justice.

He'd studied well in La Picota Prison. The facility was ancient, built with punishment in mind a generation before anyone gave thought to prisoner rehabilitation. Housed with deviants, thieves and killers, Pedilla looked to them for guidance, learning from his elders, fighting for his privacy and picking up a macho reputation on the side. Within two weeks of his arrival, would-be rapists knew enough to pass the dark boy over, moving on in search of victims who weren't prepared to die—or kill—in self-defense. Pedilla's courage won the admiration of selected older inmates, who extended him protection and instruction in return for minor favors, common courtesies.

Pedilla had viewed the prison as an institute of higher learning, but he had also realized that his professors were available specifically because each of them had failed. Successful smugglers, thieves and murderers wouldn't be found in La Picota; they were on the streets, still working at their trades and reaping the rewards of their ability to circumvent the law. Pedilla studied those around him, listening to every word they said, his mind extracting useful bits and pieces, filing their mistakes for future reference as errors to avoid at any cost.

Above all else, the young man had been determined that he wouldn't serve another stretch inside while he still had strength to run—or pull a trigger. Prison might be educational, but it was also deadening to mind and spirit. Day by day Pedilla felt himself become more and more detached from reality, more and more a part of his surroundings. For the first time he understood why certain convicts came to crave incarceration, viewing prison as their only rightful home. And he resolved that he would never let himself become like them. Before he sank so low, he would find strength to put a pistol in his mouth and end it all.

When he emerged from captivity, he had applied the lessons learned in La Picota, adding twists and turns he had devised himself, avoiding the mistakes that had betrayed his mentors. There was money to be made in contraband, specifically in drugs, and Hector's raw intelligence, his willingness to murder, granted him an edge on his competitors. With half a dozen early rivals dead or missing, Hector had secured a reputation as one who took his business seriously. He attracted allies, earned the friendship of officials who approached him with their hands out—and in time he came to dominate them all.

The Medellín cartel had taken months to organize, long years to build from scratch into a multibillion-dollar empire, but it had been worth the effort, worth the blood he had been forced to spill along the way. He had conceived the plan with Lehder and Navarro, roping in Aguirre and Raoul Ornelas to complete the hand. Ornelas had been taken by the government at Tranquilandia and was sitting out a prison sentence that would leave him old and gray upon parole—if he survived that long. The four surviving partners had discussed recruiting a replacement, but had finally decided that Raoul's share of the action, split four ways, was better than another mouth to feed.

And now the partners numbered only two, with one of those reduced to a minority position by his loss of troops and inventory. If Aguirre and Navarro had been targeted for private reasons, Hector thought he stood a decent chance of coming out on top. He might even consider killing Julio, a kind of favor to the faceless gunmen who had paved the way for his ascendancy.

If, however, Aguirre and Navarro's enemies were targeting the Medellín cartel itself, Pedilla would inevitably be the next in line. Where his companions had allowed themselves to be surprised and conquered, Hector was prepared to stand the graveyard watch himself, if necessary, to preserve all he had worked and fought for through the years.

He would not be imprisoned, and he would not let himself be frightened off by shadows in the forest, faceless rivals who didn't possess the courage to confront him as a man. They might destroy him in the end, but he would not go down without a struggle. Any victory his enemies achieved would be a bitter one, and few of them would live to celebrate.

And so he made the dawn patrol without complaint, demanding that his driver stop at this or that location on their route, exchanging words with field commanders, issuing instructions to his troops. Before he made the rounds again that afternoon, he would touch base with Colonel Rivas and request protection from the government. As a respected businessman, the leading rancher in Caquetá Province, he was reasonably certain the army wouldn't turn a deaf ear to his plea.

Not if the colonel wanted to maintain his place on Hector's payroll.

Not if Rivas valued the survival of his wife and children, safely tucked away in Bogotá.

Pedilla watched the sun rise on his empire, breaking through the trees in shafts of gold, and knew that fortune must be smiling on his face this day.

MACK BOLAN CROSSED Pedilla's borderline at noon on his eighth day in the bush. There were no signs or fences, but the soldier knew precisely where he was from studying a detailed topographic map. In front of him, and off to either side, two thousand sprawling acres formed the home base of the dealer he had come to kill.

This time it wouldn't be enough to torch the stock on hand and slip away. He had already missed Navarro—a mistake Bolan thought he still might have an opportunity to mend—and he couldn't afford to duplicate that error with Pedilla. Settling for less than total victory in this case would be an admission of defeat.

The Executioner didn't delude himself that his activities would halt the traffic in cocaine—before Pedilla's body cooled, the struggle for succession would be on; Aguirre had most likely been replaced in the cartel already. But elimination of the brains behind the Medellín cartel, destruction of its major inventory, would at least produce a temporary vacuum in the industry. As second-rankers rushed to fill the gap, the DEA and other agencies would have a shot at infiltrating syndicates or bagging dealers who were still confused, still scrambling for cover and a new source of supply.

With Lehder jailbound, most—or all—of his remaining partners dead, the Medellín cartel would be a headless viper, thrashing aimlessly until another head could be grafted to the body. Every day the cartel's operations were disrupted was a victory of sorts in Bolan's everlasting war.

The problem was that victory—unlike defeat and death—was frequently insubstantial, transitory, changing by the hour. Morning's triumph might be sour by noon, an abject loss come nightfall. Shifting circumstances made the difference, and he knew from grim experience that no success against the savages was permanent, no conquest carved in stone. A dedicated soldier had to fight the same grim battles time and time again until he lost his life or reached a satisfactory accommodation with his enemies.

For Bolan, there was no accommodation with the savages, no pretense of a cease-fire. He was in for the duration, and he would not—could not—rest as long as there were fresh replacements for his fallen enemies. Today the killing grounds were in Colombia. Tomorrow the same scenario would unfold in a new locale.

Bolan concentrated on his target, moving through the forest like a shadow, homing on the viper's lair. He crossed an unpaved road, maintained for visitors and for the delivery trucks that brought raw coca from the Cordillera, and continued following the track in the direction of Pedilla's compound. If his maps were accurate, he had a good two-hour walk ahead, and he didn't wish to draw attention on the way.

Twice, en route, he went to ground in the forest while bands of peasant workmen passed him by. He noticed that the laborers were under guard, each group of ten or twelve accompanied by two men bearing automatic weapons. Were they prisoners? Or was Pedilla gearing up for trouble, counting on an unexpected visitor?

The news about Aguirre and Navarro would have reached Pedilla's ears by now, of course. The dealer would be putting two and two together, weighing odds and angles, trying to determine if his name was next on someone's list. Before he found the answer, Bolan wanted to deliver it in person, but this strike would take more preparation than the others. He was up against a larger fighting force, for openers, and the dimensions of Pedilla's operation dwarfed those of Aguirre and Navarro.

Based on reports from informants, Bolan's target had five tons of coca and at least a half ton of refined cocaine on hand at any given time. Though considerably smaller than the operation that federal troops had sacked at Tranquilandia, it was a substantial stash. Trucks ran day and night between Pedilla's vast plantations in the Cordillera range and air-conditioned labs where men in smocks painstakingly refined coca into poison, bagging it for shipment to America and Europe.

Importation of the drug was something else entirely, and the men of DEA could handle that end on their own. Disruption of the source was Bolan's mission, one he meant to accomplish before another sunrise burned the jungle mist away.

Reconnaissance was critical, and Bolan took his time with the surveillance of Pedilla's compound. Guards were everywhere, resembling cheap extras from a Pancho Villa movie with their handlebar mustaches, low-slung holsters, belts of ammunition strapped across their chests. For all of that, he knew that most of them were hard professionals, selected by Pedilla for their willingness to kill and their ability to do the job without unnecessary frills. According to reports on file at Stony Man, Pedilla's gunners were recruited out of prisons and from the military and the police, with emphasis on violent, homicidal backgrounds. They were taught to follow orders on the basis of a simple code: obey or die. For those who toed the mark there were assorted perks, including drugs and women on the house. The stick-and-carrot combination made Pedilla's soldiers fiercely loyal, and if he suffered any problem with betrayal, word of it had never reached the outside world.

Bolan spent four hours circling the compound, noting landmarks, memorizing the position of every building from Pedilla's fortresslike mansion to the smallest shed. He charted avenues of access and retreat, including alternate escape routes in case the whole damned thing blew up in his face. He swept the long perimeter for cameras or listening devices, timed and counted the patrols, including one in which Pedilla participated personally.

Studying his enemy through long-range lenses, Bolan had an opportunity to put flesh on the skeleton contained in Hector's file at Stony Man. It might have been enough to know that he was ruthless and possibly psychotic, but an observation of the man in action granted Bolan greater insight, placing him in touch with his intended target on a different level.

It was Pedilla's eyes that were most disturbing. Once, before he climbed into his chauffeured jeep and disappeared, the dealer turned and seemed to look directly into Bolan's eyes. He couldn't have actually done so, for Bolan was concealed in jungle growth a hundred yards from where Pedilla stood, but for an instant Bolan imagined that the dealer had been staring through him, penetrating flesh and bone to probe his very thoughts.

And there was something in Pedilla's eyes, defying easy labels, that set Bolan's teeth on edge. A trace of madness, possibly. A strain of egomania, beyond the shadow of a doubt. And something else. Serenity? The kind of jaded fatalism that accrues from long exposure to a world of violent death?

He couldn't put his finger on the quality, except to say his enemy wasn't afraid. Pedilla might be on alert, prepared to cope with danger, but he wasn't frightened by the prospect.

Where Aguirre had dissolved into hysterics and Navarro had contrived a getaway while members of his crew pinned Bolan down, Pedilla was the sort of man to stand and fight, regardless of the odds.

When he finished his surveillance, Bolan knew he had the place covered to the best of his ability. The unforeseeable would have to take care of itself.

There was an hour left until sundown, but shadows were already growing long among the trees. Around the compound floodlights blazed to life, anticipating nightfall.

Outside the ring of artificial light a hunter sat and waited.

4

With nightfall, Bolan launched in earnest his preparations for the strike against Hector Pedilla. There was no need to change his tiger-stripe fatigues, but camouflage cosmetics on his face and hands would reduce the odds of anyone detecting his approach by moonlight. He spent an hour field-stripping and reassembling his weapons by touch, carefully loading the assault rifle, the Beretta 93-R with its custom silencer, the Desert Eagle automatic chambered in .44 Magnum. Extra magazines were slotted into canvas pouches, belted to his waist. The sleek Beretta nestled in a shoulder holster, and the Desert Eagle rode his hip on military webbing. Frag grenades, a few incendiaries, wire garrotes and the Ka-bar fighting knife completed his ensemble, fitting Bolan out for doomsday on the killing grounds.

The C-4 took some time as Bolan cut and shaped the plastique into charges, set the detonators and swaddled each charge in plastic wrap before he placed them back inside his satchel. He could damage or destroy nine buildings with the goop on hand, and based on his observation earlier, the Executioner had already selected several targets.

First and foremost was the laboratory, where Pedilla's coca base was chemically converted and refined into cocaine. Two charges would do the job, igniting chemicals inside the lab and setting off a chain reaction that a limited emergency response by Hector's troops couldn't contain. The warehouse complex, with its tons of lethal merchandise, would fall to thermite bombs, and Bolan could save the rest of his plastique for other targets in the compound.

Mentally he checked them off. The generator and communications shack. The Quonset huts that served as barracks for Pedilla's troops. The hangar and garage that flanked the helipad. The house itself?

He might not have the time or opportunity to goop Pedilla's mansion—and he didn't have enough C-4 to bring it down, in any case—but it was something to keep in mind, if he was able to position all his other charges safely, and there was time remaining.

He couldn't afford to lose the numbers when his very life would depend on precision timing. Once the charges detonated, planning would be out the window, and he'd be forced to play the final moments of the game on instinct, going with the flow. Above all else, he was determined to eliminate Pedilla. If he'd read the dealer wrong—if Hector didn't show himself at once—then Bolan would be forced to seek him out, regardless of the risk involved.

In normal circumstances, Bolan liked to time his raids for dawn, when biological imperatives deprived the keenest sentries of their fighting edge, but this time he would deviate from form. Assuming there would be survivors from Pedilla's garrison and that pursuit was highly probable, the Executioner preferred to make his flight in darkness, with the forest as his ally, rather than attempting to outrun an army in the rosy light of dawn. He had noted that Pedilla's sentries stood eight-hour shifts, the latest coming on at four o'clock, which indicated they would be replaced at midnight. If he made his move shortly before their relief, he would be dealing with soldiers who were tired, distracted from their duties by eagerness to finish out their shift.

At quarter past eleven Bolan was crouching in the shadow of the generator shack, alert for any sign of sentries deviating from their rounds. Unseen, he slipped inside the shed and fixed a C-4 charge against a fuel drum standing in one corner. He gave himself a good half hour on the timer, checking it against his watch to log the time for other settings, and moved on.

A separate shack housed the compound's radio equipment. This time Bolan fixed the plastique charge outside, against the wall where cables from the generator entered to provide power for the shortwave gear. When it blew, Pedilla's contact with the outside world would be eliminated—long enough, at least, for Bolan to complete his work and put the place behind him.

Setting up his charges for the laboratory, Bolan used more caution, peering in a dirty window here and there to gauge the layout of the operation. Satisfied that he had seen enough, he set charges on the northern and eastern walls. Their simultaneous explosion would demolish most of the lab equipment, which was on long tables in the northeast section of the room, and he could help them out with thermite if necessary.

Twelve minutes left. The barracks still remained, together with the warehouse, and Bolan wrote off any hope of setting charges in or near Pedilla's manor house. If he had judged his enemy correctly, Hector would emerge as soon as charges started going off around the compound, spoiling for a fight and anxious to destroy a challenger.

The sudden darkness and confusion would be Bolan's edge. Before Pedilla could assess his situation, it would be too late. But there were still more preparations to be made, and time was running short.

He gooped the barracks, listening to muffled voices on the inside, exercising special caution as he tamped the C-4 into place and set the timers. He was thankful they made no ticking sound that might have given them away. The Executioner couldn't have said how many men were inside the Quonset huts, nor did he care. They had been chosen by Pedilla on the basis of their records—rap sheets listing torture, rape and murder as the standard bill of fare—and Bolan knew that all of them were spinning out their lives on borrowed time.

Tonight their notes were coming due.

Four minutes. He wasn't far from the big house, keeping to the shadows and avoiding open, floodlit ground, when he became aware of headlights drawing nearer, following the narrow unpaved road. He ducked inside an unlocked toolshed and left the door ajar to watch as several vehicles approached Pedilla's house.

There were three trucks, preceded by a jeep. All of the vehicles bore military markings. For an instant Bolan thought he was witnessing a raid, but the approach was far too leisurely, and there had been no warning from the pickets in the forest. Clearly the new arrivals were expected, welcomed by the man in charge.

An officer dismounted from the jeep and snapped an order to his second-in-command. Another moment, and the Executioner was watching troops unload, some forty soldiers falling into double ranks beside their vehicles, all snapping to attention in the glare of interlocking floodlights.

Pedilla cleared the porch and smiled in greeting, hand outstretched in welcome to the officer, who shook it gravely. Words passed between them, out of Bolan's earshot, and another brusque command in Spanish sent the soldiers off in double time, their ranks disintegrating into two- and three-man teams as they assumed positions on the dark perimeter.

Mack Bolan cursed and checked his watch. Only ninety seconds left. There was no way on earth for him to reach the several charges, let alone to neutralize them, in the time remaining. Judgment day was coming, and the *federales* were about to join the party.

It occurred to Bolan that their officer deserved no better. He was clearly in Pedilla's pocket, using troops at his command to guard an operation that they should have been dismantling on sight. The knowledge made small difference, though; in all his years of waging endless war, the Executioner had rarely fired upon authorities of any friendly nation.

This time, it seemed, he had no options left.

Twelve seconds.

Bolan started counting down, attempting to determine the location of the reinforcements, knowing it was too damned late to save the play. Pedilla was his mark, and there was nothing he could do to save the others.

Bolan found the detonator override and keyed its doomsday signal, touching off the hidden charges prematurely. He had visualized the trigger as a backup system, for his own protection in a pinch, but now it was his only hope of bringing down the house before the *federales* wandered any closer to the danger zone.

Around the compound, marching like a giant's footsteps, thunderous explosions laced the night with fire. The generator shack disintegrated first, and all the rest went off in darkness, hellish flashbulbs capturing the scene in grim stop-motion, freezing startled sentries in their tracks.

The Executioner pushed off from cover, welcoming the darkness like an old, familiar friend. He had one chance to take Pedilla down and out. With reinforcements in the compound, there might never be another opportunity.

One chance to do it right.

Or die in the attempt.

PEDILLA HAD BEEN WAITING for the convoy, wondering if Rivas would decide to stop en route and make his entrance in the morning. There was something of the prima donna in the colonel's makeup, but he had his uses. Like tonight.

The troops had driven out from Medellín in answer to Pedilla's summons. Reasonably confident his private force could deal with any outside threat, Pedilla hadn't reached his present state by leaving things to chance. A federal presence would amuse his gunners and discourage any opposition force from striking at his compound. It would also reinforce Pedilla's image as a man with friends both powerful and highly placed.

Who else in all Colombia could call upon the army to protect his cocaine labs and inventory? Lehder might have done it once upon a time, but his excesses had overtaken him and he was facing something like a century in Yankee jails before he set foot on his native soil again. Meanwhile Pedilla was the heir apparent—no, the heir *in fact*—to everything the Medellín cartel had worked for through the years. Navarro would be dealt with in due time, but first Pedilla had to guarantee his own security and the safety of his private operation.

Rivas and his troops would help in that regard. The colonel had been hesitant, at first, upon receiving Hector's summons. He had pleaded urgent business—the pursuit of Communist guerrillas and suppression of *la violencia*—until Pedilla jogged his memory about the nature of his true allegiance. Rivas might have sworn to serve the military, but in recent years he'd been earning more under the table from Pedilla than the army could afford to pay a man of his admittedly substandard talents. Colonel Rivas knew which side his bread was buttered on, and he was conscious of the penalties for failure to respond in moments of his master's direst need.

Above all else, the recent rash of violence in Colombia had reaffirmed the universal truth that no one was immune to sudden death. A colonel's uniform was no more bulletproof than the cassock of a village priest, or the expensive suits preferred by politicians in the capital.

Of course, the colonel decided after a bit of prodding, it was possible for troops to be allotted to protect the thriving business interests of a man of Pedilla's status. Colonel Rivas recognized Pedilla's problem as a symptom of the same insidious disease that had confronted him in Medellín. There were guerrillas to be dealt with in the hinterland—most likely Communists, if one considered their assaults upon the local bastions of free enterprise—and as a military man, it was the colonel's duty to protect the law-abiding people of his country. Rivas hadn't wasted any time in transit.

Pedilla smiled when the trucks arrived, amused as always by the colonel's basic cowardice. He wondered how a man so weak and seemingly devoid of character had risen through the ranks to a position of command, deciding it had likely been those very traits that made the crucial difference. Superiors within the army could depend on Rivas to obey their orders out of fear or self-interest; they would never have to fret about a sudden outburst of initiative or independent thought. In fact, the colonel was ideal for his position as a bureaucratic middleman in uniform.

The colonel clicked his heels and shook Pedilla's hand, explaining his assignment briefly for the benefit of any troopers who were listening. It was preposterous to think that any of them bought the cover story; all of them must recognize the warehouse complex, the adjacent laboratory, for precisely what they were. But in Colombia illusions were important—even vital—to the daily conduct of affairs. Police *appeared* to go about their business energetically. Guerrillas *seemed* to wage unending war against the state and drug cartels. The courts and wardens *tried* to punish criminals. The government *pretended* to investigate the rise of rampant violence in the streets and countryside. They all accomplished nothing in the end.

Pedilla loved his country. He suspected there was nowhere else on earth with circumstances so ideal for conducting illicit business. Having dealt with politicians and corrupt police in the United States, Mexico, France and Britain, he was satisfied that orchestrated chaos made the crucial difference. If *la violencia* hadn't existed in Colombia, the Medellín cartel would have been forced to fabricate a substitute. In this case, fate had smiled upon Pedilla and his comrades, granting them the golden opportunity to build an empire and to watch it grow beyond their wildest dreams.

Except that nothing was beyond Pedilla's dreams these days. He had begun to find the Medellín cartel confining, too restrictive for his talents. He was meant to paint upon a broader canvas, act upon a bigger stage. The world at large was waiting for a man of his abilities and vision.

First, however, he would have to make his home base perfectly secure. Which brought him back to Colonel Rivas and the forty soldiers under his command.

"I hope you will accept my thanks for your protection, and agree to share my humble hospitality."

"Of course, think nothing of it." Rivas preened and strutted, ordering the captain who accompanied him to see the troopers at their posts. "It is my pleasure to cooperate with our respected citizens in the suppression of subversive forces."

"You have traveled far. Perhaps a taste of brandy would be welcome, while your men get settled in."

"A marvelous idea, Señor Pedilla. By all means."

They were proceeding toward the house, Pedilla in the lead, when sudden thunder ripped the compound, shock waves staggering both men before the lights went out. Pedilla turned to find a fiery mushroom sprouting where the generator shack had stood a second earlier. Before he could react, a rolling string of blasts demolished the communications hut, shot ragged bolts of hellfire through the laboratory and flattened the two Quonset huts that served as barracks for his men. He was surrounded by a ring of fire and rubble, sharp smoke in his nostrils, screams of dying *pistoleros* ringing in his ears.

"Guerrillas!" Rivas shouted to his scattered troops. "Take cover!"

Hector cursed and tried to drag him back, but then he saw—or *felt*—a shadow moving toward him on the dim periphery of sight. Before he turned, alarms were hammering inside his skull, insisting this wasn't a member of his palace guard, nor one of the "professionals" detailed by Rivas. Breaking for the house, he shot his enemy a sidelong glance and caught a brief impression of a large man, face and hands obscured by war paint, charging toward him with murder on his mind.

Pedilla hit the porch and slammed the heavy double doors behind him, conscious of the fact that simple locks wouldn't detain an enemy who had already leveled half his compound. Several of his guards were groping through the dark with flashlights, and he snatched an Uzi submachine gun from their leader, flicking off the safety as he spun to face the entrance.

Hector counted five beneath his breath, then held the Uzi's trigger down and sprayed the doors and foyer windows with a stream of parabellum slugs. He reveled in the power flowing through his weapon, cackling and dancing as he emptied the magazine. When it was spent, he took another from the hands of his dumbfounded guard, reloading as he moved in the direction of the scarred and punctured doors.

There was a calculated risk in stepping out while rifle fire still crackled in the compound. Through the shattered windows, he could see the laboratory burning, and behind it flames were leaping from the warehouse complex. Soldiers pounded past the window in pursuit of shadows, and a moment later members of his yard force passed the other way, grim faces equally determined.

"Shit!"

He threw the doors back, leveling the Uzi, ready to behold the prostrate body of his adversary on the porch. This one, at least, wouldn't slink home to boast about his raid on the Pedilla factories.

But there was no one on the porch, no trace of blood to indicate that anyone had suffered wounds and dragged himself away to die. Though the steps were bright with shattered glass, and wooden splinters crunched beneath his shoes, there were no further signs of a desperate battle having taken place.

But the compound was a different story. From the porch, Pedilla saw the skylights of his giant warehouse spouting tongues of flame. The cloud of rising smoke would have kept an army high for months, provided it didn't kill them first, and he was thankful for the brisk north wind that carried it away across the treetops. Let the forest sloths and spider monkeys party till they dropped; at least some living thing would have the benefit of Hector's epic loss.

He couldn't think yet of the dollar value of the loss. Instead, he felt the raid was a direct, personal attack upon his honor, upon his reputation as a man of power. Color burned in his cheeks, and he was immediately thankful for the darkness that concealed his shame.

Across the smoky clearing, on the far side of the compound, small-arms fire continued, crackling along the tree line. Hector was about to move in that direction when he sighted Colonel Rivas, dusty and disheveled, striding toward the porch.

"My men have driven off the rebels," he announced to Hector and those of his men assembled on the steps, "and they are in pursuit."

"How many?"

Rivas looked embarrassed. "Only one was seen, but from the damage—"

"One? One man did this?"

"I think we may assume, *señor*, that there were others in the forest, possibly with mortars, rocket launchers—"

"Did you hear a mortar, Rivas? Did you see a rocket fired?"

"It is entirely possible—"

"One man!" Pedilla shouted in the colonel's face, enjoying the reaction as the older man recoiled. "I want him brought to me alive. You understand? Alive!"

"I will make every effort—"

"Do it!"

Hector left the colonel gaping, didn't see the weak salute as he brushed past his sentries, handing off the Uzi, and entered the house. It was the job of Rivas and his troops to run around the jungle in pursuit of madmen; they were paid to do so by the government, and Rivas had been quick to claim his other, secret paycheck from Pedilla. Let him earn his money now, Pedilla thought, or else admit that he was worthless and retire.

One man.

It was not possible, of course...or was it? He would have to wait until the soldiers brought their quarry back for questioning.

And if they failed? If he escaped, or they were forced to kill him in the end?

Pedilla smiled. In that event, he would have to entertain himself with Rivas, teaching an incompetent the error of his ways.

THE WARRIOR'S RUSH had been aborted when his target bolted for the house, a sidelong glance alerting him to Bolan's move. Before the Executioner could aim and fire, a flying squad of uniforms closed in on his starboard flank, the frantic voice of their commander urging them to haste. Already some of them had spotted Bolan, breaking stride and taking aim.

He scattered them with half a dozen rounds deliberately fired above their heads, using the moment of confusion to retreat. The troopers might be green and poorly trained, but they still had the numbers necessary to surround him if he wasted precious time and let them have the opportunity.

A running glance in the direction of Pedilla's house confirmed that he had lost his chance to bag the dealer with an easy shot. There might not be a second chance, but Bolan saw no profit in deliberately laying down his life to play a long shot when the dogs were baying at his heels.

A bullet whispered past his ear, and Bolan veered hard right, obtaining temporary cover in the shadow of the smoking laboratory. Loping past Pedilla's warehouse, he took time to spring a pair of thermite bombs and yank the pins, delivering them overhand through frosted windows. Bolan didn't have the luxury of waiting to examine the results, but he was reasonably sure that in a pinch the compound's crew would come up short on fire-fighting equipment. Sprinting for the trees, he wished them luck. All bad.

He half expected his pursuers to give up before they reached the forest, but they took him by surprise and followed through, their noisy progress putting startled animals to flight. Ten minutes later they were still behind him, holding doggedly on course and fanning out to execute a sweep of sorts, prepared to circle Bolan if he didn't hold his pace. He thought of doubling back to meet them in the darkness, then scuttled the idea when he considered the results of being trapped, pinned down beneath a cross fire, while the hunters sent for reinforcements.

His salvation lay in speed. But there the jungle conspired against him, reaching out with ferns and creepers in a bid to snare him, bring him down. He plunged ahead, aware that he was making too much noise, unable to afford the break in stride that would permit him to proceed with caution.

Grim, determined, Bolan led the chase southward toward the river and his only chance of getting out alive.

5

It is impossible to move with speed *and* stealth at night on unfamiliar ground while twenty hostile gunners beat the bush behind you, drawing closer by the moment. Bolan had already given up on stealth, relying on his speed and trusting in the racket made by his pursuers to cover some of the noise he couldn't avoid.

Behind him they were fanning out along a curved perimeter, designed to trap him in the center, calling back and forth to one another as they tried to stay in contact. Bolan had a sufficient lead to guarantee they wouldn't encircle him unless he stopped and let them close the gap, but he couldn't be certain what would happen once they reached the river.

He had crossed the Yarí once to reach Pedilla's territory, but the crossing had been made in daylight with the luxury of time for preparation. There had been no snipers, no one bent on killing him before he got across. This time he would have to improvise. He wouldn't have the luxury of ropes and stepping stones, no chance to plan his crossing with the jackals on his heels.

And yet the river seemed to be his only hope. He couldn't simply alter course and leave the trackers groping after him in darkness; they had flung their net too far for Bolan to outrun the closing flanks. He had to find a way across.

There was a bridge, of course, but it was miles upstream, constructed to accommodate the narrow highway that had brought Pedilla's reinforcements in the nick of time. To reach it, Bolan would have had to parallel the road, allowing his pursuers ample opportunity to race ahead and cut him off. Crossing the bridge itself would be plain and simple suicide, with Bolan totally exposed to enemies on either bank.

There had to be a better way. His problem would be finding it in time before the *federales* overtook him and dispatched a call for reinforcements from the compound. Bolan had no wish to kill these soldiers, even though they obviously served Pedilla's interest. He had encountered venal officers before, and while he sometimes left them with a headache they would never forget, the soldier always let them walk. He didn't mean to break the pattern now.

He hadn't come this way on his approach to the Pedilla compound, but he kept the details of his topographic map in mind, referring to his compass twice, by penlight, to confirm his course. Another half mile should see him to the river's edge, and there he might be literally forced to sink or swim.

He had no way of measuring the river's depth or calculating the velocity of the current. From observation he knew the waters moved briskly—a guarantee, at least, that he wouldn't be threatened by piranhas. But a man could lose his footing even in the shallows. Once the river had him down, he could be swept away, and it would take a miracle to save him from the current's grasp.

In his haste, distracted by his thoughts of crossing the river and by the sounds of close pursuit, he nearly missed the boa. Draped across a branch that overhung his track, the reptile measured close to fifteen feet in length. It was hunting. Though Bolan didn't qualify as prey, in his headlong flight he rated treatment as an enemy. The snake was primed to strike when he noticed it. Recoiling awkwardly, he lost his footing.

The slide was all that saved him. Boas aren't venomous; the big snakes wrap their prey in coils of muscle, crushing out the breath and life before they start to feed. Even with its body twined around his own, he might have been able to kill the snake barehanded, but he couldn't afford the time it would have taken to grapple with the reptile. Every second counted now, and he could hear the numbers falling as he scrambled low beneath the boa's perch.

Behind him, hissing wickedly, the snake was satisfied at being left in peace. The next man on the scene might be less fortunate, and that was fine with Bolan, too. He didn't mind an unexpected watchdog on his trail.

The village took him by surprise. No more than half a dozen huts collected on the river's edge, it scarcely rated designation as a settlement, and by the time he cleared the tree line, Bolan realized the thatch-roofed dwellings were unoccupied. The blackened rocks that formed a central fire pit had been cold for weeks—or months, for all he knew— and animals had nested in the thatch of several huts. He heard them rustling at his approach, imagined rodents scurrying for cover, and moved on with only a cursory glance at the vacant homes.

What had become of the inhabitants? He couldn't say, but there was every possibility Pedilla's men had been involved in their removal. Forest Indians were bad for business in the *narcotraficante*'s world—too independent for conscription as a labor force and inclined to tell their friends and relatives about their observations of the white man's private business. Tribesmen could bear witness in a court of law as well as anyone, and Bolan was aware of cases where particularly ruthless dealers had annihilated families, even whole tribes, to guarantee their silence.

Had the people of this tiny village been wiped out, or had they opted for escape, one jump ahead of Hector's raiding party? The solution to that mystery was critical for Bolan, since a river settlement meant boats. If the villagers had been forcibly removed or slain, there was a chance their means of transportation might remain behind.

He found three long canoes upstream, prows tethered to the bank with lengths of rope. Each craft would easily accommodate four men, and Bolan saw no reason to invite further pursuit. He drew the sleek Beretta with its custom silencer and fired a three-round burst below the waterline on two of the canoes. When he was satisfied the third would serve his purpose he cut the mooring line, scrambled in, pushed off and used the double-headed paddle to move away from shore.

The racing current took the craft downstream, and Bolan made no effort to resist. Right now he needed time and space between himself and his pursuers; he could change his course and strike off overland again when he was finally free and clear. When his escape was noted, searchers might be sent ahead to comb the riverbanks, but given decent lead time, Bolan knew he could outmaneuver them. While they were looking for the boat, his footprints in the mud, he would be miles away, moving toward his prearranged rendezvous with Jack Grimaldi.

He refused to view his mission as a failure—massive losses had been inflicted on the Medellín cartel—but neither could he count it as a victory. Of three prime targets, two were still alive, and the mere destruction of their cocaine inventories wouldn't put the syndicate away. Pedilla's ruined lab might be rebuilt within a week, or two at most, and then the poison merchants would be back on line, prepared to pick up operations where the Bolan raids had interrupted them. Within a month it would be back to the status quo and SOP.

The prospect galled him, but he had no easy answers in mind. Whatever edge surprise had offered him originally, it was lost. Navarro and Pedilla would be waiting for him next time—possibly together, if they had the common sense to pool their strength in mutual defense. Opposition from the *federales* was another danger, demonstrated by Pedilla's close alliance with at least some portion of the army. The

Executioner didn't intend to let himself be captured or identified.

In 1986 Colombia's elected rulers had requested military aid from the United States in an attempt to crush their native dealers; the attempt had failed. Times had changed now; there was no reason to suppose the government would welcome covert action by Americans against the Medellín cartel. Exposure of his mission, failed or otherwise, might well provoke an international incident complete with public accusations, and the Phoenix program didn't need that kind of heat.

Downriver, then, as fast as tide and human strength could carry him. The Executioner was paddling for his life.

ORLANDO RIVAS WAS DISGUSTED with himself and his surroundings. He'd been disturbed by the initial message from Pedilla, angered by the fact that he couldn't refuse the *narcotraficante*'s summons, but that much, at least, was part of life in latter-day Colombia. The government was infamous for holding hands with dealers, even as it made a show of waging war against their networks, and the army had no corner on corruption. Rivas hadn't gained the rank of colonel without recognizing certain facts of military life—among them, the availability of healthy "bonuses" for officers who made themselves available for "special duties" as the need arose.

Most often, special duties for the Medellín cartel involved an escort, riding shotgun on the caravans that ferried coca to the labs and brought the finished product back again for shipment. There was little danger in such work, for the cartel had made its point with small competitors through years of ruthless violence. There were still a few small operators—would-be giants—who might risk a suicidal gesture, but their ranks had thinned with time and the attrition of *la violencia*.

Guerrillas were another problem altogether, though they seldom posed a problem for the members of the Medellín cartel. There were so many groups that Rivas couldn't keep them all in mind, and there was no point in doing so, anyway. The Communists believed in overthrowing the established government and setting up their own while weeding out their enemies along the way. The program of the fascist right was virtually identical, aside from certain differences in the choice of enemies to be annihilated. Sandwiched in between the two were gangs of vigilantes, smugglers and small-time cocaine cowboys offering little competition to the kingpins of the trade.

The single common trait of all these groups was *la violencia*—sàvage, lethal, often indiscriminate violence. The army tried to cope with them as best it could, but it was a losing battle from the start. As state police were hampered by the frequent calls to serve as bodyguards for this or that official, so the army was distracted from suppression of guerrilla forces by the conduct of its zany "war on drugs."

That war had been declared by men who realized that it was lost before they made their call to arms. In Bogotá and Medellín, judges were intimidated, bribed or killed. Police were either on the take or posted on a death list that was circulated and updated periodically by ranking dealers. Military officers like Rivas frequently owed dual allegiance to the state and the cartel.

In such an atmosphere, enforcement of the drug laws was virtually impossible. There were dynamic raids from time to time, eliminating minor targets, and occasional mistaken body blows against the ranking drug lords. Tranquilandia and the destruction of that massive laboratory complex had been a reaction to the murder of a cabinet minister, but for the most part, good intentions fell considerably short of action.

Colonel Rivas stayed away from violent situations when he could. He had no wish to be a hero in a casket, lying cold and stiff while so-called friends paraded past and whispered lies he couldn't hear. Some of his colleagues actively sought contact with the various guerrilla bands, but Rivas didn't share their taste for danger. Life was short enough; he risked his only in an absolutely vital cause.

Tonight's, for instance.

When Pedilla snapped his fingers, Rivas jumped, aware that failure to perform could mean much more than simple loss of income. If he chose, Pedilla could disgrace him, ruin his career by leaking information about their past association. Rivas might wind up in prison, caged with deviants and psychopaths.

Or worse. Pedilla might elect to punish Rivas privately for any show of insubordination, and the officer had seen enough to know the forms such punishment could take. A sudden burst of gunfire from the darkness would be merciful and quick. A slaughtered family was sometimes more effective punishment, leaving the survivor with the haunting knowledge that he could have prevented the killing had he only followed orders.

Rivas frankly lacked the courage to resist Pedilla. He seldom needed courage...but this was different. At first, Aguirre's death had seemed a curiosity, the raid against Navarro something of an aberration. Both events could be explained by several theories, one of which, Rivas had speculated, was that their esteemed associate, Pedilla, was the source of their misfortune.

But tonight was...something else. Pedilla might have staged an incident to cast off suspicion, but he would not have destroyed his laboratory or the warehouse complex with his merchandise inside. Such an action was preposterous. But that meant that Rivas was pursuing a determined, dangerous opponent through the jungle, absolutely ignorant of who that enemy might be, his strength, his goals.

It was a foolish move, but Rivas had no option but to forge ahead.

Their prey was making decent time, and that alone made Colonel Rivas wonder if the first reports about a single man might be correct. It seemed impossible that one commando could inflict such damage on the compound, all without a single sentry spotting him beforehand, but Pedilla was right about the mortars and rocket launchers. There had been no shelling from the forest. Someone had entered the compound and planted charges where they would inflict the maximum destruction in the minimum time.

A skilled professional.

And they were chasing blindly after him, through darkness.

When the pursuers reached the village by the river, with its clutch of empty huts, the colonel thought they must have missed their quarry in the jungle. There would be no point in turning back to search for him at night. If he had managed to elude their sweep the first time, he was gone.

Discovery of the boats had changed his mind. Two punctured recently by bullets, splinters bright and clean around the holes, with an impression on the muddy bank where someone not long ago had launched a third. The severed mooring line was still in place, wound tight around protruding tree roots.

Rivas cursed beneath his breath and wondered how Pedilla would react to the report that they had lost their man.

Six huts, but only three canoes? He thought there should be more, and sent a pair of soldiers out in both directions to scour the bank. It took a moment, but two more canoes were found half hidden in a stand of reeds along the water's edge. They were intact.

Two boats, and four men each. Rivas knew it would look better to Pedilla if he led the party in pursuit. Selecting seven marksmen, one of them a sergeant, Rivas left his second-in-command to offer explanations at the compound. Rank still had its privileges, and one of them was handing off unpleasant jobs to underlings.

They pushed away from the shore, the sergeant in the lead canoe, with Rivas bringing up the rear. There was no point in taking chances, he thought, if their prey had doubled back to lie in ambush somewhere up ahead.

The colonel understood Pedilla's wish to take the man alive; if he was killed, the secret of his sponsors would die with him, leaving the cartel—or its surviving members— open to attack on other fronts. But while it might be possible to overtake their prey, Rivas had his doubts about securing a prisoner. It would be so much easier to simply kill the man and claim his death was unavoidable.

Pedilla would be furious, of course, but in the circumstances he could scarcely criticize. And, in any case, Rivas was prepared to blame the shooting on his careless men. A dead assailant would minimize the colonel's risk, and if Pedilla's enemies dispatched another killer—or an army— it would be the dealer's problem.

Smiling to himself despite the queasiness he felt upon embarking in the old canoe, Orlando Rivas settled back and waited for his men to overtake the enemy.

He did his finest work when he was looking out for number one.

THE RIVER CARRIED Bolan swiftly out of earshot, and he soon lost touch with his pursuers, concentrating on the current, watching out for logs or other obstacles ahead. He used the double-headed paddle sparingly, content to let the river set his pace.

They couldn't follow him without a boat. Inevitably they would find the two he had disabled and realize a third was missing; if they were thinking clearly, they would have to know he'd gone downstream.

No matter. If they tried to follow him along the bank on foot, he would outdistance them with ease. He had only to maintain his course and let the river carry him for several miles, effectively beyond their reach, before he went ashore.

The soldiers wouldn't follow him indefinitely. Somewhere, sometime, they had to count the race as lost and give it up.

The Executioner relaxed a bit. His work was done, and if the job was less than perfect . . . well, perfection was a goal more frequently aspired to than attained. Pedilla would be piling on security precautions now, and Bolan knew it might be weeks—or months—before he found another golden opportunity to make the tag.

Too long. He couldn't linger in Colombia and put his life on hold, in hopes Pedilla might reveal himself next week, next year. The warrior had prepared himself for every reasonable outcome of his probe, but the federal troops had been completely unexpected. There was nothing he could do about it now, and Bolan doggedly refused to dwell on failure.

He was coming out alive, and that was all a combat soldier in the midst of everlasting war could hope for.

Far behind him he heard something like a shout, and Bolan shipped his paddle, swiveling to glance along his track. A speck of something trailed him by half a mile or more, and as he watched the speck divided, making two.

Canoes? He had destroyed the only other boats he had seen—which meant nothing if his enemies had found others. His night vision tried to pick out details, caught a hint of movement in the lead boat, and the shout was repeated, barely audible above the night sounds of the forest.

They were after him.

Somehow they had found transportation and were closing on him. He cursed and dug in with his paddle, bettering the river's pace, which now seemed almost lackadaisical. He heard the distant echo of a rifle shot, immediately followed by another and another. If the bullets reached him, they were off their mark and passed unnoticed in the darkness.

Speed was everything to Bolan now. He couldn't turn and fight without surrendering control of the canoe. If it dumped him now, he might drown before the troops got close enough to shoot him. But if they weren't deterred from sniping at him, he could be hit.

More reports, in rapid-fire, and this time Bolan heard bullets slapping water on his flanks. A hundred yards ahead, the river curved, and Bolan paddled harder, intent on gaining temporary cover, which would grant him time to pick up speed and increase his fragile lead. The soldiers must have had the same idea, for he was forced to duck as they increased their fire, attempting to disable him or sink his boat before he was out of range.

A wild round grazed his ribs. He cursed and lost a stroke before recovering. The pain was minor, but he felt warm blood beneath his arm as he dug with everything he had.

Beyond the river's curve a new sound captured his attention, momentarily distracting him from the perils of pursuit. It was a rumbling sound, like distant thunder, drawing closer as he leaned into the paddled strokes. It took him another moment to place the sound, but recognition didn't put his mind at ease.

A waterfall.

He couldn't judge its height from where he sat, would have no final estimate until his boat had tipped the edge, but from its sound he judged the drop to be substantial. If he rode it out, he'd be thrown from the canoe, perhaps disarmed; the odds were fifty-fifty he would drown. And if he put ashore, the enemy would spot him, land upstream and resume their foot pursuit.

A spit of land thrust out from shore on Bolan's left. He saw his chance and paddled for it, battling the current's pull. Another twenty yards, and his pursuers hadn't cleared the bend. If he could make it while the beach and jungle lay between them, he would have a fighting chance.

Precision timing was the key. When his efforts placed him ten feet off the spit, still moving, he jumped, employing every ounce of strength at his disposal. The canoe slid out from under Bolan's feet, reducing his momentum, and his legs were in the water as he landed, riptide sucking at his feet and spinning him around.

He found a purchase on the spit, his fingers digging into sand and rock, gripping solid ground. With trembling arms he hauled himself out of the water and scrambled a dozen yards on hands and knees before he gained the beach and made it to his feet. Behind him, his canoe sailed on toward its appointment with the waterfall, unmanned.

He reached the tree line, found a hiding place and hunkered down to wait.

6

The darkness was a friend that Bolan used to hide himself from hostile eyes. He used a camou cloth to wipe the Colt Commando dry and started on the Desert Eagle while wondering where in hell they had discovered the canoes.

It was often said that you could never be too careful. Bolan knew that to be false—excessive caution could delay a soldier's move until the crucial time was lost, and any stroke became a suicidal gesture of futility. But he had been guilty of a careless indiscretion. It would have taken him a minute, less, to make a superficial search for other boats, and by so doing, Bolan could have prevented the pursuit.

The lead canoe, then the second one, slid past him—two boats, four men in each, straining at their paddles. He caught a glint of an officer's insignia. Pedilla's military puppet hadn't been satisfied to send his troopers down the river after Bolan; he'd joined the chase himself, yet more evidence of the power Pedilla held over the organs of the state.

The pursuers had Bolan's craft in view again, and he hoped it was holding steady on its course. A spattering of automatic fire told him the hostile troops were buying it—so far. Their officer exhorted them to greater speed, and in another moment they were past his vantage point, slipping out of sight.

He took the calculated risk of leaving cover, moving to the river's edge and raising his night glasses, watching three ca-

noes en route to the apocalypse. From where he stood the
rumble of the waterfall was simple background music, as
pervasive as the night sounds of the forest.

Bolan knew that some of them—perhaps the lot—could
drown if they were swept across the falls. He drew a narrow
mental line between destroying "friendly" enemies and letting those same enemies destroy themselves. Their officer,
at least, was guilty of corruption and malfeasance in his
dealings with Pedilla, and the grunts presumably had some
idea of what was happening. The Executioner would raise
no hand against them, but if they should run afoul of
Mother Nature while pursuing him, it wasn't his place to
meddle with the cosmic scheme of things.

He stowed the glasses, wondering if he hadn't already
crossed the line. He could have saved them with a warning
shot, but then they would have put ashore and pursued him
yet again. He had elected to protect himself. It was done,
and he would have to live with it. And if he meant to live at
all, he had to move.

Regardless of what happened at the falls, he had to move.
The wound beneath his arm was still seeping blood into a
hastily applied compress, and while the blood loss wouldn't
immediately slow him down, he had no time to waste.

His enemies would have to look out for themselves. The
Executioner had miles to go before he could afford another
rest.

"CEASE FIRE, goddamn it!"

Colonel Rivas strained his ears against the aftershocks of
rifle fire, attempting to identify the other sound. At first he
had mistaken it for thunder, irritated by the prospect of a
rain squall in the midst of their pursuit, but now he realized
he had been mistaken. This sound emanated from the river,
becoming louder by the moment as the current swept them
onward.

Rapids?

Rivas felt a sudden rush of panic and nearly called out for the sergeant in the lead canoe to turn his boat around, but they were gaining on their quarry now and Rivas couldn't let him slip away. The colonel's dread of going back to face Pedilla empty-handed rivaled his instinctive fear of anything the river had to offer. He was safer on the water than he would be in the compound if Pedilla decided to punish someone for the damage suffered by his plant and personnel.

The crew of the second canoe had faltered, listening with Rivas, and the point vessel had surged ahead, maintaining the pursuit. Now the colonel snapped an order at the paddlers, startling them back to action, and another moment saw them gaining on the sergeant's boat. About a hundred yards ahead their quarry had slumped in his canoe, no longer paddling, allowing the momentum of the current to propel him forward.

They could take him now, perhaps before they reached white water. It occurred to Rivas that their target might be wounded, even dying, but he didn't care. It was enough to have the man within their grasp, and Rivas urged his men to greater speed, intent on pulling even with the enemy's canoe before it reached the next approaching bend.

He hadn't memorized the river's course, knew nothing of what lay ahead beyond the sound of brooding thunder, so much louder now. For all he knew the rapids might be miles away, and then again—

He blinked, almost stood up, but caught himself when the canoe began to rock. His mouth fell open, gaping. He couldn't believe his eyes.

Their quarry and his boat had disappeared.

The colonel blinked again, glanced toward the nearest shore to clear his head and scanned the river once again. The empty water stretched before him like a piece of slate, the sergeant's lead canoe still racing on in hot pursuit of nothing.

Toward a *waterfall*!

He understood, too late, and snapped an order at his soldiers. They began to paddle backward, making for the shore, but it was difficult to fight the current now, as it accelerated toward the falls. Rivas's stomach lurched. He clamped his knees together in a desperate but unsuccessful effort to control his bladder, unwilling to disgrace himself before he died.

He shouted to the sergeant and his paddlers, knowing that his words were lost beneath the rumbling of the waterfall. It took a moment for the soldiers in the lead canoe to recognize their danger, then they started paddling hysterically in the direction of the opposite shore. Somehow they slowed their boat to a momentary standstill, turning—and then suddenly they lost control.

Dumbfounded, Rivas watched the long canoe begin to rotate, picking up momentum as it spun. The soldiers dug in furiously with their paddles, trying everything they could think of to arrest the dizzy spinning, all in vain. Still twirling, they were swept downstream in the direction of the roaring falls.

He saw them go, a final twist before they lost it, and the sergeant catapulted from his seat, lips ovaled in a scream that Rivas couldn't hear. The boat was there...and then it wasn't.

In all his life Orlando Rivas hadn't felt such terror. Even in the compound, under fire, with shrapnel whistling around him, he hadn't experienced such paralyzing fear. He clutched the sides of the canoe, his knuckles white and cracking from the pressure he exerted, praying feverishly to a forgotten God.

He would reform, quit drinking, break off with his mistress—or his wife, whichever God preferred—if only they could reach dry land alive. He didn't even care about the others; death could take them all, a living sacrifice, but surely Rivas could be spared this time. He was a relatively young man, in his prime, with so much living still ahead of him.

It was all bullshit. Even as the silent prayers took shape, the colonel knew they were worthless, wasted. Any deity would see through his pathetic pose at once and shun him for the cheat and liar he was. Although he hadn't been to church for years, he thought it would be worse to die with false prayers on his lips than with no prayers at all.

He concentrated on the shore, encouraged by the fact that it was closer now...or was that mere illusion? Were they really gaining, or was he hallucinating in the depths of his despair?

Behind him, in the stern of the canoe, one of the paddlers alternately cursed and exhorted God to lend a hand in their extremity. The combination seemed to work. In another moment their prow was grounded. One man leaped from the boat to drag it farther up on shore; another splashed overboard behind and shoved from the stern.

All three of his companions were ashore before the colonel dared to move. He tottered from the boat, glanced down at clammy trousers, hoping river spray had soaked them through and hidden his cause of shame. It hadn't. The earth beneath his feet seemed frail, unsteady for a moment, but he soon regained his equilibrium.

They would be walking back, of that much he was certain. Dawn would break before they reached the compound, but it didn't seem to matter now. They were alive, if empty-handed, and Pedilla would be forced to vent his anger on the river if he sought a scapegoat for their failure to return with prisoners.

It was enough, for now, to stand on solid ground and know he wouldn't have to go out on the river for the long trip back. Rivas would rather have hiked a hundred miles through stinking jungle than return to the canoe for half a mile of easy, risk-free navigation.

"Come," he told the others, breaking through the spell of silence. "We must go."

They glanced at one another, coming back to life and forming up abbreviated ranks. With all that they had seen tonight, these men were soldiers first. *His* soldiers.

Rivas was about to offer them a rare word of congratulation when the automatic weapons opened fire.

THE YOUNG MAN had been waiting, watching, since a jungle breeze carried the initial sound of gunfire to his ears. Adept at picking out directions in the forest, he had recognized the shots as coming from upstream. The next burst was closer, and he settled down to bide his time.

He had been watching when the first canoe appeared, its solo pilot veering toward the opposite shore a hundred yards upstream from where the young man waited. This wasn't a military man—at least, he bore no obvious resemblance to the *federales*—and the young man studied him with interest as he leaped to reach the sand spit, scrambling ashore and disappearing into the forest shadows. His canoe, unmanned, swung back to the center of the stream and held its course.

The next two boats were filled with soldiers, four men each, and it required no special talent to detect the officer, surrounded by his troopers in the rear canoe. They seldom took the lead, these heroes of the state; instead, they found it safer to allow their peon privates to precede them and take all the risks, while honors were reserved for those with stars and oak leaf clusters on their caps.

The young man hated soldiers generally, but he saved his worst contempt for officers. Officers gave orders for an execution, an interrogation, the destruction of a peaceful village. He knew they, too, took orders, from civilians in the government and private enterprise, but they allowed themselves to stand as symbols of the military.

The young man dealt with them accordingly. Whenever possible he cut them down on sight.

Tonight he chose to watch and wait before he made his move. The first canoe glided past him, making for the falls, and soldiers sprayed a scattering of rifle shots, without effect, before their leader called them off.

The officer would be listening by now, the young man thought, attempting to interpret unfamiliar sounds. The rumble of the waterfall would puzzle him at first, then panic him as recognition struck. Would he be quick enough to save himself? The men of his command?

Secure in his hiding place, the young man eased the safety off his AK-47, sliding one scarred finger through the trigger guard. It would be simple, at this range, to rake the soldiers with a tracking burst and kill them where they sat, or sink their boats and pot them as the current whisked them off downstream.

But he held his fire, content to see what happened next. There would be time for killing later if the river failed to do its job.

The first boatload of uniforms was past him now, the second closing fast. He saw the officer as clear as day, a ferret of a man with pencil-thin mustache and sunken cheeks, his face made laughable by sudden fear. The bastard *knew*, and knowing didn't help him in the least.

An order to the paddlers, and they started paddling for shore, the young man's side, this time. The officer was shouting now at his soldiers in the lead canoe, but if they heard him, they made no response. The current had them, and by the time they realized their danger, it might be too late.

He stood and moved slightly out of cover for a better view. The first, unmanned canoe had vanished, and the soldiers closest to it got the message finally. They dug in frantically with paddles that seemed like matchsticks in the rushing tide, successful for an instant in arresting forward motion. But they couldn't seem to turn their craft for shore, and as he watched the current spun them dizzily around, the long boat twirling like a pinwheel, soldiers screaming, thrashing with their paddles.

He watched them go, a final tilting, bodies airborne as the stern tipped skyward, then disappeared. The second boat was having better luck, already gaining on the shore. With a muffled oath, the young man moved to greet them.

Born and raised within the forest, he possessed the skill of traveling in nearly perfect silence through the undergrowth by night or day. They wouldn't hear him coming over the thunder of the falls. It should be easy to surprise them in their present state, and he would need only a moment to complete his task, fulfill his duty.

They had beached their craft some thirty yards downstream, bedraggled scarecrows standing on shore and staring at the falls, incredulous. Their officer had wet himself, a sight that made the young man smile. He loved it when the leaders were revealed in all of their pathetic weakness, standing naked for the world to see.

The young man had a fair idea where they had come from, but it made no difference to him at the moment. They were here, and they were his. He would not let them slip away.

The officer was ordering his small squad into line, their rifles slung, preparing for a long walk through the jungle. They were obviously near exhaustion, but their leader clearly didn't trust the river, memories of near disaster causing him to tremble where he stood. The young man circled for a better angle on his human targets, settling behind a fallen log. He set the selector switch for automatic fire and raised the AK-47 to his shoulder.

His first rounds dropped one private in his tracks, the others breaking randomly for cover. Squeezing off precision bursts, he dropped a second and a third, not caring if they died immediately, only concerned that they were down and out of action.

He saved the officer for last.

The weasel didn't even try to draw his pistol, but sprinted for the safety of the trees without a backward glance or second thought about his men. A burst across the ankles brought him down, all thrashing arms and legs and pleas for mercy.

Standing over him, the young man saw a creature worthy of contempt. The rodent eyes swam into focus, then widened as they saw the AK-47 in the strong, scarred hands. The officer—a colonel—tried to speak. The word came out sounding like a whimper. "Who?"

The young man shook his head. "My name is not important. You are charged with crimes against the people of Colombia. The penalty is death."

"I beg of you—"

A single 7.62 mm full metal jacket round between the eyes cut off the rodent's pitiful entreaty. Moving back along the riverbank, the young man found one of the privates still alive and finished him, as well.

He checked the boat for any sort of traveling supplies, found none and doubled back to strip the colonel of his pistol belt and extra magazines. Three rifles might have been a valuable prize, but he was traveling alone just now, and they would only weigh him down. He tossed them in the river, one by one, and watched them sink.

He thought about the man they'd been chasing, wondered who he was, what his offense had been against the state. From what he had observed, their quarry was a man of skill and courage; he had tricked the soldiers handily, sent four of them to meet their fate beneath the roaring falls.

With skill like that, he could have been a valuable addition to the movement . . . but the young man stopped himself before that train of thought went farther. He wasn't on a recruiting mission, and he should be thankful for the opportunity to kill four soldiers and observe four more in the final moments of their lives. It had been a treat. And he was one short step closer to repaying all he owed the government, the *others*, hidden in the shadows, who controlled the law, the military, the police. Full payment might require a lifetime, but he drew his satisfaction, meanwhile, from collection of the individual installments.

It was all he had.

Aware that he couldn't risk making camp here, the young man gathered up his sparse equipment, shouldered his Kalashnikov and struck off through the forest. He had promises to keep, a rendezvous to make, and he was late already. When his comrades heard what had delayed him, he hoped that they would understand.

And share his pleasure in the kill.

THE EXECUTIONER HAD PUT a slow kilometer behind him when he heard the sounds of muffled gunfire from the general direction of the river. He was curious, but not curious enough to double back and check it out, now that he had successfully eluded his pursuers. Time was of the essence, and he didn't mean to sacrifice his lead.

Still moving, Bolan mulled over solutions to the puzzle. He eliminated signal shots at once. The bursts had been too short and too irregular, the final shots too widely spaced, for anyone to use them as a sound reference in the darkness.

Judging by the report, they had been military weapons, or a single weapon, probably in the possession of the soldiers who had chased him down the river. Once again the question rose to taunt him: Who had been firing, and at what . . . or whom?

A stitch in his side reminded Bolan that he was injured, and he slowed his pace. The compress taped against his side was saturated now, and he took time to change it for another, keeping one hand pressed against the aching wound as he continued, following a forest game trail.

The wound was superficial, really, but the bleeding was a problem. It would stop for a while, then some fresh exertion would begin the flow anew.

Another klick, still bleeding, and the soldier knew what he must do. He stopped and shed his gear, then collected twigs and bark to build a fire, aware of all the risks involved. He had no options; if an enemy sighted his fire and came calling, he would have to cope with that threat in its turn. Just now his life was leaking out by slow degrees, and Bolan had to stop the flow while he had strength enough—and blood enough—to carry on.

He added larger sticks and fallen branches, stoking up the fire until he had a bed of glowing coals. When he was satisfied with the degree of heat that radiated from the fire, he drew the Ka-bar, slipped its blade into the minifurnace and settled back to wait. His mind remained alert, ears straining to identify the forest night sounds.

When at last the blade glowed dull red, Bolan carefully picked up the knife by the handle and applied the metal to the oozing wound. The pain was startling, well remembered from other operations in the field. No matter how he braced himself, initial contact always sent a tremor through his screaming flesh. The smell of cooking meat was ripe and heady in his nostrils.

Finished, satisfied he wouldn't begin to bleed again when he resumed his trek, the soldier cooled his knife by stabbing it repeatedly into the earth. He wiped the warm blade on his camou trousers, sheathed it, then pulled himself erect with the assistance of a handy sapling. Shaky on his feet at first he spent a moment ambling in circles, testing out his legs until his equilibrium was restored.

So far so good. The wound would hurt like hell for days, but he wouldn't bleed to death by slow degrees. If he was careful, took his time, he should have no problem with his scheduled rendezvous.

Twelve miles. No problem.

He covered three before the darkness overtook him in a rush and brought him down.

7

The day began well for Ramona Hernandez. She woke to the first light of dawn feeling rested and fresh, giving thanks that the nightmares, for once, hadn't troubled her sleep. It was rare that she slept through the night, rarer still that she woke feeling that something unique, something new and exciting, might happen.

It was silly of course. Nothing new had occurred in the village for nearly two years. Not since—

Frowning, she cut off the thought at its roots, let it wither and die. There was no point in living the past every day of her life. She could no more change history than she could conjure a miracle out of the rich forest soil.

Village life, for the most part, was strictly routine. Life and death, work and leisure—though free time was a rare commodity, coveted widely, secured by a few. When Carlos was alive, there had been time for love, but in the past two years . . .

That aspect of her life could be resumed, Ramona knew, if she would let Virgilio have his way. Her brother-in-law wasn't unattractive: slim and muscular from working in the fields, with straight dark hair and hazel eyes that sometimes caught her by surprise, reminding her of Carlos, making her feel weak inside. But there were crucial differences, as well.

Virgilio Hernandez didn't have his brother's fire, the sense of outraged justice that had finally taken Carlos to untimely death. Virgilio was capable of compromise on any issue, even when his honor and his manhood were at stake. Where Carlos stood defiantly against injustice, fighting for what was right, his brother bowed and offered thanks for any crumbs that might be tossed his way. It was an attitude that kept Ramona from regarding him as any kind of man.

Unfortunately her reaction didn't stop Virgilio from thinking of her as a woman.

He had lusted for Ramona in the days before she married Carlos, quarreling with his brother in the early days of courtship, later making lame attempts to hide his feelings in the interests of propriety. While Carlos seemed oblivious, Ramona had been conscious of Virgilio observing her with more than casual interest in the three years of her marriage, making up excuses for interminable visits, sometimes even dropping by when Carlos was away from home. Virgilio had never touched her, fearing the reaction of his younger brother and the scandal that would force him into exile, but his very presence had set her teeth on edge.

When Carlos had been killed—no, murdered—it had seemed Virgilio was always at her side, supplying her with extra food or firewood, offering his services for any task, however menial. Initial gratitude was swallowed by revulsion when Ramona saw the way he looked at her, especially when he believed she didn't notice his eyes undressing her and traveling along her curves like filthy hands.

Virgilio had noted her reaction, but hadn't been put off. His confidence was rooted in the fact that he had no real competition in the village. Of the dozen men Ramona's age or older, all except Virgilio were safely married; younger men—those old enough to stir her blood and interest—had a way of disappearing from the village at the first real opportunity, abandoning the rural life with all its rigors to pursue their fortunes in the city.

Not that she could blame them for deserting. Rather, she applauded their initiative, their courage. What had once been home, now felt more like a prison, stifling Ramona with its daily sameness, a monotony that was disrupted only by occasional bad news.

Ramona would have fled, herself, but she possessed no money, had no marketable skills. She would have been a friendless stranger on the streets of Bogotá or Medellín, reduced to begging—or worse—for her daily bread in cold, hostile surroundings. It was better, in the long run, to endure monotony, when loss of self-respect and honor was the sole alternative.

But she would never grant Virgilio his fondest wish, no matter how she longed for Carlos, craved his touch at night . . . or, lately, any time throughout the day. No yearning of the flesh would ever tempt her to debase herself before Virgilio. Above all else, she hated his subservience to their common enemy.

But life went on. Her clapboard house had been erected on the outskirts of the village—Carlos had remarked, a twinkle in his eye, that newlyweds should have their privacy—and she had few visitors. A widow, and especially a woman widowed through an act of violence, was regarded as a jinx of sorts by village wives. She wasn't ostracized or abused, but other women seemed uncomfortable in Ramona's presence. One or two of them had dropped broad hints that she should think about remarrying. While she remained alone, Ramona was a living incarnation of their own worst fears.

The last thing she expected to discover on her morning search for firewood was a man. The path she followed was the same one she had used a hundred times before, collecting twigs and branches the forest had discarded in a bid for growing room. She walked a hundred yards into the forest, following the trail, before she set to work, one eye continuously on the undergrowth around her.

There were jaguars in the forest, vipers lurking in the ferns and drifts of fallen leaves. She knew the forest predators, respected them without experiencing abject fear. A lifetime in the jungle had convinced her that the most vicious animal was man.

This morning her discovery came quite by accident. Ramona was returning to the village, picking up selected sticks and placing them inside a canvas carrier, when her attention was attracted by a rustling in the shrubbery to one side of the trail. Approaching cautiously, a stick of firewood ready in her hand, she nudged the undergrowth aside, prepared to strike or leap away if she was suddenly attacked.

The man lay curled up on his side, knees drawn against his chest. Initially, considering his dress, the weapons he carried, she mistook him for a *federale*, but a second glance dispelled the notion. There were no insignia, his weapons weren't standard issue, and beneath the war paint she could see that he wasn't Hispanic.

An American? If so, what was he doing here?

At first she thought he was merely sleeping, then her eyes took in the crusty bloodstains that had soaked through the fabric beneath one arm. It didn't seem to be a fatal wound—indeed, the man was breathing heavily, as if caught up in some unpleasant dream—but with infection, loss of blood, such things were difficult to say.

Ramona's instinct told her she should flee and alert the people of her village to the presence of an armed and wounded stranger in their midst. It was the only rational response, and yet...

In sleep, the painted face possessed a quality that made Ramona wish she could see the man awake. She sensed a certain strength within him, knew with inexplicable conviction that he wouldn't be her enemy. If she was wrong, Ramona knew the error might cost her life, but she had always been a decent judge of character. She had selected Carlos, after all—and shunned Virgilio. So far her native common sense hadn't betrayed her.

Aware of all the risks involved, she crouched beside the man and gently prodded him awake.

PEDILLA WASN'T ONE to take bad news with grace. When he was balked in any way by his subordinates—a swiftly growing class that now, in Hector's mind, included nearly everyone—he often flew into a rage, lashed out at those around him, sometimes smashing furniture. The tantrums were a throwback to his childhood, but he owned the furniture and those who served him; he was free to treat his chattels as he pleased.

This morning members of the scouting party who returned with news of the disaster on the Yarí River had expected nothing short of pandemonium. The death of Rivas and his soldiers, coupled with the disappearance of four troopers and the quarry, was the kind of bulletin that might have provoked Pedilla to a new plateau of fury. Those who had observed him in the past when minor problems came his way were betting secretly among themselves that Hector would annihilate the scouts and throw their bodies in the forest, food for scavengers that prowled around the compound night and day.

But they were wrong.

He seemed to take the news with equanimity, a stiffening of posture and a tightening of narrow lips the only signs that he was disappointed. It was a miracle, the veterans agreed.

In truth, Pedilla had expected something of the sort, and he had braced himself for the inevitable news of a disaster almost from the moment Rivas led his soldiers out of camp. It had been obvious to Hector—obvious to anyone with eyes—that their assailants were professionals, with combat skills refined through frequent use. The raiders had no more in common with Orlando Rivas and his *federales* than a tiger had in common with a weasel.

Still, when witnesses insisted the raid had been conducted by one man alone, Pedilla had allowed himself to hope, however briefly, that the colonel might succeed. In vain, he had imagined that superiority of numbers could compensate for the ineptitude of Rivas and his men.

So much for miracles.

The scouts hadn't returned with Rivas's remains. They had returned with Polaroids of four dead soldiers, obviously cut down in their tracks by automatic weapon fire. The colonel's pistol belt and the soldiers' rifles were missing.

Four dead, four missing—and survivors of the sweep reported that the chase team had been using two canoes. His scouts reported that the shooting had occurred some fifty yards upstream from a prodigious waterfall, and only one canoe had come ashore. Pedilla thought he understood the workings of the trap, and he was properly impressed. His enemies were clever—certainly too clever for the likes of Rivas—and he wondered if they might come back to finish what they had begun.

One man. Pedilla was disturbed by the persistence of the rumor, angered by the fact that he could offer no substantial argument in contradiction. He wouldn't have thought a single man could wreak such havoc and escape unscathed, but neither could a fighting team dismantle weapons and obliterate all traces of themselves within the time it took for Rivas and his soldiers to retaliate in force.

Pedilla paced his study, pausing now and then to scan the smoking ruins of his lab and warehouse complex through a window. If a single man could do all that, elude pursuit through darkness in the jungle and destroy the chase team that pursued him, he would truly be a formidable enemy. An enemy worth more attention than the average peasant or guerrilla.

He was well acquainted with professional assassins, knew their names and capabilities, the prices they charged. At one time or another he had dealt with mercenaries, terrorists, fanatics brooding over causes that were clear to them and to no one else on earth, but he was confident that he had never met a man of such ability. A group of them together, possibly, but one man, serving as a solitary fighting unit? Never.

That left Pedilla with a narrow range of possibilities. A new, incredibly professional assassin might be hiring out his services selectively, or else his enemy had been dispatched from some official governmental source.

He jettisoned the first idea immediately. His intelligence-collecting network was superb, and the arrival of a major hit man in the country would have reached his ears before the object of his interest got through customs. On the other hand, who had the raw material and the ability to field a one-man army of such capabilities? Pedilla instantly dismissed the governments of Colombia and her several neighbors. None of them could manage to eradicate the unarmed Indians within their borders, and their "crack commando units" were a sorry joke. Such skill was the result of arduous instruction, and combat experience, with superior equipment to support the soldiers.

Pedilla had done nothing to upset Fidel, his Russian patrons or their numerous "advisers" in Managua. If the Communists were after him, he thought, they would have waited for a personal appearance on the streets of Bogotá or Medellín and gunned him down in style.

What government, then? The United States? Great Britain? Canada? France?

He dealt cocaine and other contraband in all those countries, reaping tax-free millions for himself, but they were law-abiding nations, bound by treaties and conventions to respect the sovereignty of smaller countries. They might try to extradite him—there were warrants pending in Miami even now—but would they attempt assassination?

Certainly the British and Americans had people who were capable enough. The SAS had proved itself in tighter situations, and the States could field a wide variety of SEALs and Rangers, Green and Black Berets. The CIA might even try its hand . . . except its hands were dirty at the moment.

Hector shook his head, still pacing. Covert operations in the eighties lacked the flair of ten or fifteen years ago. The Russians and their puppets were the only ones now who freely used assassination, and any raid conducted by the British or Americans on foreign soil invited public scrutiny that might do damage to their ruling power structure.

Someone private, then, supported by the British or Americans.

His mind was blank. The weary roll call of professional assassins was complete, and he was staring at a cold brick wall.

He didn't require descriptions, date of birth and blood type for his enemy. He would announce a general alert for any strangers in the province, and expand that bulletin to Bogotá and Medellín, if need be. With his contacts in customs and passport control, he could shut down the airports on two hours' notice, grill every damned Yankee in sight before embassy lawyers horned in on the show.

Such a blatant display might bring heat in reaction, but Hector was willing to risk it, as a last resort. Meanwhile, barring acts of God or access to an aircraft, his assailant must be in Caquetá Province, trudging through the jungle in an effort to escape the coming storm.

Too late.

A single call would close the province's borders, sealing every road and track. There was the jungle, yet, and Hector's enemy had proved himself extremely capable of traveling by night or day, but he couldn't outrun an army. By the time Pedilla finished mobilizing peasants, *federales*, trackers from the local forest tribes, his adversary would have nowhere left to turn.

The government would have a stake in seeing justice done, with Rivas and his soldiers lying dead beside the river. Later, if he had the time, Pedilla thought he might send out a party to retrieve their bodies—but why bother? Rivas was a failure who had perished as he had lived—without a trace of dignity or honor. Let the army waste time hauling carrion; Pedilla's troops had more important things to do.

Like clearing off the rubble from the compound and beginning rapid reconstruction of the cocaine lab and his warehouse complex. While the plant was out of operation, he was out of business, street supplies diminishing with every sale in Bogotá, Miami, New York or Los Angeles.

How long could he supply the needs of countless addicts while his laboratory lay in smoking ruins? One day? Two or three at most? Before the week was out his secret stockpiles would be empty, drained, and every moment he remained inactive gave his competitors an opportunity to reach out for customers who might prefer Pedilla's merchandise but were agreeable to any source in time of need. And once those contacts were established, once his customers had turned away in disappointment, how would he regain supremacy?

Pedilla shook himself and grabbed the telephone. The line was dead, and he remembered the explosions that had shattered both the generator and communications shacks. The CB units mounted in some of the vehicles downstairs would never reach Florencia across a hundred miles of jungle. For the moment, Pedilla was isolated from the outside world.

A runner, then. He would dispatch a message to Florencia and let his people make their calls from there. He could have all the necessary lab equipment on its way from Medellín tomorrow morning, with delivery at the compound by evening if they pushed it. In the meantime he could organize a work detail and get construction started on a new facility to house the operation.

Materials weren't the problem. Hector had been looking toward expansion, and he'd collected most of the equipment in advance. He would be short of workers, though; the barracks blast had seen to that.

He counted twenty-seven corpses under camou tarps, lined up beside the smoking ashes of the Quonset huts. There would be others, in all probability, but even twenty-seven left him badly understaffed. There were perimeters to guard, patrols to mount, a search to be conducted in the forest—and he had to launch construction on the new facility without delay.

A hundred extra men wouldn't have been too many, and instead, he might wind up as much as forty short. Without a fresh supply of able hands, he had no hope of meeting his imaginary deadline. Hector needed workers, but he dared not call his soldiers off from combat readiness.

As always, there was a solution, and Pedilla smiled at its simplicity. He was embarrassed that he hadn't thought of it before.

MACK BOLAN STIRRED, the sounds and smells of food preparation bringing him around. It took a moment to remember where he was, and even then he slid a hand across the floor and sleeping pallet to confirm his gear and weapons were securely in their place. That done, he settled back to watch the woman cook.

She had discovered him, unconscious, in the forest; Bolan knew that much. He had reacted to her touch instinctively, recoiling out of sleep, a pistol in his hand before his conscious mind had recognized the need for self-defense. She had been frightened, momentarily, but had recovered in an instant, and he gave her points for courage under stress.

The walk back to her hut had been a hazy fever dream in Bolan's mind. His side had throbbed in rhythm with his footsteps, and his forehead had been on fire. He'd kept one arm around the woman's shoulders to support himself, and had found it vaguely pleasant. She had promised him that the people of her village would be unlikely to come calling unannounced.

She'd helped him shed his harness and the pistol belt, arranging them to Bolan's satisfaction, with his rifle placed in a corner of the small hut's single room. She'd checked his wound, applied a homemade salve and changed the dressing. When his Spanish had failed, she'd spoken to him in English.

He knew her name—Ramona—and he knew she lived alone. The rich aromas now filling Bolan's nostrils told him she could cook, eliciting a rumble from his stomach in response. He spent another moment watching her and then began to take stock of himself.

Still weary, Bolan had regained a measure of his energy. Two hours, at most, had passed since she discovered him and brought him home, but in the meantime he had lost the fever and queasy feeling that had sapped his strength. The wound in his side still ached, but it no longer felt as if a red-hot blade was probing there.

He knew he could travel, felt an urge to rise and leave at once, but hunger held him back. If any further cautionary word was needed, Bolan told himself he couldn't risk leaving in the daylight, when he might be spotted by Ramona's neighbors in the village.

Even so, each moment spent beneath her roof brought danger to them all. Pedilla would be hunting him by now, beyond all doubt, and while the Executioner was shaky on the details of his present whereabouts, he knew the village must lie well within Pedilla's sphere of influence. He hadn't traveled far enough, by any means, to shake the jackals off.

His presence in the village, in Ramona's home, was a destructive time bomb, ticking down to doomsday. Assuming he could trust the woman—and there had been ample opportunity for her to sell him out by now—he still couldn't assume she was capable of coping with surprise patrols, interrogation by Pedilla's troops. He had no right, in any case, to put her through that living hell. The soldier made up his mind to depart as soon as possible—by nightfall at the latest—and allow her to resume her life in peace.

It was the least he could do in payment for her kindness. Meanwhile he would do his best to keep them both alive.

8

Virgilio Hernandez straightened gingerly to ease the aching muscles in his back. He'd been chopping weeds for what seemed hours now without a break, and though the morning breeze was cool, he still had beads of perspiration on his face. Leaning on the handle of his hoe, he watched the others moving in a ragged line across the field, and once again his thoughts were with Ramona.

There were some—a very few, and they his closest friends—who said he thought of nothing else. The joking statement was inaccurate, of course, but as a measure of Virgilio's obsession with his late brother's wife, it was a close approximation of the truth.

Hernandez dealt with all the day-to-day details of life, he worked and earned a living for himself, but when his thoughts had time to stray from mundane pursuits, they always centered on Ramona. Or his brother.

Carlos had been younger, by a year, which put him closer to Ramona's age, and though Virgilio could understand their mutual attraction, it had still been embarrassing to have the baby of the family marry first. And if that slight wasn't enough, Carlos had settled on the very woman who had stunned Virgilio and claimed his heart the day they'd met.

Of course Ramona had done nothing to encourage the attention of Virgilio Hernandez. He had been attracted by her beauty, like a moth by flame, but he was slow to speak his mind, intimidated by the depth of his emotion. Carlos had been quicker and more confident, his personality and easy patter serving as a bridge that he could cross to steal Ramona's love. As for Virgilio, who loved his younger brother with the fierce devotion of a parent once removed, he had made himself a promise that he wouldn't interfere.

There had been times, of course, when he couldn't prevent himself from staring at Ramona, lingering around his brother's house, sometimes inventing errands that would take him there when Carlos was away. Virgilio had never touched Ramona, never voiced his innermost desire, but there were moments when he thought she knew and understood. Those moments were the worst of all, because her eyes had shown him he couldn't expect her to respond in kind.

He recognized her loyalty as a wife, admired her for it, but subconsciously, within the dark recesses of his mind, Virgilio had come to wish that Carlos didn't stand between them. If Ramona had been alone, he'd thought, without commitments to another man, she would have reciprocated his feelings, made his dreams come true each night in bed.

Carlos was gone now, and the past two years had taught Virgilio his error. Even after Carlos died, when the obligatory year of mourning had elapsed, Ramona still showed no romantic interest in her dear late husband's brother. It appeared to make no difference that the village was devoid of eligible bachelors. Married men, or boys, were scarcely worthy competition for Virgilio Hernandez... but the god of love refused to smile upon his face.

He knew Ramona didn't have another man outside the village. On the rare occasions when she traveled to Florencia with others, he contrived to tag along on this or that fabricated errand, maintaining a discreet surveillance of her movements there. He was gratified to see she spoke with no one on the street, kept no clandestine rendezvous, met no one on the sly. She simply did her shopping, bundled up her purchases and traveled home again.

And she ignored Virgilio whenever possible, as if he were a stone or stick.

Sometimes, in a masochistic effort to arouse himself, he wondered if her sex life with Carlos had been so fantastic that Ramona had no need of other men. Could she be satisfied for life, or merely stricken by the loss of one whose talents she deemed irreplaceable?

He often pictured them together, naked, making love, and suffered in the knowledge of their pleasure like a lover scorned. More frequently, of late, he took the place of Carlos in those fantasies, his own skills overpowering Ramona, sweeping her away.

This morning he had seen her briefly as she carried back a load of firewood from the forest. Usually reserved, defensive, this time she had shown him frank suspicion. He wondered if she might have sensed his impatience, his resolve to share her bed. Virgilio believed that women possessed strange gifts of nature that their mates could never share. They seemed to know when death was coming to the village, and his mother—God preserve her soul—had several times predicted whom the Reaper would select to join his congregation. Women could detect the early warning signs of love, or lust, before men recognized those feelings in themselves.

It didn't surprise him, therefore, to discover that Ramona recognized his feelings; he would have been startled if she hadn't. What disturbed Virgilio was her reaction to them—bland, lack of interest, tinged more recently with traces of contempt.

But he would teach her. One day soon Virgilio would force Ramona to accept the love that only he could give. If necessary, he might even let her know the truth about her husband's death. She might despise him all the more, at first, but she would realize in time that he had saved the village.

And his sacrifice had been no less than hers.

A brother and a husband lost. No words could fill the gap Carlos left behind, but wife and brother could still hold each other, seek a relief from pain in mutual enjoyment. One day they might even manage to forget. Together.

Virgilio was smiling as he set to work again. Ramona would be his no matter what she thought about him at the moment. He could feel it, with a certainty that tolerated no denial.

She would be his for the taking. Soon.

THE BREAKFAST was delicious. Bolan ate a double helping of the eggs and thick, fresh bacon while Ramona watched him, barely picking at her food. She passed the time with small talk and vignettes of village life until he finished, the plates were cleared away and fresh coffee was poured. Within an hour, Bolan felt he'd been adequately briefed on the inhabitants and background of the settlement.

For openers the village had no name. At one time, years before, one of the leading families had tried to christen it El Corazón—the Heart—but they had been defeated by a public vote of seventeen to six. Since no alternative was suggested, then or later, people of the village and surrounding forest had continued their daily business, content to leave their settlement anonymous. They knew precisely where it was; they knew one another. What more did they need?

Before he finished breakfast, Bolan learned that the men and boys—eighteen in all—were working the communal fields that fed their village. Decent land for cultivation was a rare commodity in that part of Caquetá Province, where the jungle clung tenaciously to every foot of soil, every hillside. It had taken all one spring to clear the fifty acres they farmed, long years of constant work to hold back the forest. Ramona's people weren't socialists—indeed, if she was an example, they were totally indifferent to politics—but it didn't require a genius to determine that division of the hard-earned land, its meager produce, would inevitably hurt them all.

And so they worked the land together, men and boys responsible for plowing and cultivation, while the girls and women did their share with planting and at harvest time. It was a system that had served them well for years, and no one showed an inclination to "improve" it now. They were apparently content with life, as with their nameless village, willing to continue on the timeless path their ancestors had trodden.

Their lives were relatively free from interference by the outside world. The villagers paid taxes to the government in Bogotá, but there had been no major local crime in living memory, and so they had no contact with the police or the courts. Conscription to the military hadn't touched the young men of the village lately, since they tended to seek their fortunes in the city on attaining their majority. If life within the nameless settlement was static, even stale, at least it had the added benefit of being reasonably safe.

Until the *narcotraficantes* came.

He recognized the style. A pair of scouts with money in their pockets, pistols on their hips, had turned up in the village on a Sunday afternoon to look for able-bodied men. They had unspecified construction work in progress, and they needed laborers. The pay they offered wasn't much, but it was more than any young man of the village stood to earn while working the communal fields.

The elders had discussed the offer, and they had declined it. There was something in the bearing of their visitors, an aura that they emitted like some low-grade radiation, warning anyone who met them of impending danger. They had taken the refusal with a smile, a shrug, and they had gone away.

Until the next morning, when their jeep was followed by an army surplus truck with riflemen in the back. This time there would be no negotiation, no discussion of the daily wage. The gunmen had collected what they'd come for, taking every boy twelve or older and all men less than the age of sixty-five.

All men but one.

"My husband was a stubborn man," Ramona said. "A proud man. He would not submit. He fought them, and they killed him in the street . . . out there."

The soldier didn't offer his condolences. This lady had already come to terms with pain and loss. He waited, giving her an audience.

"The other men and boys were gone six days. When they returned, they had no money, nothing for their labor. We found out they had been used to build a warehouse and a laboratory for the *narcotraficantes*."

Bolan could have told her that their work had been destroyed, but he didn't want to interrupt her while she felt like talking. For the moment, he was content to watch her face and listen to her voice.

"We have had no trouble with them since," she told him. "I believe that we were fortunate. In other villages there have been many deaths."

"And the police?"

"I traveled to Florencia and spoke with officers who promised to investigate. A few weeks later we were told the killers of my husband were identified as Communist guerrillas. It was then a matter for the army."

"And the army took no action?"

Putting on a bitter smile, Ramona shook her head. "The army, in Caquetá Province, is a tool the *narcotraficantes* use when they are tired of killing people for themselves. The officers receive two paychecks—one from Bogotá, and one from smugglers who tell them when to look the other way."

He couldn't argue with the lady, having seen the system work firsthand, but Bolan clung to the hope that she was overstating the extent of general corruption in the military. If the rot was so pervasive that it spread from top to bottom, he was dealing with a hopeless situation.

"The men who shot you . . ."

"Soldiers," Bolan answered. "Smugglers."

Ramona nodded. "So you understand. You are American?"

"By birth. My business here is, let's say, unofficial."

Frowning, she refilled their coffee cups. "Your government is interested in cutting off the drug trade?"

"Very much so."

"But you take no action."

"Washington gets nervous when you talk about invading other countries. Fifty, sixty years ago, it might have been all right. Today we wait for invitations, and we've tried that once already."

"Yes, we heard about your 'military mission.' I believe it was unsuccessful."

"You could say that, yeah."

"What brings you to Caquetá Province, Señor . . ."

"Blanski. Mike. You might say I'm a bill collector."

"I am afraid I do not understand."

He shrugged, rewarded for the effort by a stabbing pain beneath his arm. "You've got some animals out there who've run up quite a tab in human misery. Aside from victims like your husband here at home, they've murdered thousands and addicted thousands more in the United States and Europe. They've been operating free of interference too damned long. It's payback time."

"You kill them?"

Bolan nodded. "When I can. I didn't do so well last night."

"About last night," she said. "Your enemy . . ."

"A dealer named Pedilla."

"Yes." Her lips were tight. "I know the name."

"Your husband?" Bolan thought he knew the answer, but he had to ask the question anyway.

"Pedilla's men. I buried him alone. The men and boys were gone. The other women were . . . afraid."

"Why do you stay?"

"This is my home. I have no money for an apartment in the city, and no training for employment. Here I work the land and not the streets."

"Why did you take me in?"

His question seemed to catch her by surprise. She studied Bolan for a moment, then gave a little shrug. "You needed help."

"I could have been an enemy."

Ramona shook her head. "I know my enemies. Besides, I saw that you were American."

"That doesn't guarantee a kindly disposition."

"I have learned to trust my judgment in these matters."

"Well . . . I owe you one."

"If you have harmed Pedilla, then your debt is paid."

"I may have slowed him down a little, but he's still in business."

"Never mind. If you had killed him, there would simply be another after him. We have been cursed with coca in Colombia. The plant that makes our leaders and the *narcotraficantes* wealthy men condemns us all."

"It doesn't have to be that way," he told her earnestly.

"Should we create a revolution, Señor Blanski? There are fewer than thirty of us in the village, most of those too young or old to fight. What difference can we make, when fighting men with guns are being slaughtered by the hundreds?"

"You can take a stand. Resist."

"My husband took a stand against Pedilla. He is dead, and now I am alone." She stared at Bolan for another moment, and her voice was softer when she spoke again.

"There are men who believe as you do, that the *narcotrafi-cantes* and their running dogs must be destroyed."

"What men?"

"Guerrillas. Victims of *la violencia* who fight back for themselves."

"I see."

She caught his tone and smiled. "They are not revolutionaries, *señor*...at least not yet. The fat men up in Bogotá would tell you they are radicals and Communists—and some may be—but there are others also."

Bolan played a hunch. "You know such men?"

"A few. They pass this way occasionally."

"Can you get in touch with them if necessary?"

"It is difficult. Their camps are secret. They move frequently. The government has prices on their heads."

"But if you tried—"

Ramona shrugged and he was conscious of the way her breasts moved under the simple peasant blouse. "It might be possible."

"If I could speak to them..."

"I doubt they have the strength to move against Pedilla's compound."

"I've already tried that." Bolan knew his time was growing short. He had a date with Jack Grimaldi and he meant to keep it, but if there was any chance of salvaging his mission, striking one more solid blow against Pedilla... "I had something else in mind."

"I will see what I can do."

"How soon?"

"Tomorrow, perhaps the next day."

"And tonight?"

"You must stay here. I cannot have my patient sleeping in the forest."

"Doctor's orders?"

"*Sí.*"

"Your neighbors—"

"Will not bother us," she finished for him. "Not un-less—"

"A problem?"

"It is nothing. Rest now. I have work to do."

When she was gone, he lay back on the pallet, cradling his head on one bent arm. He thought about the woman, recognized the risk she was taking, and offered up a silent plea that nothing would go wrong.

He hoped the universe was listening. He didn't want this woman's blood on his hands.

RAMONA DID HER WASHING with the other women of the village at a spring located fifty yards outside the settlement. The spring arose from solid rock and formed a pool where deer and other forest creatures sometimes came to drink. The stones along one bank were smooth due to the tons of laundry that had been pummeled on their surface over several generations. In a village that had no electric power, it was still the most efficient means of washing clothes.

She saw three other women at the pool and considered turning back, but finally decided to proceed. The others raised their eyes at her approach and nodded silent greetings.

Still a threat, she thought. *I still remind them of the killing.*

She dismissed the thought and concentrated on the task ahead of her. Concealing the American wasn't a problem, since the other villagers took pains to guarantee Ramona's solitude. The only difficulty she foresaw might be an unexpected visit from Virgilio. He'd been dropping by more frequently of late, inventing duties for himself, and so far she hadn't been able to devise a foolproof means of keeping him away. If he came by her house tonight . . .

Ramona shrugged. She would take care of that eventuality when it arose. Meanwhile she had another problem on her hands, more urgent that the possibility of an unscheduled visit from Virgilio.

She had to get in touch with the guerrillas, and it had to be tonight. The tall American was restless, nearly well enough to travel on his own. Ramona knew he wouldn't wait indefinitely while she tried to reach her contact in the underground.

Her contact.

It was strange to think of Jaime in such terms. He was a young man, barely twenty, but he had already seen and done so much that he seemed vastly older, more experienced than one his age had any right to be. Their meeting had occurred a short time after Carlos was murdered. Jaime had been told, somehow, about her visit to Florencia, her talk with the authorities, and he'd known instinctively that she would help him if he asked. They shared a common sense of loss, the pain of loved ones murdered by the *narcotraficantes*, and she hadn't hesitated when he asked her to become his eyes and ears inside the village.

There was little she could do, in concrete terms, to help the armed resistance movement. Any news that reached her village was invariably out-of-date, a week or more behind the times, but she provided Jaime with whatever help she could. On two or three occasions she had sheltered members of his band as she was sheltering the American today, and no one in her village was the wiser.

Sometimes, she decided, ostracism had its advantages.

For all of that, approaching Jaime's group wasn't a simple matter. They had no fixed base of operations, and they traveled widely, striking at the army when and where they found an opening. They seldom left Caquetá Province, but Ramona couldn't cover every trail and village by herself, inquiring after Jaime like a jealous wife gone looking for her husband.

Husband. Memories of Carlos pierced her heart and brought tears to Ramona's eyes. She kept her head down, concentrating on her laundry as she waited for the sudden dizziness to pass, determined that the other women not notice anything peculiar in her attitude or her behavior. She was rinsing out a cotton skirt when she decided on the course of action she must take.

Outside the village, living on their own with minimal connections to the settlement, a family named Ochoa owned a hut and a tiny plot of land. Their sympathy for the guerrillas was well-known, though never spoken of aloud. More to the point, the oldest son, Miguel, had what the Yankees might have called a crush on Ramona. On their past few brief encounters, she had caught him staring at her, blushing when she caught him at it, smiling sheepishly. What if she approached Miguel and asked him nicely?

It was worth a try, at least. He might know how to get in touch with Jaime and the others. If he did, and if he agreed to help her, there might still be time to help the American complete his task.

She had no firm conception of his mission, nor was she concerned with details. For the moment, any move against Pedilla's operation was a victory of sorts. Ramona pledged herself to help the American if she could, and never mind the danger to herself.

The rest of the village was another matter, but she didn't think her actions on behalf of the man called Blanski would jeopardize her neighbors. They lived in peril every day, regardless, with the *narcotraficantes* close at hand. Whatever she might do to end Pedilla's reign of terror would ultimately benefit the men and women who had chosen to regard her as a walking memory of death.

And if she failed? What did she really have to lose? Her life, of course.

And what was that? Not much these days.

Her mind made up, Ramona concentrated on her laundry, hurrying to finish. She would have to catch Miguel before he left home for the day to hunt or pass the daylight hours lazing in some forest hideaway. She counted on his shyness, hoping he wouldn't demand a price for his cooperation, but she was prepared to pay in any case.

Pedilla, and his ultimate destruction, took priority. Her modesty and reputation were nothing in comparison.

She thought that her beloved Carlos would have understood.

9

Discovery of an intruder sent a ripple through the paramilitary camp. A runner brought the word, and twenty minutes later, sentries marched a slender boy into the firelight. Waiting near the jungle lean-to that saw double service as his field CP and sleeping quarters, Jaime Vargas rose to greet the new arrival.

He had known Miguel Ochoa for approximately eighteen months. The family had sheltered members of his small band in the past, and the Ochoas could be counted on for help whenever Jaime's people needed their assistance. Too young for fighting when they met, Miguel had grown throughout the months of their association. Jaime thought he might soon be fit to take an active role in the enduring struggle.

Today, however, he was merely bearing information. Jaime greeted him with warmth and tried to put the boy at ease, surrounded as he was by men with weapons.

"So, Miguel, you told the sentries that you have a message from Ramona?"

"*Sí.*" Miguel glanced nervously at the armed guards who stood on either side of him. "She told me I should give the message to you, personally."

"Here I am," Jaime said. "You may speak before these men in perfect security. They are my brothers."

The two gunners smiled, but Miguel remained hesitant. "Well—"

Jaime frowned. "You insult me by doubting my judgment, Miguel. If you have words to say, let me hear them."

"As you wish." The young man tried to choose his words carefully. "You are invited to visit Ramona and speak with a guest in her home."

Jaime smiled at the notion, Miguel's choice of phrasing. "A social call? Sadly I have no free time."

"An American soldier," Ochoa informed him, his voice coming out as a whisper now. "Injured, but healing. Ramona believes you have something in common."

"Such as?"

"Your opinion of Hector Pedilla."

The dealer's name wiped Jaime's smile from his face. One scarred hand gripped Miguel by the shoulder and pulled him in close. Jaime smelled the boy's fear and did nothing to calm him. "Explain yourself."

"I . . . I was told nothing more," Miguel whimpered, and Jaime decided he wasn't soldier material yet. "Nothing."

"I'm fond of your family, Miguel. If you're lying . . . well, let us say I will regret what my duty compels me to do."

"I deliver the message, no more and no less."

"Very well. And this message came when?"

"Just this morning. Ramona insisted I find you at once."

"Do your parents know where you have gone?"

Miguel glanced left and right at his guards, then shook his head. "They suppose I am hunting."

"Of course." Jaime smiled. "But your mother expects you at home for siesta?"

Miguel saw his chance, nodding rapidly. "*Sí.* She might worry if I am delayed."

"We must not let her worry. My brothers—" he smiled at the sentries "—will see that you get home safely. They may spend some time with your family while I go see this American soldier. If all is in order . . ."

His meaning was clear, and he didn't belabor the point. Miguel knew that his life and the lives of his family were riding on Jaime's blind date with a man neither one of them knew. If Ramona had made a mistake, been deceived by Pedilla or one of his cronies, the outcome might well be disastrous.

"My family is loyal to your cause," Miguel said, his tone pleading.

"I know that. If there was a doubt in my mind, you would not be alive. As it is, I am sure you will understand why I must take every precaution. The world is a treacherous place these days."

He didn't doubt the boy's dedication, the family's loyalty, but traitors were everywhere, posing as patriots, men of respect. You couldn't always tell who your friends were, and in war one mistake could be fatal.

He trusted Ramona Hernandez, had learned of her loss before making first contact himself, but in spite of her personal loyalty he knew that she might be deceived. This American—if he was truly American—might be an agent dispatched by Pedilla to infiltrate Jaime's guerrilla band, shatter the troop from within. There was always that chance.

But he owed her the effort, at least. He would take every possible step to ensure that no trap had been laid for himself and his men. He would stake out the village, stand ready to fight at the first sign of ambush. But he couldn't simply ignore the request from Ramona. He owed her too much.

When his family and neighbors were slaughtered on orders from Hector Pedilla, Ramona Hernandez had found Jaime roaming the forest, half-dead from exposure and hunger, his mind balanced delicately on the fine edge of madness. Her heart had gone out to him, and she'd taken him in, nursed him back to a semblance of health. She had sheltered him, put him in touch with a few other boys and young men like himself, the beginnings of what Jaime now called his army.

Their mission, quite simply, was total destruction of Hector Pedilla, his allies and stooges, including the soldiers who sullied their oath of allegiance by working for murderers, smugglers and thieves. He'd killed four such rodents last night, and the incident merged in his mind with Ramona's report, giving Jaime another good reason to trust in her judgment.

Coincidence? Possibly. Still...Jaime thought of the chase he had witnessed, the tall man who had scrambled ashore while the soldiers had swept past him toward death and the falls. It was possible, Jaime supposed, that the man had been wounded in flight, though he hadn't displayed any visible weakness. Escaping westward on foot, he might well have encountered Ramona, as Jaime himself had once done—and it would have been like her to take the man in.

Jaime's mind was made up. He would send two men back with Ochoa this evening. Tomorrow, with plenty of guns at his back, he would visit Ramona and meet the American soldier whose life she had saved. They would talk, and if Jaime was satisfied by what he heard, they might join hands to punish Pedilla for all he had done.

Jaime flexed his scarred hands, warming up to the prospect. How long he had waited to strike at the heart of his enemy's world. And how weary he was of quick raids on the outskirts, brief clashes with soldiers and smugglers whose death meant no more to Pedilla than dust in the wind.

It was time for the dealer to learn that he wasn't immortal. If wounded, Pedilla would suffer and bleed like the lowest of peasants. His money and arrogant pride wouldn't save him this time.

Jaime Vargas was anxious to get one more look at the dark man. This time, when they met, only one would survive.

VIRGILIO HERNANDEZ SCRUBBED his face and hands until they tingled, drying off with brisk, impatient strokes of a threadbare towel. His hair was standing up in spikes, and he combed it flat against his skull, taking several moments to experiment with the part before he was satisfied.

There wasn't much he could do about his clothes. Ramona had seen every stitch of clothing he owned, and it was no good trying to impress her with a fancy getup. Thinking of Ramona in conjunction with his tiny wardrobe made him wish she could see him naked. Maybe then she might be willing to consider him more seriously, break her vow of chastity.

Virgilio had once seen Ramona naked. Aware that she was bathing in a stream, he had concealed himself to spy upon her, studying her almost clinically for what seemed like hours. Other women had been with her, and Virgilio had seen them all, all naked, but he'd been fascinated only by Ramona. Every move she'd made was fluid grace personified, but she had belonged to Carlos, and the tears that filled his eyes had owed as much to rage as guilt or longing.

Now Ramona was alone, but Carlos still remained between them. When he pondered various solutions to his plight, Virgilio occasionally tried to put himself inside Ramona's brain. He understood—or thought he understood—at least a part of her resistance to his obvious desire. For her, relations with the brother of her dear, departed husband would be incest, once removed. She couldn't see Virgilio without recalling thoughts of Carlos, and if they were lovers, she might feel that she was cheating on his memory each time they went to bed.

This made sense to Virgilio, but it didn't provide him with an answer to his problem. He couldn't change his identity, but if he tried his best, perhaps he might eventually change Ramona's mind.

And there was no time like the present to begin.

When he was reasonably satisfied with his appearance, and after he had practiced several different smiles, Virgilio set off to see Ramona. He didn't lock the door of the small frame house where he had lived alone for seven years. In fact, it had no lock, but he wasn't concerned about thieves. The villagers looked out for one another, and the last young man with sticky fingers, caught red-handed in the act some eighteen months before, had been so soundly beaten by his father in the village square that he was forced to stay inside and hide his battered face for more than a week. It was the kind of lesson that impressed the young and kept them out of trouble.

Moving past the other houses toward Ramona's on the outskirts of the village, he was conscious of a growing nervousness, the kind of sexual excitement he imagined was experienced most often by a generation younger than his own. Ramona did that to him still, although she seemed to have no inkling of her power. On the street, in casual conversation, she appeared completely ignorant of the effect her very presence had upon Virgilio.

Tonight, he thought, might be the perfect time to tell her. Guile had failed him up to now; perhaps sincerity was called for. It wouldn't destroy him if he had to bare his soul, and in the end he might find it was worth the effort.

This would be a social call and nothing more—unless he was presented with an unexpected golden opportunity. He wasn't bearing gifts. That, he believed, would be too obvious. But he intended to declare himself…if only he could find the nerve.

Ramona's house, he saw, needed a few repairs. Perhaps he should visit more often, working there, spending time where she couldn't avoid the odd, coincidental contact.

Standing at her door, Virgilio at once forgot the little speech he had memorized. Determined to proceed despite his mental block, he rapped on the wooden door with heavy knuckles, squaring his shoulders as he waited, putting on a smile so wide that he thought his face might crack.

Ramona didn't seem so much surprised to see him as annoyed. He felt his smile begin to slip and saved it only with an effort. She was cooking—he could smell the spices—and he hoped she might invite him in.

Instead, she speared him with a glance and asked, "What is it?"

He began to stammer, caught himself and said, "I see that you could use some work around the house. This siding here . . . the window frames. I thought . . ."

"I've been too busy. I'll take care of everything when I have time."

"You shouldn't have to do it by yourself. I mean, if I can be of any help . . ."

Her smile had more in common with a grimace, cutting to the soft meat of his ego. "No, that won't be necessary. I appreciate your offer, but I like to do these things myself."

"You work too hard."

"We all work hard, Virgilio."

"I'm sorry if I interrupted dinner." He could do no more in terms of asking for an invitation. Begging was beneath his dignity.

"I've only started, but I should get back to work."

"Of course." He made a final, desperate bid. "If you have any need for me at all—"

Her eyes frosted over. "Thank you. I'll remember that. Good night."

The door closed in his face, and he could feel his cheeks on fire. His teeth were clenched so tightly that they ached. At first Virgilio's anger focused on himself, his mind replaying every nuance of their conversation, taking him to task for clumsiness, timidity. A real man would have told Ramona how he felt, perhaps reached out to take her in his arms without awaiting invitations.

But, no.

Returning to his one-room house, he felt his anger change by slow degrees, acquiring different form, a new direction, as it focused on the one who was, in fact, to blame for his humiliation.

Carlos.

It was Carlos's fault that Ramona wouldn't give Virgilio a chance to prove himself. Except for Carlos, she would almost certainly have yielded to his manly charms. How else could she resist, except by clinging to a ghost?

He hated Carlos in that instant, felt the guilty aftershocks of his disloyalty preparing to assault his mind, his soul. But at the moment rage and lust were stronger, louder, than his conscience.

Suddenly Virgilio was thankful for his brother's death. In time, he thought he might discover how to slay a ghost.

RAMONA FELT Bolan's eyes on her as he left the huddled corner, moving toward his pallet. *His* place. It was strange the way she had already started thinking of him as a fixture, something *in* her life instead of merely passing *through*. She realized it was a serious mistake and forced herself to concentrate on her cooking as she spoke.

"Virgilio—my husband's brother—tries to help me when he can."

"I think it's more than charity."

So obvious, she thought. The tall American had merely overheard a snatch of conversation, and he knew Virgilio as well as or better than she knew the man herself.

"I think so, too. He watches me sometimes."

"And you don't like it."

It wasn't a question, and she merely shrugged, afraid words might betray her if she tried to offer him an explanation. Would he understand that she still loved her husband? *Could* he understand the yearnings that she felt sometimes when she was all alone with no man to console her?

Consolation. A reward that was acknowledged as second best, reserved for losers. Having known the best in Carlos, she was prone to wonder if another man could ever satisfy her needs, emotionally or physically. Of late she'd stopped wondering, content to lead a nun's life, interacting with her neighbors on a superficial level, helping Jaime Vargas's guerrillas when she could.

Except that now the question had returned to haunt her. She could feel the old familiar stirrings, and she didn't have to ponder on their source. The American had done this to her, simply by his presence in her home—the house she had never shared with any man but Carlos.

She had never lived beneath that roof with any man who didn't love her, who didn't *possess* her. By intruding on her life, her private space, this man had awakened old desires she had thought were safely dead and buried.

The dilemma, simply stated, was that he hadn't intruded, after all. She had invited him to share a portion of her life, however limited, when she could just as easily have left him in the forest to fend for himself. Compassion was her undoing, but Ramona knew that there was more than pity in her heart.

She wondered if Miguel had passed her message on to Jaime yet, and if Jaime would respond. The American might resist the notion of cooperating with guerrillas—his compatriots were unpredictable in that regard, sometimes supporting liberation fighters, other times condemning them as Communists—but she would have to take the chance. He plainly couldn't stay with her beyond tonight, when he might be found out.

And if he did stay, if her neighbors didn't know... what then?

Ramona grudgingly admitted to herself that she was frightened of her own reactions, the intensity of feelings she had long suppressed, now struggling to life in this man's presence.

He would have to go before she started weaving fantasies around him, driving out her memories of Carlos and the passion they had shared.

Their meal was ready—rice and beans, with stringy meat from forest game birds. She was tempted to apologize, but Bolan smiled and dug in zealously as if a banquet had been laid before him.

He was smiling at her as he finished and pushed his plate back. "I've been wondering," he said, "where you picked up such fluent English."

Blushing, she replied, "I went to a mission school outside Florencia. Eight years. The sisters were American, and they insisted we use English in a number of our classes. I suppose I was challenged by it. It does not make sense, like Spanish...all the words that sound alike, with different spellings, different meanings."

He smiled. "I'd say you've got it hacked."

"I beg your pardon?"

"That's a compliment. I mean you speak the language very well."

"But I still have a problem with the slang."

"You've got a lot of company there. I think it changes every hour, on the hour."

No time like the present, she decided. *While he feels at ease.*

"I've sent a message to a friend. A member of the underground."

She felt him tense. "A message?"

"He can help you, I believe. He hates Pedilla, everything he stands for. If you cannot work together, he can offer you safe passage through the forest."

"No one has safe passage these days."

"You are better off with friends than by yourself."

"These friends...they wouldn't be from M-19, by any chance?"

She shook her head emphatically. "They have no name, and they are not political. Most of them have had friends or family murdered in *la violencia*. They seek revenge against

Pedilla and the others like him who have made our native land a place of fear and shame."

The tall American was silent for a moment. She could see him weighing the potential risks against rewards, his dark eyes staring through her as if he could scrutinize her very soul.

"I'll see them," he decided, "but I can't make any promises. We may not click. If things get heavy—"

"There will be no trouble. They respect me. I have helped them in the past. They are my friends."

"They're not *my* friends. Not yet."

"I guarantee your safety with my life."

He frowned. "I hope that won't be necessary."

Was she imagining the caring in his eyes? It seemed to go beyond mere gratitude, and for an instant she allowed herself to hope. Could this man care for her, the way a man cared for a woman? Could he want her, in the way her Carlos had? The way Virgilio did?

Embarrassed by the color blooming in her cheeks, she changed the subject, tried to make her mind a blank. "They should be here tomorrow morning after all the men have gone to work the fields."

"Tomorrow morning," he said. "That leaves tonight."

Ramona forced herself to meet his gaze. "You need your rest."

"I don't feel sleepy," he replied.

"Your wound—"

"Is superficial. I've had worse."

She could believe it. When she changed his dressing, she had seen the scars that marked his chest and back. Before she could arrest the thought, Ramona wondered if he might have other scars she hadn't seen.

"You should save your strength."

His smile was cunning. She was certain he could read her secret thoughts. "For what?"

"Tomorrow..."

He looked disappointed. "I suppose you're right. It isn't proper to abuse your hospitality."

"Abuse?"

"By taking liberties."

She shifted toward him, moving closer, hoping that it looked more subtle than it felt. "What do you mean?"

His fingers brushed her cheek, then traced the outline of her jaw. A shiver raced along Ramona's spine and struck sparks in her loins.

"We really ought to get some sleep," he said. Their lips were separated by an inch or less.

"I don't feel sleepy, either."

When he kissed her, as she felt herself responding, she couldn't believe the suddenness with which events were moving. This couldn't be happening, and yet—

His hands had found the buttons of her simple peasant blouse, and she didn't resist as he slipped them open. She wore nothing underneath, and when he touched her breasts, her nipples, she felt feverish, consumed with primal heat. She let him slip the garment from her shoulders, lying back across his pallet, kissing him until his lips were pulled away. They traveled lower, following the outline of her body, and Ramona caught her breath.

It was irrational, the strength of her reaction to this almost total stranger. It couldn't be happening, she told herself again, but she couldn't deny the feelings burning through her body. It had been so long....

She raised her hips to help him when he slipped her skirt off, kept her eyes closed as he stripped himself. He was beside her in a moment, strong and hard, his body lean and flat where hers was plump and round, his battle scars and curly hair in contrast to her own sleek flesh.

He moved above her, and Ramona arched her back to welcome him and let the warm sensations carry her away.

10

The troops returned with Colonel Rivas and his three companions shortly after dawn. Pedilla watched with absolute unconcern as the bodies, wrapped in ponchos, joined the others on the ground outside. He felt no sympathy for Rivas or his men. If anything, the officer deserved his fate as punishment for crass incompetence.

Pedilla had to deal with Rivas's successor now, the worried-looking captain, and convince him that his duty lay in holding his position, tracking down the traitors who had murdered eight brave men. It might be difficult—the younger officer was clearly nervous, wishing he had never followed Rivas to this outpost in the jungle—but the dealer had his ways. If he couldn't appeal to duty, there was always greed, and he'd found the latter motivation to be most effective in the past.

Rebuilding on the compound would begin as soon as he collected workers from surrounding villages. Pedilla had no qualms about inducting peons to perform the labor. He would offer them a living wage, and if they turned him down... well, he would have their help, in any case. He didn't call upon them often—it had been a year or more—but they remembered how he dealt with those who dared refuse, the few who offered him resistance or reported him to the police. His vengeance was immediate and absolute.

A few hours earlier he had dispatched two runners to set the wheels in motion. One would stop off in Florencia to order by phone the material needed to reactivate Pedilla's lab. The other had been sent to Navarro at his hiding place in Medellín. Before he left he was to secure Navarro's full cooperation in a war against their common enemy...or to eliminate the coward on Pedilla's orders and assume command of Navarro's surviving troops. In either case the reinforcements should be on their way by early evening at the latest.

Satisfied that he had done his best for now, Pedilla stood on the veranda of his house and watched his soldiers, working side by side with men in uniform to clear away the debris from the attack. From time to time another body joined the double rank of silent forms, but he ignored them. Men were pawns in Hector's game, and there were always more available.

His eyes picked out the slender captain, standing to one side by himself. Pedilla was a self-styled student of humanity. He liked to think he could read a man, anticipate in advance the responses and objections to any questions he might ask. Just now he knew the captain was both angry and afraid. The officer would be resentful of Pedilla and of his late superior for placing him in a precarious position, and he would undoubtedly be questioning his own ability to cope. Manipulation of the young man would require expert handling on Pedilla's part, a combination of iron fist and velvet glove at which he normally excelled. Now seemed a good time to begin.

Pedilla felt the captain tense at his approach, but noted that he didn't snap to attention as Orlando Rivas might have done. Nor was his manner properly subservient. Not yet.

The smile Pedilla plastered on his face was sympathetic and entirely artificial. "I am happy that the bodies of your comrades were recovered, Captain..."

"Munoz." The name was printed on his tunic, but by forcing him to speak, Pedilla took control. The captain scowled. "And four weren't recovered."

"Ah, the waterfall." Pedilla's feigned commiseration was as phony as his smile. "The Yarí can be treacherous."

"Why are we here?"

The question was predictable. The captain surely knew its answer, but he wanted verbal confirmation from the horse's mouth.

"Your colonel was assigned to help protect my...business...from guerrillas who have plagued our area in recent weeks. He was a zealous soldier—and, perhaps, the least bit hasty in his eagerness to do his job."

"Perhaps. And these guerrillas? You have no idea of their identity?"

"Suspicions, nothing more. The sort of rebel trash who constantly subvert our lawful government."

"Of course." The captain didn't sound convinced. "It is apparent that we will not find them now."

"Apparent? On what basis, Captain?"

"They escaped from Colonel Rivas, killed him in the bargain, and we have no way of tracking them."

"A search—"

"Would surely be a waste of time," the captain interrupted. "My soldiers are in danger here, and I must speak to my superiors without delay."

"The orders from your colonel were specific, I believe."

"The colonel is no longer in command."

"Of course." Pedilla smiled in recognition of the captain's new, inflated status. "I am certain you would wish to carry out his mission."

"It is not for me to say, *señor*. When I receive my orders—"

"By that time, we may all be dead! I can't believe you would leave my men and me defenseless."

Smiling, Captain Munoz scanned the compound, picking out the sentries with their automatic weapons at the ready. "You have more men under arms than I do," he replied. "I wouldn't say that you are helpless."

"You have seen how the guerrillas fight, attacking without warning, firing rockets from the trees. What chance have simple peasant laborers against such trained professionals?"

"Precisely what are you suggesting?"

"Simply that you carry out the colonel's orders and protect my business while these men rebuild. Just a few more days."

"You're aware of the penalties for trafficking in drugs?"

"I am a simple businessman."

"I think, perhaps, that Colonel Rivas owed as much to you as to the military."

"Let us not speak harshly of the dead."

"The truth can scarcely harm him now."

"And if your supposition is correct?"

The captain faced him squarely, solemn now. "Then he'll have to be replaced."

"I've been thinking in those terms myself."

"And with the new apparent risks..."

"A raise in salary is indicated?"

"I would not presume to ask."

"There's no need. Cooperation must be based on mutual respect."

"Of course."

"Shall we say three thousand pesos a month?"

The captain hesitated. "I was thinking..."

"Four?"

"We have a deal."

Pedilla's smile was genuine this time. He shook the captain's hand and knew he had bought himself another friend, another lackey who would do his bidding. Once the fish had tasted bait, the hook was set. There could be no wriggling free.

Pedilla had his edge, the extra bit of personal insurance he preferred when dealing with an unknown enemy. As for the inability of troops to find the trail of his attackers…well, he would discuss that with the captain in due time when it was light enough to start another search.

The captain owed him now, and he would dance when Hector called the tune. For some, Pedilla knew that it would be a dance of death.

GERALDO MUNOZ WATCHED Pedilla from the corner of his eye and smiled. He had known about the link between Pedilla and the late but unlamented Colonel Rivas for some time, and though Pedilla had no way of knowing it, Munoz had volunteered to join the force that Rivas had led to guard the *narcotraficante*'s compound. He had hoped to cut himself in on their bargain somehow. Though he hadn't expected Rivas to be killed, he wasn't sorry, either.

All things came to those with the ability to wait.

Acceptance of command and the continuation of the search for Rivas's assassin wouldn't guarantee Munoz promotion, but that scarcely mattered. Even if he stayed a captain all his life, with Pedilla on his side he would earn more than many members of the army's general staff. The cocaine business was a gold mine, and he meant to glean his share while he was young enough and bold enough to enjoy it.

Munoz had no particular opinions on cocaine. He knew the drug was both addictive and destructive, but it scarcely touched his private world. If Indians were prone to chew the coca leaf and thereby mute the pangs of hunger, what was it to him? If rich Americans destroyed themselves, their families and their careers, why should he care? To Captain Munoz the narcotics trade was nothing more than golden opportunity laid out before him, ripe and ready for the taking. He'd be a fool to pass it by.

Corruption in Colombia bore little of the stigma that attached to dereliction of official duty in America. As in the other Latin American states, *mordida*—bribery—was an accepted fact of life. It greased the rusty wheels of government and kept things moving more or less on course. And if the grand ideal of justice was occasionally subverted, sometimes, Munoz thought, it might be for the best.

Americans had come to view Colombia as one large shooting gallery. Munoz wouldn't argue with their general assessment of the ravages inflicted by *la violencia*. What Americans refused to realize, however, was that crime still carried heavy penalties throughout Colombia. The punishment for murder ranged from twenty years in jail to death by firing squad, and random killers—those involved in street crimes—were pursued most energetically by the police. Likewise with rapists, thieves and deviants, the castoffs of society who had no business walking up and down the streets in freedom.

The traffic in cocaine was punished, too, by federal forces. Munoz had participated in a score of raids that had landed men and women—even children—in the custody of *federales*; he'd seen many of them sentenced to hard labor for their crimes. If certain wealthy *narcotraficantes* were effectively above the law, Munoz could live with that. His country, after all, had more important problems on its hands.

The Communist guerrillas were a prime example, spreading their subversive poison through the hinterlands with full assistance from the Cubans, Sandanistas, Soviets. A die-hard anti-Communist, Munoz was totally committed to eradication of the rebels. If he faced a choice between pursuing leftists and harassing wealthy coca merchants, there was no contest.

Captain Munoz was a patriot. And he wasn't a fool.

He didn't mind dispatching troops to search for Rivas's assassins. If he found them, he would kill them on the spot and win a commendation from his superiors. If not...well, it would appear that he had done his duty to the utmost, pleasing both the army and Pedilla. With both his employers happy, Munoz wouldn't suffer any unexpected interruption in his cash flow for the month.

And with Pedilla happy, he would also sleep more soundly.

It was not unheard of for an army officer to be eliminated by the *narcotraficantes*. Personally Munoz thought the victims generally brought destruction on themselves, by making promises they couldn't keep or stepping over bounds that had been clearly drawn by their employers. If a soldier tried to go in business for himself, competing with the dealers who were paying him to guard their stock, it was entirely logical for him to suffer retribution somewhere down the road. In the coca trade such retribution was inevitably fatal.

In another hour, when they had full light, Munoz would lead his troops into the forest. He didn't expect to find the killers of his late CO; the hunters had already wasted too much time, and even with a clear-cut trail they would be hours behind their prey. But if he got lucky and overtook the criminals—or anyone who might *appear* to be the killers— he would do his duty and eradicate them instantly. There would be no survivors to contest his claim that he had bagged the killers, and if Rivas's assassins surfaced later somewhere else, he would dismiss them as a different band of cutthroats preying on the people of the countryside.

Another hour.

Munoz was a city boy at heart. He didn't enjoy these forays through the jungle. Irritated by the heat and the humidity, afraid of snakes and spiders, still he swallowed personal concerns and offered no complaints when he was ordered to the field. A soldier served where he was sent, regardless of his private preference, and on occasion, if he kept his eyes wide open, even the most noisome duty had its rewards.

He cast an eye in the direction of Pedilla's house, unscathed beyond the damages done to doors and windows by the dealer's own wild firing at the height of the attack. It was a palace in comparison to quarters occupied by lowly captains of the army, and Munoz aspired to owning a more fashionable home before another birthday rolled around. Of course he couldn't occupy a house as grand as this while still a captain; he would need promotions. He suspected Pedilla could assist him there, as well. In any case, it couldn't hurt to ask.

But not just yet—later, when his brand-new *patrón* had more reason to be cheerful, generous. When he had seen the bodies of his enemies stretched out before him on the ground, perhaps.

Munoz decided he *would* discover Rivas's assassins, even if he had to camp out in the bush for days. He wouldn't be especially particular about his choice, but in Caquetá Province there were bandits and guerrillas in abundance. Surely some of them would fit the bill, and if he came up empty, there were always peasants he could arm before he executed them for treason. It was simple. He had seen it done before in similar circumstances.

Invigorated by the notion, caught up in a daydream of his own advancement through the ranks, Munoz climbed into the nearest truck and seated himself, prepared to wait.

Less than an hour now until they had full light.

Until the hunt began.

RAMONA SLEPT within the circle of Bolan's arms as he lay awake, eyes fixed upon the ceiling of her one-room house. Her warmth, communicated through the flesh, stirred Bolan, but he held himself in check. He needed time to think, to lay a working strategy, if he intended to survive.

His moments with Ramona had been serendipitous, a wholly unexpected moment in the sun, but he couldn't pretend there was any future for him here. His war lay elsewhere, and he hoped it wouldn't touch this peaceful village, tainting the lives of innocents who wouldn't even recognize his name. He had to leave, for he was fit enough to travel now. But he'd made a promise to the woman. He'd told her he would wait and meet her contact with the underground.

The Executioner had no intention of enlisting with a local ragtag army to pursue its special goals. At Ramona's urging, he had agreed to meet their spokesman, but he wasn't signing on for any unexpected duty in the field. If they agreed to help him make his pickup, that was fine. If not, he hoped they could part on equitable terms.

A firefight with guerrillas in the middle of a nameless village wasn't on the Executioner's agenda. If it came to that, he would face the problem, but in the meantime he was thinking through alternatives, still hoping for the best...and planning for the worst.

He knew Pedilla might be tracking him, although he doubted the federal troops would muster much enthusiasm for a hot pursuit. Four of their number had been lost on the river and he still had no idea who had fired the shots he'd heard as he'd retreated through the forest. Were the other soldiers dead, as well? If so, who had dispatched them?

With a mental shrug, he let the question slide away. Whatever else had befallen them in the jungle, he wasn't responsible, and the troops had known the risks before they'd made their move.

If there was any heat at all, he thought, it would be applied by Pedilla's private troops. When they had pulled themselves together, sorted out their dead and called for reinforcements, they might wish to even up the score a bit.

And how much time did Bolan have before his enemies were ready for the road? Not much, he reckoned, squinting at his watch and realizing it was now completely dark outside. Most of a day had passed since his attack upon Pedilla's compound, and he still hadn't escaped the dealer's sphere of influence.

He shifted slightly, turning toward Ramona. She murmured something in her sleep. Stark, cold images invaded Bolan's mind against his will. He knew precisely what Pedilla's men would do if they suspected villagers of harboring an enemy. Ramona knew the risks as well—she had been widowed by the *narcotraficantes*, after all—but her unselfish willingness to take a chance didn't ease Bolan's sense of guilt, his feeling of impending doom.

He was a lightning rod, attracting danger to her home, her village. People he had never seen were now in jeopardy because of him. He didn't like the feeling that gave him.

He should be out of there, and never mind his promise to Ramona. If he angered her by leaving, anger was still preferable to death. The longer he delayed, the likelier the danger to her and to the village.

He watched Ramona's face in sleep and felt the pressure of her breasts against his ribs, the weight of one leg thrown across his own. Their coupling had been a primal affirmation of survival in the killing zone, and he didn't regret it for a moment.

Despite himself, the soldier felt himself reacting to her warmth, her closeness. He bit his tongue and tried to make his mind a blank. It didn't help.

Time enough to think about leaving in another moment, Bolan thought, or another hour. For the moment, affirmation of survival was his only goal. He couldn't have placed a fast, coherent label on his feelings if he tried.

Outside, the forest was a world of darkness rife with predators that would destroy him. Inside Ramona's tiny house, a different sort of darkness sheltered Bolan, soft and warm and caring. In the middle of the killing fields, he'd discovered an oasis where the primal laws of kill or be killed, punch and payback, temporarily didn't apply.

11

Virgilio Hernandez heard the trucks as he made ready for another day of labor in the fields. At first the sound was faint and distant, but he recognized the growl of engines, as alien to his surroundings as a jaguar's cry would be in the streets of Bogotá.

He'd been shaving, studying his reflection in the tiny mirror. Now he laid his razor down and wiped the lather from his face, then stepped outside. He could hear the sound of two engines, maybe three, approaching rapidly along the narrow track that linked the village with Florencia and the world beyond. A worm of apprehension wriggled in his stomach, and he swallowed hard to keep it down.

The last time trucks had visited their settlement...

He thrust the image out of mind before it could undo him. Standing in the hard-packed dooryard of his tiny house, Virgilio sensed trouble coming toward him on the one-lane road. He felt a sudden urge to run and hide, to observe the new arrivals from the shelter of the forest. But he was a man, and men couldn't be driven from their homes like children, scurrying before a nameless dread.

The little village square was filled before the jeep came into view, two flatbeds laboring behind it on the rutted track. Virgilio couldn't profess to recognize the driver, or the man who rode beside him, but he knew their type. He wished now he'd surrendered to his urge and hidden in the jungle. Now, when it was patently too late.

The jeep rolled ten or fifteen feet past him, one of the flatbeds parking just outside his door. The men who scrambled from the cab wore pistols; one of them carried a shotgun with the barrel sawed off short, for hunting men.

A quick scan showed Virgilio that while the new arrivals wore no uniforms they all bore arms. His worst suspicions were confirmed.

Pedilla.

Villagers had gathered to observe the new arrivals, curiosity and apprehension in their faces as they studied men and trucks and guns. The scene was painfully familiar, bearing novelty for toddlers only. The adults knew what was coming, but they waited silently to hear the words.

The driver of the jeep spent several moments scanning faces, counting heads and shanties. Having satisfied himself, he turned to face the natives with a crooked smile.

"Amigos," he began, "it is my pleasure to inform you that your village has been chosen for a most prestigious honor. Able-bodied men, and boys more than ten years old, are invited to participate in the construction of a modern scientific complex right here in Caquetá Province."

The word *science* meant cocaine production in the backwoods of Colombia. Any doubts Virgilio had had about the intentions of the visitors were wiped away.

"Each worker will be paid an hourly wage of four pesos. Meals will be provided, as will transportation to and from the job site. Señor Pedilla offers you this golden opportunity because he loves Caquetá Province and its people."

"But our crops..." The voice was weary, cracked with age. Virgilio picked out the old man who had spoken, even as Pedilla's gunner cracked a hungry smile.

"The work should take four days, no more than five. Your crops will not be damaged if the women do their share." He slid an arm around the old man's shoulders, squeezing hard enough to make his captive wince. "And you, *viejo*, may remain at home. Our work needs able-bodied men, not mummies."

His companions snickered, nudging one another. The villagers were silent, for no one else saw fit to protest.

Then a teenage boy had nerve enough to raise a question. "When must we begin?"

"At once," the gunner answered. "Men and boys above the stated age should board the trucks within five minutes." Nodding toward his men, he added, "We will guarantee that no one is accidentally deprived of such an honor."

As he stepped back into his house to fetch his hat, Virgilio seethed with mixed emotions. He could picture Carlos, lying in the middle of the dusty road, blood pooling into crimson muck beneath his body, and the image turned his stomach. Guilt crept up to catch him by surprise and wouldn't let him go. But at the same time there was anger toward the bastards who would make him crawl once more before Ramona.

She would certainly despise him now for knuckling under in the face of guns a second time. Her man—his brother—had been brave enough to stand and die when called upon to be a slave. It made no difference that his blood had been spilled in vain, a foolish, wasted gesture. Carlos had become a martyr and a hero, while Virgilio lived on. Alone.

No matter. Living was the key. With a few more pesos in his pocket, he might be able to shop in Florencia. A gift might soften Ramona's heart of stone, begin the slow task of persuading her that mere survival didn't make him any less a man.

In time, Virgilio hoped, he might convince himself.

Emerging from his house into the sunlight, he found several men and boys already seated in the first truck. The second would be almost empty, but there would be other villages along the route that would "contribute volunteers" to the construction effort. By the time they reached Pedil-

la's compound, the trucks would hold about forty men, and
no doubt other teams were scouring the province, fanning
out toward all points of the compass.

In his heart Virgilio wasn't surprised to see the raiders in
his village once again. Pedilla had been bold the first time;
now he merely called upon experience, remembering tech-
niques that had proved successful in the past. Instead of
surprise, Virgilio felt a growing curiosity. Two years ago,
when men with guns had come the first time, workers from
the village had been forced to build a laboratory and warehouse for the *narcotraficantes*. Had Pedilla's operation
grown to the point that it had outgrown those sizable facil-
ities? Would the recruits be building an addition to the
compound... or was some new development under way?

Virgilio didn't waste time or energy attempting to sec-
ond-guess the gunners, but found a seat in the flatbed.
Leaning back against the slats that formed one side, he
waited for the journey to begin. As he remembered, it was
something like three hours to the turnoff, roughly half an
hour more until they reached the compound. They would be
home late tonight—if they came home at all.

Four days, or five at most. He hoped they wouldn't have
to spend that time inside Pedilla's jungle camp. Last time,
they had been driven back and forth between the village and
the work site, leaving close to dawn, returning hours after
dusk.

A movement drew his gaze in the direction of Ramona's
one-room house, positioned on the outskirts of the settlement. The driver of the jeep was halfway there, a gunner
trailing for protection. Momentary apprehension welled up
in Virgilio's breast, and then was gone.

Ramona would be safe. She had no man to lose.

He had already seen to that.

ANTONIO YBARRA FOUND IT awkward and distasteful dealing with the forest peasants. Born of lowly stock himself, he

had succeeded in escaping from the dead-end drudgery of village life. He had position now, respect, in part because he worked for the Pedilla syndicate, and partly from his reputation as a killer. Put the two together and you had a man of means.

Ybarra had been killing from the age of twelve, at first to guarantee his own survival, later as a method of transacting business and occasionally as a sport. He had no more regard for human life than for the lives of the insects he daily trod beneath his feet, but he was wise enough to understand that violence must be held in reserve on some occasions, promised rather than displayed.

The people of this nameless village and a hundred others were like children, putty in his hands. He flattered them with lies that none of them took seriously, but the threat of violence that resided in the holster on his hip and in the guns of his companions made the peasants fall into line like sheep. Ybarra gloated over the sense of power he derived from stepping in and channeling their lives in new directions, almost on a whim.

The whim, of course, wasn't his own. He thought the ultimate achievement of his life would be to stand in place of the *patrón* and choose himself which lives would be disrupted, which destroyed. What absolute, apocalyptic power that would be.

He had detailed his men to sweep the village while the sheep were loaded onto the trucks. He wouldn't put it past the villagers to hide a man or two, perhaps some children, in an effort to deceive him and avoid contributing their all to the construction effort. He wouldn't begrudge them the attempt, but neither would he let them make a fool of him. If an example was required, Ybarra was prepared to leave the slackers with a memory to haunt them all their days.

It seemed to him that every hovel in the village had been emptied by the sounds of their arrival, save for one. A solitary house in need of repairs was situated at the far end of the village, separated from the others by some yards, as if the occupants had tried to set themselves apart, avoiding constant contact with their fellow peons. No one had emerged from this house to observe the trucks or listen to his little speech, and this peculiar lack of curiosity immediately made Antonio suspicious.

Calling on his shotgun rider, he approached the house without a hint of hesitation. He recognized potential danger but refused to let it cow him. If a peasant crouched beside the hovel with a shotgun or a muzzle-loading rifle, he would take his chances, counting on his reaction time and expertise to make the difference. And woe to anyone inside if the first shot wasn't on target.

Ybarra had a dozen yards to go when he was startled by the opening of the front door. A woman stood revealed before him, reasonably young and attractive, with a figure he thought might be enticing once her peasant clothes were stripped away. She didn't close the door behind her, and he caught no hint of shadows or subtle movement, which might have indicated another presence in the house.

"Hello, *señora*. Is your man at home?"

Her eyes drilled into him like bullets. "No."

"Where has he gone?"

"Your memory is short," she answered, fairly sneering at him.

Anger flared inside Antonio. "I have no time for riddles, woman. I demand to see your man at once!"

She stabbed an index finger toward the forest. "As you wish. His grave is with the others of our village. A reminder of another golden opportunity to serve Señor Pedilla."

Ybarra was momentarily confused. He hadn't been a member of Pedilla's team the last time the raiders struck this nameless village. His sidekick whispered to him, hastily explaining that the woman's husband had resisted them and had died as a result.

Ybarra's anger faded as he moved closer to the house.

"You have no sons?"

"We had no time."

"A pity. And a waste for someone like yourself to be alone."

"Your sympathy is out of place."

"And you forget yourself, *mujer*. If I should snap my fingers..."

"Snap them, then. What have I left to lose?"

"Your life, perhaps."

"Too late. A weasel stole it long ago."

He forced a smile. "Your courage does you credit. I admire a woman who is not afraid."

"You flatter me." She turned her face away and spit into the dust.

Ybarra felt the angry color rising in his cheeks. He glanced over his shoulder toward the village proper. Several of the sheep were watching him, but he was confident that none of them was close enough to catch the woman's words. If they had heard her, dared to smile at his discomfiture, he would have felt compelled to kill them all.

It was a grave temptation, even so, but he was under orders from Pedilla to return with hostages, employing violence only as a last resort. If he allowed himself to kill the woman for a mere display of arrogance, it might mean heat, and he would have to answer for his error at the compound. Fear of the *patrón* prevented him from acting on his instincts, and he forced a cocky smile instead.

"Your solitude has made you bitter," he declared, "a circumstance with which I sympathize. You need a man to keep you happy in the night, and curb your tongue by day."

"A man? If only there was one available."

"Your insolence is unbecoming."

"It is all I have."

"Not all."

"Then let us say that it is all I offer you."

"No offer may be necessary. Men are known to take what they desire."

"As rats do, under cover of the darkness."

"I believe you need an opportunity to reconsider. When you realize the value of my offer, you will be more grateful."

"Will I?"

"I believe so. Possibly when I bring back these sheep tonight we may discuss it at our leisure."

"There is nothing to discuss, tonight or ever."

"You might be surprised."

She laughed aloud. "Amused, perhaps, but not surprised."

"Tonight, then."

"Don't forget your gun. You'll need it."

Clinging to his plastic smile with a supreme exertion of his will, Ybarra thought it might be wonderful to sweep the bitch aside and search her house, ransacking everything she owned, providing her with work until he paid her another visit.

Tonight.

He would have taken her at once, in front of everyone, if he had only had the time. Unfortunately he was on a schedule, and Pedilla wouldn't understand—wouldn't forgive—a deviation motivated by his wounded ego.

There would be another time, and soon.

Antonio Ybarra was looking forward to it.

BOLAN WATCHED the gunners turn and head back to the flatbed trucks. The narrow gap between two sheets of plywood siding had allowed him a restricted view, but he'd been near enough to take them with his Colt Commando if they'd advanced another step toward Ramona. After that . . . well, he was thankful it hadn't come to killing, with the odds so long against him and so many innocent civilians in the cross fire.

He laid the Colt Commando down beside his pallet as Ramona closed the door behind her and leaned against it for a moment with a weary sigh. He saw she was trembling and would have gone to take her in his arms, but the move would have forced him to pass the single window in the house, and he wasn't prepared to give Pedilla's gunners any reason to return.

"That took some courage," Bolan told her, stating fact, avoiding flattery.

"I do not fear them," she informed him. "They have killed me once, already, when they murdered Carlos. There is nothing they can do to hurt me now."

I wouldn't be so sure, the soldier thought, but kept it to himself. "They mentioned coming back tonight?"

She shrugged. "Last time, when they abducted workers from our village, they would come each morning with their trucks, and then return the men and boys some hours after sundown. This time... who can say?"

"If I were you, I wouldn't hang around to wait for Romeo this evening."

"I am not afraid," she answered stubbornly, but Bolan read a different message in her eyes. "Perhaps, however, it would do no harm for me to go away."

"If you need help—"

She shook her head. "I know a family not far from here. They have befriended the guerrillas and we keep in touch. If I request it, they will find a place for me to stay."

"Okay, then, if you're sure."

"I'm positive."

The trucks were pulling out, and Bolan watched them go, the fat tires raising rooster tails of dust. The village was a dead end on the narrow jungle track; the jeep and flatbeds had to turn around and grumble back the way they'd come in order to escape the cul-de-sac of jungle.

"They'll need more hands than that if they're rebuilding the Pedilla compound."

"They will find more 'volunteers' in other villages. The forest has no shortage of potential slaves."

"They're not afraid of someone notifying the police?"

"We have no easy method of communication here," she said. "It takes two days to reach Florencia, another two to come back home. In any case, the men and boys are hostages. If anyone complains to the authorities, they will be murdered. If we wait for them to finish with their work, Pedilla's *pistoleros* will come back at night and raze our village."

Bolan recognized the mark of terror in action. It was possible for the Pedilla syndicate, the Medellín cartel, to hold a province in its clutches through selective application of the carrot and the stick. An individual or village that cooperated was rewarded, publicly, for all to see. Resistance would be punished savagely—and every bit as publicly—to serve as an enduring lesson for the rest.

Obey or suffer.

Yield or die.

It was the kind of savage mind-set Bolan had been fighting since he'd joined the infantry, fresh out of high school. He'd seen the method used in Vietnam and in America, where savages wore different skins, spoke different dialects, but otherwise were indistinguishable. He'd seen the tactics utilized by right and left, by Caucasians, blacks and Orientals, by fanatic cults and godless terrorists. It all came out the same, with ruthless jackals preying on society—until a bullet brought them down.

"You mentioned the guerrillas," Bolan prompted her.

Ramona nodded. "I would be surprised if they are not in the vicinity already. They will see the trucks and wait until the danger passes. We will know when they are ready."

"And your neighbors?"

"They will talk awhile, then go to work the fields. What else have they to do?"

"Should you go with them?"

"Yes, but they will not expect me now. A woman must fulfill her role, and they will be expecting me to spend the day inside, with memories of Carlos." There was sorrow in Ramona's face, all right, along with something else. "I must be truthful," she informed him. "Mourning does not recommend itself, just now."

"I understand," the soldier said. Ramona turned to her household tasks, and Bolan began to consider what he had learned that morning about Pedilla's activities.

The dealer's raid on the village manpower might not be an obstacle in terms of Bolan dusting off on schedule, but it did mean the compound would be back in action, cranking out more coke, sooner than expected, perhaps before the week was out. Bolan had known his victory was short-term at best, but it was galling to have to watch the reconstruction of his recent target starting underneath his very nose.

It was a challenge, and he wondered if he could afford to walk away.

Ramona's friends in the underground were wild cards, unknown quantities. She had informed him they weren't political, but that could mean a hundred different things within Colombia's chaotic climate of unrest. They could be apolitical and still despise Americans on general principles.

They might, he thought, decide to murder one particular American for kicks.

And yet, theirs seemed to be the only game in town. Ramona hadn't failed him so far, and in the absence of convenient options, he had to trust her judgment. He would meet with the guerrillas when they came, and would be prepared for literally anything that happened afterward. If they proved hostile, and it came to killing, he would take as many of them with him as he could.

Ramona wouldn't knowingly betray him. She'd promised him that much, in secret ways that put no stock in spoken words, and he trusted her implicitly. But he couldn't afford to extend that trust to her friends and casual acquaintances, at least until he met them for himself.

He watched Ramona's graceful movements as she accomplished her domestic chores. That afternoon he might face death, but for the moment he was living, and she was just the friend a lonely soldier needed in the hour before the storm.

12

Jaime Vargas crouched beside the game trail, waiting, watching, every sense alert for signs of danger. Something had gone sour in the village—he knew that—and nagging apprehension warned him that Pedilla was the author of the trouble. Jaime didn't smell a trap, not yet, but caution was required.

He'd observed the girls and women working in the fields at tasks usually performed by men. Where were the men and boys? Their absence sounded an alarm in Jaime's mind and set his teeth on edge.

The nameless village had a single street, and that was empty now, deserted save for one or two lean dogs that idled in the morning sun. On any normal day he would have seen women bustling about their daily tasks, or children playing, but they had been called away to do the work of absent men. If any had remained behind, they kept indoors and out of sight.

Jaime hadn't seen Ramona in the fields. He stared at her little house for several moments, studying the door and window, checking shadows and the forest that surrounded her abode. The widow wouldn't willingly betray him, but she might not have a choice. If any of Pedilla's men had learned her secret . . .

Jaime finished his reconnaissance and whispered orders to his two companions. They would cover him as he approached Ramona's house, assist him if a trap was sprung, and try to save themselves if he was clearly lost. It was imperative that one of them, at least, survive to warn the rest of his guerrillas. If the *narcotraficantes* cracked Ramona, they would quickly move on the Ochoa family, and from there against the rebel camp.

It was an easy twenty yards between the game trail and the house, with cover all the way. But the young man took his time, evaluating every move before he made it, pausing frequently to look and listen, finger on the trigger of his AK-47.

If enemies awaited him, he decided, they wouldn't be *federales*. The troops might well be searching for the killer of their comrades by the Yarí, but they had no finesse, no guile. They would have barricaded off the village, set up gun emplacements and waited for a blind man or a fool to blunder in and give himself away. Their very negligence would doom them, in the end, but for the moment he was glad he wasn't dealing with the army.

It was always better, sweeter, to fight the *narcotraficantes*. They were closer to the heart of his vendetta, one step nearer to the man he must eventually kill in order to avenge his family, his village. While Pedilla lived, there was an open wound in Jaime's soul that time could never heal.

Someday. Perhaps this day.

He covered five more yards, fell prone behind a rotten log and counted off a minute, two, before he moved again. If there were snipers, it was possible they hadn't seen him—or they might be waiting for a perfect shot, until they satisfied themselves that there were no more sitting targets in the shooting gallery.

Accustomed to the sights and smell of death, he didn't fear its sting. Jaime Vargas's only fear of death lay in dying prematurely while Pedilla and his cronies still survived. To lose his life before he had Pedilla in his sights, the young man thought, would be a waste. Beyond that private victory, he was indifferent to his fate.

A glance over his shoulder found the others watching from concealment, automatic rifles trained on Ramona's house. One of the weapons was a captured M-16, with M-203 grenade launcher mounted under the barrel. At a signal from Jaime—or at the first sign of an ambush—his men were prepared to level the small house, tracking on from there to rake the village street if need be.

If Jaime Vargas died here, he wouldn't go down alone.

Another scurry, five more yards, and he took cover in a stand of ferns. They wouldn't stop a bullet, but by this time he was more or less convinced there would be no opposition in the village. Something certainly had happened, but the source of fear had passed away. No more than sorrow lingered in its wake.

He played a hunch and stood erect, revealed to any sniper who might have his nest within a range of fifty yards. He would be visible from half the houses in the village, but if anyone was watching him, they gave no sign.

So far, so good.

He moved along the tree line, circling toward Ramona's house, no longer taking care to hide. If hostile guns were waiting for him, they would certainly have spoken by now. His curiosity was playing tag with caution, making Jaime almost reckless in his haste to meet Ramona's guest and learn his business in Caquetá Province.

An American, according to Miguel Ochoa. Someone sent to fight the *narcotraficantes* on the level where they lived and breathed.

He'd been unimpressed with the exalted "expeditionary force" dispatched from the United States in 1986 to help the *federales* crush the traffic in cocaine. Forbidden to participate in the gritty business of arrests and seizures, the Americans had been employed as mere "advisers," offering suggestions on suppression of the drug trade. It was funny when you thought about it; they couldn't eradicate cocaine at home, and yet the proud Americans were eager to supply advice to other nations, stretching out a feeble hand in aid.

The effort, as expected, had been less than successful. There had been arrests, some seizures, inventory burned, but for the most part, members of the Medellín cartel had wriggled through the net unscathed. The American troops had been withdrawn in record time, avoiding accusations of "another Vietnam" in South America, and drug traffic had returned to normal in a day or two.

But if the gray-haired men in Washington had learned their lesson, if they had decided to supply assistance on a different level, maybe there was hope.

It was a dream of Jaime's, cherished as a secret even from his comrades, that their guerrilla movement might secure assistance from outside Colombia. Cocaine was grown and processed in his own backyard, but the recipients, the wealthy addicts, were Americans, Canadians and Europeans. Leaders of a dozen governments had pledged themselves to crush the traffic, each in turn retreating as illicit profits and corruption proved untouchable, but Jaime Vargas still clung to fading hope.

One government would be enough, supplying cash and arms to aid his fight against Pedilla and the Medellín cartel. The group Vargas led was neither Communist nor rightist; it took no position on internal politics, except where politicians and policemen reaped profits from the cesspool of narcotics. If the *narcotraficantes* could be routed, killed or driven from the country, Jaime would be more than glad to lay down his weapons and seek a peaceful life among the scattered remnants of his people.

First, however, he'd have to kill Pedilla. There could be no negotiation on that point. Pedilla had to die, as Jaime's family and friends had died.

At last he reached Ramona's house, relaxing with an effort. He slung his rifle, knowing it would do him little good at this range. If his instincts had betrayed him and a trap was waiting, he would have no time to answer fire.

He circled to the front, took care to pause before the open window, then knocked softly on the door. A moment passed before Ramona opened it and stepped aside to let him enter.

"I was worried that you wouldn't come," she said, addressing him in English.

"I am here," he answered, frowning.

"Everybody's here."

Jaime swiveled toward the source of the unfamiliar voice, a corner of the room where a tall man stood dressed in camouflage fatigues.

The stranger held an automatic rifle leveled at his chest.

BOLAN SIZED UP the guerrilla. He was young, his jungle costume patchworked out of olive drab and denim, with a pistol belt around his waist and a bandolier across his chest. His weapon was an AK-47 of uncertain origin. His hands and forearms were a map of scars, as if he might once have plunged both fists through a heavy plate-glass window.

His reaction to Bolan's Colt Commando was a smile. The soldier gave him points for cool. Just points; no slack.

Ramona moved between them, offering a cautious smile designed to calm Bolan and reassure Jaime. "There is no need for violence here," she said.

Bolan read the young man's eyes and said, "Okay." Before he lowered the Commando, Bolan made damned sure the new arrival heard him flick the safety on.

"Where are the men and boys?" Jaime asked Ramona.

She made a hasty recon of the empty street, then closed her door and the shutters on her window. She briefed the young guerrilla on that morning's visit by the Pedilla crew. Bolan noted that the stranger didn't seem surprised.

"Mike Blanski," she began the introductions, "Jaime Vargas. I believe the two of you have much in common."

"Oh?" The young man's voice was deeper than expected, strong.

"You both make war against Pedilla."

"Ah." The young man turned his eyes on Bolan, frowning. "This is true?"

"I trashed his compound night before last," Bolan answered. "He got lucky. There were federal troops on hand."

And there was something in the young man's eyes now, something that made him smile. "I thought you looked—how should I say?—familiar."

"Familiar?"

His English wasn't polished, like Ramona's, but it served his needs. "I saw you from the riverbank, above the falls. Your boat went over, then some soldiers." Grinning, Jaime made a gesture imitating a canoe in free-fall. "There were others who escaped the trap, but I was waiting for them."

The gunshots. Bolan understood at once. "Pedilla was supposed to be my last target before I split," he said. "I'm running late."

"Your last? Have there been others?"

"I've visited a couple of Pedilla's friends."

"Aguirre and Navarro." Jaime's smile was ear to ear by this time. "Señor Blanski, you have not been lucky. Julio Navarro also lives."

"I play them as they're dealt. So far I've had to satisfy myself with inventory and some shooters."

"There will always be cocaine, and *pistoleros*."

"Maybe you'll get lucky, find yourself a better shot."

"And you?"

"I'm looking at an eighteen-hour walk to make my scheduled dust-off. *If* I make it. Otherwise I have to exercise my fallback options."

Bolan said no more about his plans, and Jaime didn't ask. The fallback called for him to try the rendezvous a second time, next day, and failing that, to reach a covert friend of Able Team's in Bogotá. The latter would be risky, if it came to that; he would be forced to jettison his gear and weapons, slipping into civvies in a country where he wasn't fluent in the language.

The young man faced Ramona. "You would like me to provide an escort?"

"*Sí*. And transportation if you can."

He frowned at Bolan. "Eighteen hours? Where are you supposed to meet your friends?"

"Is that important?"

Jaime Vargas shrugged. "If I am to escort you, I must know where we are going."

"Close to San Vicente del Caguán."

"There is a road. If you possessed a vehicle..."

"Too risky. If Pedilla's men aren't covering the highways, they'll have *federales* on the job. Especially now that soldiers have been killed."

The young man made an airy gesture of dismissal. "Never mind the *federales*," he responded. "They are paid to take their chances—by Pedilla *and* the state."

"You don't like soldiers?"

Jaime shot a swift glance toward Ramona. She nodded, urging him to speak. "Two years ago," he said, "the people of my village were 'requested' to supply Pedilla with a labor force, much like the scene you witnessed here today. A group of men and boys were taken to assist in the construction of a house and other buildings in the forest. What you call the compound, I presume."

"Where you among them?"

Jaime nodded. Sudden inspiration hit the Executioner, but he consigned it to a mental shelf and concentrated on the young man's story.

"There were men and boys from several villages," he said, "and older men—professionals—to do the finer work. Pedilla wanted peasants to replace machines for digging ditches, raising walls and so forth. We were paid three pesos for a day."

The soldier scowled. "The going rate's four pesos now."

"A cost of living raise, perhaps?" The young man laughed. "It is a pittance, but my people were unarmed and isolated, frightened to refuse. The project was completed after several weeks, and then a member of our village made complaints to the police."

Bolan could guess the rest of it, but he let the story run its course.

"Investigators came and questioned everyone. A few were still too frightened of Pedilla to admit the truth, and while their stories were in conflict . . ."

"No arrests."

"Precisely. At first it seemed Pedilla might take no revenge for the impertinence. A month went by, then two. One morning I was wakened early by a call of nature. I was in the forest when the helicopters came, with men in uniform and *pistoleros* riding side by side. I watched them do their work, and now I have no love for soldiers."

Bolan couldn't blame him. He was studying the young man's scars, and Jaime caught him at it, holding up his hands.

"I was alone, with more than forty graves to dig. At that, I nearly finished. Four were left when darkness fell and the scavengers came. Wild dogs, a jaguar, following the scent of meat."

"You fought them off?"

"I tried."

The soldier was impressed. "I'd say you owe Pedilla something."

"*Sí.* And one day I will pay my debt in full."

"I wish you luck."

The young man waved it off. "No luck is necessary. You have done enough by killing Aguirre and disrupting their operations for a time."

"I'd hoped for more."

"Destroying the cartel is not an easy task." Jaime shrugged. "It may be more than anyone can manage."

"I don't see you giving up."

"Nor you, but we must each fight in our separate ways, I think."

"You'll help him, then?" Ramona asked.

"Of course." His smile was genuine. "For you, this favor is a small thing."

"Thank you, Jaime. *Muchas gracias.*"

"De nada." He turned back to Bolan. "We should leave at once."

"I'm ready."

"Muy bien. We go."

There were a thousand things Bolan could have told Ramona, but he didn't have the time for any of them now, and he knew none of them would matter in the long run. She had helped him, maybe saved his life, and they had shared a welcome respite from his everlasting war. Beyond that point his presence in her life was nothing but a liability, a source of danger she wouldn't survive if any of Pedilla's gunmen learned the truth.

The best way he could thank Ramona for her kindness was to get the hell away from there and not look back.

The warrior shouldered his gear and took the only option he could find. His bivouac was over. He could hear the hellgrounds calling.

Ramona watched the two men disappear from sight beyond the tree line. There was much she had wished to tell the American, but she had been inhibited by Jaime's presence and there had seemed to be no point, no time. The feelings that had passed between them were transitory; she hadn't lost her memories of Carlos.

She thought Bolan would be safe with Jaime—or as safe as anyone could be in Caquetá Province while Pedilla was seeking the man who had attacked his laboratory. Given half a chance, Ramona would have torched the place herself, but she didn't possess the skill, and so she tried to help the cause in other ways.

Before she stepped inside and closed the door, Ramona scanned the empty street again. The dogs had changed position, moving with the sun, but otherwise the village might have been uninhibited, dead. Ramona wondered whether anyone had caught a glimpse of Jaime or Bolan, finally deciding that it made no difference. They were gone now, and her neighbors weren't likely to report her to Pedilla.

If they did...well, she'd taken care to learn as little of the underground's activities as possible. She couldn't show them Jaime's hideout on a map, although she knew that under torture she might give Pedilla the Ochoa family. If it came to that, she would resist with all her strength, but there were limitations she recognized and understood.

Her Carlos had been lucky, in a way. He had acted as a man, and he had been murdered outright in the moment of his glory. If he had been beaten, tortured—or if threats had been directed toward his bride—Ramona thought he might have been remembered differently. The mental picture of her husband broken, pleading with Pedilla's *pistoleros*, left a bad taste in Ramona's mouth, and she dismissed it from her mind.

Who could anticipate a monster like Pedilla, or the tactics necessary to destroy him? After Carlos was killed, Ramona's faith had been tested to its limits by her neighbors and their platitudes, the priest who offered vague condolences and useless words of reassurance. She was pleased that Carlos had a place in heaven, but couldn't deny her feeling that she needed him on earth, to share her life and kiss away her tears.

Ramona tidied up her one-room house in record time, removing every trace of Bolan's visit and the passion they had shared. She left the door and shutters open, airing out the place against the chance a faint aroma hinting of his brief presence might remain. There must be nothing to betray her secret when Pedilla's men returned.

The sudden thought transfixed Ramona. When the *pistoleros* came again, the driver of the jeep might try to make good on his threats. Ramona had no doubt of his intentions; he had greedily undressed her with his rodent eyes, and she believed that only time pressure had held him back from trying worse. Bolan would have stopped him, certainly, but she wouldn't allow herself to think about the consequences of a firefight, with the unarmed people of her village milling in a cross fire.

Next time, when Pedilla's people came, there would be no one to protect her. She couldn't rely upon her neighbors for assistance in the face of arms. Virgilio? Despite his obvious preoccupation with her, he would be of little help. When Carlos died, Virgilio hadn't found strength enough to lift a hand against his brother's murderers. Why should he risk himself to help a woman whom he merely lusted after when he wouldn't protect his own blood kin.

Ramona stepped outside herself a moment, wondering how Virgilio might have reacted had she been his wife. The prospect made her vaguely ill, and she dismissed it from her mind, preferring to consider her options and responses to future threats.

She could vacate her home and stay with the Ochoas for a time. They would be happy to receive her, generous with food and sleeping space despite the fact that their house was overcrowded now. But her absence might provoke suspicion, prompt the *pistoleros* to begin a search. She wouldn't call danger down upon good friends to save herself.

When the men and boys returned that evening, if she remained indoors, there was a chance she might be overlooked, forgotten. It was even possible her nemesis might not accompany the column, though she thought the odds were slim.

A combination of approaches, then—avoid him if she could, and be prepared to fight if he tried anything beyond mere threats and bluster. Picking up an eight-inch carving knife, she tried its edge against her thumb, decided it could use a decent honing. There were hours yet before the men and boys returned—if they returned at all that night—and she would give the blade a razor's edge before she finished.

You could never tell, Ramona thought, when someone unexpected might drop by to get a shave.

From ear to ear.

13

"And you are not an agent of your government?"

The man Vargas knew as Blanski shook his head. "We share some common interests on occasion, but I'm self-employed."

"A mercenary?"

Bolan's smile contained a hint of irony. "That's close enough, I guess."

The concept puzzled Jaime Vargas. In Colombia the men who trained with guns and hunted other men were *federales*, outlaws or guerrillas. There were no such things as "self-employed" commandos lending their assistance to the government on piecemeal terms. The young man couldn't comprehend a system that would tolerate such operations.

"You enjoy the full protection of the state?"

"On work like this? Hardly. If I'm made down here, it's all she wrote."

The slang was unfamiliar, but Vargas got the drift. Whoever had assigned Mike Blanski to attack the Medellín cartel, they were determined to absolve themselves of all responsibility in case the mission failed. If it succeeded, on the other hand, he had no doubt they would be swift to claim the credit.

"Governments, I think, are all the same."

"I wouldn't go that far."

"Your people use you, but they are ashamed to claim you as their own."

"They can't afford an incident between Colombia and the United States. We're talking politics, diplomacy."

"It is the same," he said again, and Bolan shrugged, refusing to be baited.

They were following a game trail through the forest, northbound toward the base camp Jaime's troops had recently established. Fifty yards ahead of them Luis had the point, while Mateo hung back to guard their flank. If there was trouble fore or aft, they ought to have sufficient warning.

Above them brightly colored birds exploded into screeching flight as Bolan, Jaime and his men intruded on their feeding grounds. Monkeys chattered a chorus in the background. Vargas did his best to tune out the distractions, concentrating on the man he'd agreed to shepherd through the jungle on a trek to San Vicente del Caguán.

Beyond the shadow of a doubt, he thought, Mike Blanski was a slick professional. His age was indeterminate, his face weathered by exposure to the elements on countless battlefields. The ice-blue eyes had seen their share of pain, and more, but there was still compassion in their depths. His hands were large and strong enough to crush the life out of a man, but Jaime sensed they could be gentle, too.

How gentle had they been when they were handling Ramona? Jaime had not missed the looks that passed between the widow and the tall American as he made ready to depart. There had been passion in the air. Under other circumstances he would have excused himself, allowing them some time alone, but there had been no time, no place for him to go.

He felt no jealousy toward Bolan over Ramona. There had been times, of course, when Jaime viewed Ramona as a man may view a woman, taking silent pleasure in the beauty of her face, her form, without a prayer of bringing fantasies to life. His own young love, Teresa, had been slaughtered with his family and neighbors by Pedilla's animals, and in the past two years there had been little opportunity for romance. If Ramona, two years widowed, had found solace for a moment in the arms of this American, it wasn't Jaime's place to criticize her choice.

Whatever else Ramona's passion might have done, it hadn't spoiled her judgment. Jaime was a decent judge of men, compelled by circumstances to select his allies on the basis of immediate, instinctive trust, and he found nothing to be wary of in the American's deportment. The man's reticence to talk about his sponsors in the States was understandable—no, mandatory—for a man who made his living by the gun. A mercenary who betrayed the confidence of his employers wasn't worth the price he might demand.

And yet, despite Jaime's urge to pigeonhole Mike Blanski, file him in a mental category where his talents seemed to fit, the tall American didn't strike him as a mercenary in the common sense of the word. Whatever else might have happened, it was obvious that the man cared about his mission. He was privately committed to the destruction of Pedilla's empire in a manner that no simple gun for hire could hope to emulate.

That made him a crusader, and for all their many differences, Jaime Vargas understood that state of mind too well. Crusaders were more dangerous, at times, than paid assassins. They couldn't be counted on to cut and run when odds were hopelessly against them.

"You are returning to America?" he asked when they had passed some time in silence.

Bolan nodded. "I've about worn out my welcome here," he said. "And there are wars to fight back home."

"My war will not be finished while Pedilla lives."

"I hope you nail him."

"*Sí.* I will, but it takes time."

The soldier frowned. "It's not my place to interfere—"

"You have already joined our struggle. Please, feel free to speak your mind."

"Okay. Pedilla's shaky at the moment. I won't say he's on the ropes, but he's got plenty on his mind, with the destruction of his lab and everything that's happened to his buddies in the past two weeks. It figures he'll be beefing up security around the compound, but this still could be your best time for a tag before he gets his act together."

"There is truth in what you say. My force is small, but we are organized." The young man risked a cautious smile. "If you would care to show us how..."

"I had my shot," the tall American replied. "I missed Pedilla, as you know. Besides, I'm out of time."

"Of course. I merely thought—"

A burst of automatic fire sliced through his train of thought, and Jaime's words were lost forever. Dropping to a combat crouch, Bolan at his side, he scanned the trail ahead for any sign of Luis.

More firing, closer now, as gunners drove the point man back along his track. Behind them Mateo was pounding up the trail to join the fight, when other guns erupted from the rear.

"A cross fire!" Bolan hissed. He dived off the narrow trail in search of cover as the bullets started whispering around them.

Jaime fired a short burst from his AK-47, lacking solid targets, as he followed the American in flight. They were surrounded and cut off by unknown enemies, and they had nowhere left to run.

THE GUNFIRE TOOK Mack Bolan by surprise. Within the fraction of a second left before his combat instincts took control, he wondered if he had allowed his mind to stray, distracted by his conversation with the young guerrilla leader. No, he thought, the ambush had been well laid, with nothing to betray the gunners at a glance. As for the who and why, he had no time to dabble in the politics of raw survival at the moment.

Flattening himself in jungle undergrowth beside the trail, he caught a glimpse of Vargas fading back along the other side. Ahead of them the point man, Luis, was running for his life. Behind them Bolan heard Mateo, their backup, attempting to catch up and lend support.

Another burst of fire erupted on their flank, and Bolan realized they were boxed in. His grudging admiration for their adversaries was increased. The gunners in the rear had let four targets pass and never once betrayed their own position with a sound or movement. That took practice, and he wondered who their adversaries had been fighting up to now.

Luis nearly made it. He had less than fifteen yards to go when streams of automatic fire converged and found him, spinning him around like a disintegrating dervish, bits and pieces of him exploding into the steamy forest atmosphere. Responding from his cover, Jaime Vargas sprayed a burst in the direction of the hidden gunners, but it would have been a miracle if he had scored.

There was a gasp, then someone thrashing in the brush, and Bolan pivoted, his Colt Commando rising, just as Mateo slid into cover several yards uprange. The slender partisan was carrying an M-16 with an M-203 40 mm grenade launcher mounted under the barrel, and he unlimbered his artillery now, spraying their backtrack with 5.5 mm tumblers, unleashing a high-explosive can for good measure. The forest erupted there in smoke and fire, with the ghost of a scream tangled up in the midst of thunder.

So far they were holding. But holding was suicide here in the middle of nowhere surrounded by hostiles in numbers unknown. They would have to retreat if they could, but from what? And to where?

Bolan signaled to Jaime, a whistle he feared might be lost in the racket of gunfire. The young man responded with the flick of one hand barely seen in the forest's half light. Then

Bolan was moving, a shadow in transit, exposed for an instant while crossing the trail.

He was covered by Mateo, spraying their flank and unleashing another grenade. No more screams, but the sound of hot shrapnel impacting on tree trunks and slicing through ferns might serve to keep their attackers at bay for a moment.

And a moment was all they had.

He found Jaime by touch, ducking low as a fresh swarm of incoming bullets hissed over his head. Bolan couldn't count the guns, had no inkling of numbers, but he drew strength from the knowledge that they weren't completely surrounded. Though the hostiles had cut off their trail, fore and aft, they had no men here, where the targets had been forced to ground. That meant one of two things: they had run out of soldiers, or their slick strategy still had some loopholes.

Whichever, Bolan knew the enemy would waste no time correcting their mistake. That meant frontal assault, unknown numbers attacking the scant foliage that served as cover for Bolan and the young guerrilla.

The smart move would be a withdrawal at speed, laying down cover fire as they split, killing some of their enemies, sucking the rest into aimless pursuit that would rebound to kill them. He had done it before, with the Cong, and it worked like a charm.

But he wasn't alone. Escape without Jaime or Mateo smelled like desertion from where Bolan sat. He would have to convince them, or stick to the end.

"We're cut off and outnumbered," he told the young rebel. "They blew it, not spacing their men, but they know that by now. They'll be coming to get us. It's only a matter of time, and we shouldn't be here when they hit."

Jaime faced him and frowned. "I will not leave Luis behind."

"He's dead."

"He is . . . he was my friend."

Bolan wasn't inclined to argue. He'd viewed the world from the perspective of a man whose friends were scattered on a battlefield, and he knew desertion of the dead could sometimes strike a soldier in the midst of combat as the rankest kind of cowardice. If Jaime meant to stay and fight, the die was cast.

And *die* might be the operative word.

"We're too spread out," he said resignedly.

A whistle and a yelping cry brought Mateo across to join them, ducking hostile fire. He paused once to shred more foliage with a high-explosive round. Before the ringing echoes faded, Bolan heard someone cry out in pain.

A ruse? He doubted it. The opposition might be competent, but there was clearly not an Oscar winner in the pack. If Mateo had thinned the ranks, they could be grateful for one or two fewer guns to face when the inevitable banzai charge rolled over their position.

And they wouldn't have to wait much longer, Bolan thought. The random bursts were fewer now, sporadic single rounds replacing wasteful automatic fire. The enemy would be saving ammunition for the rush when they would need to spray the undergrowth without specific targets, pinning down their quarry while they closed in for the kill.

The Executioner felt along his belt for extra magazines, made certain he could find them instantly at need. He had one frag grenade remaining, plus his side arms and the Ka-bar fighting knife. If it came down to hand-to-hand combat, however, he was convinced they wouldn't have a chance.

Their hastily chosen position was by no means fortified. A fallen log provided minimal concealment on one side, but they were shielded on the other only by ferns and a wall of hanging lianas. The foliage might be fine for camouflage, but it was far from bulletproof, and Bolan felt exposed, vulnerable, as he huddled in the weeds and waited for the enemy to come.

How long?

The firing had stopped by now, and he thought he heard rustlings in the forest off to either side. Was he imagining sounds, his ears still ringing from the noise of combat? Was the enemy advancing even now?

Then there was an unexpected flicker in the trees to Bolan's right. He turned his head to follow it and caught another furtive movement out of the corner of his eye. It made good sense, the hunters circling, spreading out to ring their prey and close the perfect trap.

"They're trying to surround us," Jaime hissed.

"Be ready. It could come from any side or all at once."

The young man whispered brief instructions in Spanish to their flanker. Bolan watched as Mateo reloaded both his rifle and the M-203 launcher. When the slender man caught Bolan's eye, he smiled, revealing silver front teeth. Bolan answered with a grin.

They might be going to die, but there was no rule that they had to go out whining.

From the forest all around them whoops erupted, rising, trilling, peaking with a sound that made him think of jungle birds in pain. A thrashing in the undergrowth, a wall of automatic fire descending on three sides, and the assault was on.

JAIME VARGAS PICKED his target, squeezing off a 4-round burst that dropped the runner in his tracks. Behind the fallen gunman, others were advancing steadily, still firing as they came. Jaime held the trigger of his AK-47 down, prepared to stop them in their tracks if possible.

Beside him Bolan pitched a hand grenade in the direction of the game trail, then hunched down as it exploded, watching as it sent jagged twists of shrapnel singing through the half light of the forest. Mateo alternated bursts of automatic fire with rounds from his grenade launcher, but Jaime knew he must be running low on high-explosive shells. He'd already cranked off half a dozen; the jungle floor was smoldering in front of his position. Vargas heard the screams of dying men, and they were music to his ears.

How often he had lain awake at night and listened in his mind to the screams of women, men and children—the cries of relatives and neighbors, those he knew from childhood, some of whom he loved, cut down in their tracks like cattle led to slaughter. He couldn't escape those sounds, those memories, but he could balance them with other screams— the death knell of his enemies.

Jaime fed another magazine into the Kalashnikov and shifted his position, wriggling along the rotten log to find a better vantage point. More of the enemy were visible now, and he fired upon them when they showed themselves. One fell, another and—

The second body was in uniform.

He felt the old, familiar rage begin to smolder. For a moment he had thought they might have crossed the path of smugglers or bandits, but now he understood. They had walked into an ambush mounted by Pedilla's *pistoleros*, and the bastards were supported by at least a token force of *federales*.

Had the enemy been hunting his guerrillas, he wondered, or—as he believed more likely—were they searching for the American? He had wrecked Pedilla's compound, an affront that couldn't be ignored. Such insolence demanded a response in kind, and the Pedilla syndicate was known for paying off its debts in blood.

Vargas wondered briefly if their stumbling upon the trap had been a mere coincidence. Were gunners watching every well-used game trail in the area? Or had attention narrowed to the portion of Caquetá Province near Ramona's village, near the camp Vargas had established for his men?

A sudden chilling image entered Jaime's mind: his meager force surprised by raiders at the base camp, slaughtered as they ran for cover, the survivors taken prisoner for cruel interrogation. Were the raiders even now aware of Jaime's mission to the village? His liaison with the tall American?

This was no time for such desperate thoughts, he realized, and firmly he thrust them aside. The enemy was on the attack now, crashing among the trees betraying ten or fifteen men at least. An order, passed along the line, had brought them forward in a rush, their weapons rattling, and Jaime knew that only concentrated fire would turn them back.

He struggled to his knees, teeth clenched around the fear that tried to flatten him against the spongy forest floor. Beside him Bolan caught the move and hesitated for a heartbeat, then followed before his conscious mind could offer up a hundred different reasons to abstain. The last to rise was Mateo, reloading as he lurched erect and chambered his last grenade.

Surrounded on three sides, each man picked out his field of fire instinctively, his weapon set on automatic, blazing from the hip. There was no time to aim, no clear-cut targets available. They hosed the forest, shredding ferns, palmettos, lianas, cutting off slim saplings, splintering bark from larger trees. The concentrated din of firing deafened Jaime, muting the explosive *crump* of Mateo's grenade.

Hot rounds whispered around him, tugging at his camouflage fatigues. Knowing he might die at any instant, Jaime held his ground, emptied out his magazine and replaced it in a single fluid motion, feeling heat radiating from the barrel of his weapon.

Had they killed a dozen yet? How many more remained?

As if in answer to his silent question, three men broke the tree line just in front of Jaime, rushing his position. He caught the first one with a rising burst across the legs and lower torso, nailed the second with a line of slugs across the chest.

And lost it on the third, his hammer falling on an empty chamber.

Frozen for an instant, Jaime's enemy was slow to realize he was still alive. Recovering, the *pistolero* gave a shout of triumph, squeezed the trigger of his submachine gun—and it jammed. Panicked, he threw himself at Jaime, shrieking like a wild man, clubbing with the useless weapon in his hands. A butt stroke from Jaime's AK-47 smashed his jaw, followed by another smash against his larynx, cutting off the flow of oxygen to straining lungs. Still unsatisfied, Jaime savagely pounded at the purple face with driving blows that pulped the gunner's lips, his nose, cracked his forehead like an eggshell.

Suddenly Jaime realized he was laboring in almost total silence. There was no more gunfire, no more heavy bodies crashing through the undergrowth. Panting, he snapped another magazine into the receiver of his AK-47 and chambered a round, but there were no more targets to attract his fire.

The charge was broken. Somehow they had survived.

He glanced around the clearing that the concentrated fire had carved out of the forest. Twisted bodies lay where they'd fallen when bullets had found them, cutting short their lives. He picked out five in uniform. There would be others back among the trees, but he didn't bother with a body count.

Beside him Bolan was examining the fallen soldiers with a sick expression on his face. It suddenly occurred to Vargas that the American might have some qualms about eliminating *federales*. It scarcely mattered now, though. The deed was done, and they were still alive.

A muffled groan from Mateo brought Vargas to his side. The man had taken two hits: one, a superficial graze beneath his arm, would quickly heal; the other, where a slug had drilled his thigh, was bleeding heavily. Jaime used a makeshift tourniquet to stop the flow. There was a medic at the base camp, an hour away, if they met no further opposition. He thought Mateo could make it there with assistance.

If the camp was still there. Again the nagging premonition of disaster perched on Jaime's shoulder, whispering of treachery and death. He shook it off and turned to Bolan.

"We must carry Mateo," he said.

"No problem."

But obviously there was a problem. Bolan's voice was distant, strained, as if he was nursing some concealed pain of his own. Yet he bore no sign of injury.

"We go."

It was a riddle Jaime could decipher on the trail. His doubts and fears were coming back, full force, and they wouldn't be laid to rest until he saw the camp again, his soldiers safe and unmolested.

"Por favor," he whispered. "Please."

14

Bolan smelled the acrid smoke a quarter hour before they reached the camp. The double canopy of forest ruled out any possibility of visual detection, but the smell grew stronger as they pushed along the game trail, taking turns carrying Mateo, the free man walking point.

A proper burial of Luis had been aborted by the wounded Mateo's need, but they'd stripped the soldier of his weapons, scraped out a trench, then covered the shallow grave with stones and a rotted log for camouflage and marginal security. Their exit from the killing grounds was slower than Bolan would have liked, for Mateo was losing blood despite the tourniquet, and could only hobble with assistance. They kept to the game trail, which they realized might hold another ambush.

Two hours passed, and they were working on a third when Bolan caught the first faint whiffs of burning on the air. Vargas had been edgy since the ambush, muttering in Spanish when his wounded comrade slowed them down, as if the clash with hostile guns had flicked a paranoia switch inside his mind. Bolan knew the young guerrilla was anticipating further trouble, anxious for their journey to be over, needing reassurance that his men were safe.

The firefight had left a bitter taste in Bolan's mouth, as well, although his reasons differed. He hadn't noticed the federal uniforms while he was fighting for his life, and as the smoke had begun to lift, he couldn't say with any certainty if he had killed any of the soldiers scattered on the field of fire. Even if he had had time and gear to dig out the bullets, he still would not have been sure, for Mateo had also fired 5.56 mm tumblers at the enemy. It would have taken a forensics lab to sort things out.

A realist with pessimistic overtones, Bolan automatically assumed the worst. What if he was responsible for one or more dead soldiers in the midst of godforsaken nowhere? Military men who stood with criminals and terrorists were worse than criminals and terrorists themselves. They had no mercy coming to them in the universal scheme of things.

And who would ever know?

A simple answer. *He would.*

And if he hadn't killed the *federales*, if they'd been slain by Mateo or Jaime, did it make a difference in the long run? Was coincidence the best excuse he could offer to himself? Next time he faced a mirror, would he see the stains of murder on his soul?

He put the morbid train of thought behind him, concentrating on the trail, the wounded man whose arm was draped across his shoulders. He would deal with pain and doubt some other time when he had time to spare. Just now his mind was fully occupied with the mechanics of survival.

And the smell of burning.

He was watching Jaime as the stench grew stronger, knew that it came from the camp before his guide gave orders for a rest stop, several hundred yards short of their established destination. They left Mateo armed and propped against a tree, with orders to remain alert and guard himself while they crept forward to inspect the damage.

It was every bit as bad as Bolan had feared.

There had been perhaps two dozen men in camp, and from the carnage it was obvious they'd been taken by surprise. The several tents were little more than blackened scraps of cloth, still smoldering. The bodies lay in twisted attitudes of death, where automatic fire had cut them down.

Vargas and Bolan entered cautiously, prepared for trouble, though it seemed apparent the raiders had moved on. Had some of them lain in ambush on the game trail? It didn't seem likely, but Bolan couldn't rule out the possibility. In either case he had no doubt that all the guns—and federal troops—involved were on Pedilla's payroll.

Jaime Vargas moved among the corpses, turning over those that lay facedown, identifying each in turn. There seemed to be no weapons in the camp, although the forest floor was bright with cartridge casings. Bolan picked out 5.56, 7.62, 9 mm—all the silent residue of mortal combat, like a sprinkling of glitter for the dead.

A movement in the trees arrested Bolan's scan of the encampment, brought him to a crouch, the Colt Commando seeking targets. Jaime Vargas raised a hand, his AK-47 also leveled at the trees, as several men emerged from hiding there.

Survivors.

Five in all, and two of those had suffered only superficial wounds. They all began to speak at once, and Bolan left assimilation of the story to his host, along with explanations of his own identity and presence in the camp. He concentrated on the dead, alert for signs that some had outlived others, possibly enduring interrogation at the hands of their attackers.

But from appearances the fallen men had been killed outright, shot from ambush by the raiders or annihilated in a brief and furious exchange of gunfire. If they had inflicted any casualties, the dead or wounded had been carried off by healthy comrades, who had also stripped the camp of arms.

Scorched earth. It was Pedilla's game, but two could always play.

And if the Medellín cartel had this much life left in it after Bolan's raid, he had been premature in thinking of evacuation from the battle zone.

His mission in Colombia was obviously not completed.

He had work to do, and there was no time like the present to begin.

ANTONIO YBARRA PARKED his jeep and waited for the drivers of the flatbed trucks to kill their engines. Motes of road dust swam like insects in the headlight beams before those lights were finally extinguished, bringing darkness to the village street. In homes on either side, the fitful light of lamps and candles did its best to keep the hungry night at bay.

He waited while the men and boys unloaded, straggling toward their hovels. No one ventured out to greet them, though he knew the girls and women would be waiting just behind their flimsy doors, afraid to show themselves and thus invite more trouble. He enjoyed the godlike power he felt in dealing with the peons when they bowed before him and trembled at his touch.

The widow was alone in her defiance, and he called her image back to mind, enjoying both the lust and anger he felt. She was a wild one, drawing on the courage of a woman who believed she had nothing left to lose.

Her husband had been killed, the firm foundation of her life disrupted in an instant, and she thought that if the world rolled over on her in its sleep, she wouldn't mind. But she had much to learn about reality, the give-and-take of life.

Tonight it was her turn to give, and his to take.

The lesson would be valuable to the woman and her neighbors. Defiance in the face of overwhelming force was risky business. If the woman hadn't learned that much from witnessing her husband's death, then it was time she had the lesson driven home.

Ybarra chuckled. Driving lessons home was something of a specialty that he had cultivated over time. He liked it best when women were the students; the exercise was so much more rewarding. When he finished with a woman, he was pleased to think he left her better off, in terms of wisdom and experience, than when he found her.

Smiling as he moved along the street, Ybarra viewed himself as something of a public servant. It was his crusade to banish rudeness from the female sex, restoring the servility that had once made Latin women prizes to be cherished rather than aggressive dragons to be feared.

A light was showing in the widow's house. Antonio Ybarra spent a moment dusting off his clothes and straightening his gun belt. It was only proper to present a neat appearance when you came to call, and it was doubly important in his role as teacher so that he could make a strong impression on his student. She might not pay close attention to the nuances at first, but by the time he paid a second visit, and a third, she would appreciate the time he took to make himself presentable.

Remembering her husband, he took time to check his pistol, fastening the thumb-break strap that held the gun securely in its holster. It would slow her down if she attempted to disarm him, leaving him with ample time to draw and fire at need.

But he didn't anticipate that kind of action here tonight. A different kind, perhaps. Most definitely.

Ybarra was forced to knock three times before she answered. He was annoyed by her discourtesy, but chalked it up to normal nerves that any student might experience upon enrolling in a brand-new class, a class that was about to change her life.

She wore a different blouse and skirt tonight, although the styles were much the same. Ybarra shouldered past her, tired of waiting for an invitation, conscious of the fact that he must seize control, assert himself at once, without allowing her to take the lead. He felt her eyes on him, frightened, wary eyes, and knew he had broken through her mask of grim indifference.

"I promised I would see you."

"So you did. Now you have seen me. Please get out."

"Where is your hospitality? Your courtesy? Are women in your village always rude?"

"I save my courtesy for gentlemen," she said. "I have none left for you."

He struck her with an open palm, the sharp report as loud as pistol fire inside the tiny one-room hovel. The impact staggered her, but she didn't fall. A sign of strength. His palm print was emblazoned on her cheek.

"You have so much to learn."

"And who will teach me?"

"It appears I have been chosen for the thankless task."

She forced a laugh. "I fail to see what I can learn from you."

"Respect . . . and other things."

She telegraphed the move, a quick glance toward the stove before she lunged to reach the carving knife. Ybarra cut her off, a solid backhand bloodying her nose and knocking her off balance. While she tried to right herself, he casually thrust the knife blade down inside a burner of the stove and snapped the handle in half.

"You won't be needing that tonight."

"*You* may."

He caught her as she tried to back away. Hooked fingers snagged in the neckline of her peasant blouse and ripped downward to reveal her breasts. She made no move to hide herself, intent on searching for a weapon, lunging for a broomstick as he sprang upon her.

She was strong, he gave her that, but after he used his clenched fist twice, she melted in his arms. He recognized surrender, knew that women sometimes feigned unconsciousness in a misguided effort to preserve their precious dignity. He marveled at the way they managed to suppress their yearnings on a first encounter, biting back the cries of passion that he knew must come, unbidden, to their throats. It angered him, as well, and drove him to more strenuous exertions as he sought to break the final wall of her resistance.

Never mind. He knew the game, and realized she would come around when she had a second lesson, or a third. Ybarra seldom had to beat them after two or three sessions, and his students rarely fainted in the absence of a solid clout across the skull.

For now, it was enough that she know precisely what was happening, and why. When he left her, satisfied with one night's work, she could discard her pose and privately relive the fantasy, anticipating his return tomorrow night. And the next.

At the present rate it might take several days, perhaps a week or more, for reconstruction of the compound to be finished. Ybarra thanked his lucky stars, and wondered idly if there was any risk-free way for him to stall the job, allow himself some extra time with this most stimulating student.

Maybe, if she showed real promise, he'd take her home to study at his quarters for a while. If she was very, very good.

All things considered, he believed that she would do.

THE MEDIC HAD BEEN KILLED in the attack on the base camp. Jaime left Mateo and one of his walking wounded at the new camp. Crude patchwork had eventually stopped the bleeding from Mateo's leg, but he was weak, delirious and feverish. Without transfusions, medicine, it seemed unlikely he would last the night.

Another life, among the hundreds—thousands—that Pedilla had to answer for. It was regrettable that he couldn't be made to suffer for them one by one, enduring the agonies of hell for each before he died.

As it was, his death would have to be enough—if they could find him, break through his defenses, strip him of his guards.

The tall American had fallen in with Jaime's plan at once. He had been free to go, of course, understanding that Vargas could no longer spare the time or men to guide him. After only moments in the ruined camp, he had agreed to join the guerrillas' move against Pedilla, following the trail of those who had annihilated Jaime's men. Along the way he had added an embellishment or two to their plan.

It could be futile—maybe even suicidal—to engage a larger force in open combat. Bolan had suggested instead that they bide their time, hang back, give the murderers a taste of the guerrilla warfare they had used on Jaime's men. If the Pedilla team was hunting, chances were they wouldn't return immediately to the *narcotraficante*'s compound. They would likely make camp in the forest, even lay another ambush on a different trail, and they wouldn't expect to be the prey themselves.

Following the enemy had been fairly simple. Pedilla's men were cocky in the wake of their resounding sweep, apparently unaware that their associates had been wiped out in an abortive ambush. Jaime thought it likely they were heading for a predetermined rendezvous, and his suspicion was confirmed toward dusk as they approached the enemy encampment in a forest clearing.

Crouching in near darkness, Bolan at his side, the others hanging back to wait for orders, Jaime counted heads and weighed the odds against survival. Nineteen gunners made it roughly three to one, and he could live with that quite nicely. If the guerrillas' first move was decisive, they would cut those odds in half before the *pistoleros* knew they had a problem on their hands.

He watched and waited while they posted sentries, two men on the first watch, taking the perimeter, while others huddled near the fire and cracked their rations for the evening meal. He couldn't hear their conversation from a distance. He wondered if it might concern the missing troops, their failure to appear on schedule. He could be wrong, of course; there might be several hunter teams at large, all watching different trails and seeking contact with elusive enemies. The gunners they had killed that morning might have no connection with the group at hand.

There were no *federales* with the present team, and Vargas noticed Bolan visibly relaxing as he scanned the enemy encampment. The American would never qualify as squeamish, but he obviously had his reasons for avoiding contact with the regulars. No matter. They were dealing with Pedilla's *pistoleros* now. Jaime had no doubt the big man would perform his part with competence and skill.

Elimination of the posted sentries was their first priority, and that would have to wait until the gunmen bedded down. Already they were finishing their makeshift supper, spreading ponchos, dragging blankets out of rucksacks. In an hour, maybe less, they would be his.

The young guerrilla settled down to wait.

THE SENTRY MIGHT HAVE HEARD him coming, Bolan couldn't say, but there was no time for the guard to react before a big hand closed his mouth and nostrils, twisting to expose his throat, the juncture of his skull and spine. The Ka-bar's eight-inch blade slid home unerringly, its full length buried in the fissure the Chinese call the "wind gate," entering the trooper's brain and stirring briskly for an instant, shorting every possible command to vocal cords and hands.

The gunner died without a hint of understanding, never realizing what had happened to him. All in all, the Executioner believed it was a decent way to go.

Across the clearing he couldn't pick out the other sentry, but he thought Vargas might have made his move already. Bolan's watch showed sixty-seven seconds remaining as he sheathed the Ka-bar, shifting his position for a better field of fire and easing off the Colt Commando's safety.

Seventeen, without the sentries. Most of them, he thought, must be asleep by now. He and the guerrillas had selected targets before they moved out to take up positions on the clearing's wide perimeter. His four were lined up near the fire, two men in sleeping bags, two more with ponchos pulled up to their chins.

He set the Colt's selector switch for semiautomatic fire to conserve precious ammunition. Several of Pedilla's men were packing M-16s, and if the ambush evolved as planned, he would replenish his supply from captured stores.

Relax, he told himself. It was a classic setup. He couldn't let the images of soldiers lying in the forest cloud his judgment. What was done was done. There was no turning back; he could only forge ahead and prosecute his war as best he could. If there were psychic repercussions later, he could damn well keep them to himself.

Ten seconds.

Bolan started counting down, committed to proceed on time no matter what the others did. If the second sentry had been disposed of, fine. If not, there would be time enough to take him once the firing started.

Lining up on his initial target, Bolan heard the numbers falling in his head. It was like sniping from a distance, more or less, except that less precision was required for openers.

And there were realistic chances of the targets shooting back.

Four seconds.

Bolan took a deep breath, let part of it go and held the rest. His hands were steady on the rifle as he verified his aim.

Two seconds.

From the corner of his eye he saw a stirring, a gunner wrestling with his poncho, maybe rising to relieve himself. Too late.

Fire!

He squeezed off two quick rounds, already tracking as his target twisted in convulsions and the tree line came alive with winking muzzle-flashes. Jaime and the rest were squeezing off on automatic, raking the encampment with converging streams of fire.

The Executioner finished number two, then tracked on as his still-surviving targets struggled back to consciousness. Too late for number three already, as a tumbler drilled his forehead and erupted through an exit wound the size of Bolan's fist, behind one ear. The gunner folded like a rag doll, facedown on the forest bed of fallen leaves.

The *pistolero* he'd marked as number four was on his knees and cradling a weapon in his arms when Bolan squeezed off two quick rounds from fifteen yards away. The impact punched his target over backward, boot heels drumming on the poncho he had spread out to make his pallet. Dying fingers triggered a convulsive, aimless burst in the direction of the stars.

The firing lasted for a few more seconds, Jaime and his men unloading on the hostiles even after they were down and out, releasing pent-up anger and frustration through the muzzles of their weapons. Bolan let the outburst run its course, emerging from his shelter only when the storm had passed, the five guerrillas rising and advancing on the camp.

A hasty mop-up finished three survivors, echoes of the final gunshots battering among the trees before dying away at last. Without a word they set about relieving corpses of their ammunition belts, side arms and a few pineapple-style grenades. One of the young guerrillas traded in his ancient M-1 carbine for an M-16 that had been customized by the addition of a 12-gauge shotgun mounted underneath the barrel.

Jaime found Bolan in the middle of the carnage. "We have made a start," he said.

"Pedilla won't sit still for this. His reputation's on the line."

"Agreed. He must strike back. But where?"

They both knew the answer almost simultaneously. Bolan's eyes locked with Jaime's in the faint light of the dying fire.

"The village?"

Bolan nodded. "That would be my guess."

"We have no time to waste."

And he was right of course.

They had no time at all.

15

Bolan half expected smoking ruins when they reached the nameless village, but the narrow unpaved street looked familiar in the darkness. He didn't rule out the possibility of ambush, but a tour of the perimeter convinced him there were no outsiders hiding in the settlement.

Not yet.

Ramona's house was dark, but he'd have to wake her. Bolan had no other contacts in the village, and he and Jaime were agreed their plan would need support from local spokesmen. Or spokes*persons*, as the case might be.

His knock was gentle, scarcely a tapping, but he knew it would be audible inside the tiny one-room house. He picked out footsteps in the darkness, waited for the door to open, but instead a muffled voice came to him from somewhere just inside. Soft words in Spanish, gibberish to Bolan, but he recognized the sound of pain.

"Ramona? It's Mike Blanski. Let me in."

She hesitated, then finally told him, "No. You must not stay here."

"Jaime's with me, and some others. We've come back to help you, if we can."

"There is no help."

"Ramona—"

Suddenly she stood before him, clutching at the front of his fatigue blouse, pulling him inside. She didn't light the lamp or candles; he was momentarily reduced to speaking with a silhouette.

"You must not stay," she said again, and he thought there was something different, something thick about her voice.

He palmed a pencil flashlight and pinned her with the beam before she had a chance to turn away. Both hands came up to cover her face, but Bolan had already seen enough. He found the lamp and lit it, turning down the flame to radiate a muted glow.

Ramona tried to hide from him at first, but finally dropped her hands. One eye—her left—was swollen nearly shut; her lips were puffy, split in places where a fist had flattened them against her teeth. A dark bruise stained one cheek.

She recoiled when Bolan reached for her, a whimper rising in her throat, and she clutched the shawl around her shoulders like a cloak of mail. He scanned the room and found a little pile of shredded clothing in a corner.

"He came back?"

Ramona nodded stiffly, holding back the tears with God knows what reserve of inner strength. She didn't flinch this time when Bolan slid a gentle arm around her shoulders, but the warrior felt her trembling against him.

"We'll be waiting for him in the morning."

"No! You will be killed. You must not—"

"Jaime's camp was hit this afternoon by Pedilla's people. We've already made a small down payment on the tab, but I don't have the pull to throw Jaime off this plan...even if I wanted to."

She seemed to understand. "How many are there?"

"Six. It should be even money if they come in like this morning."

"Who will tell the others?"

"Well, I don't know enough Spanish, so I guess it falls to Jaime."

"No. It must be someone from the village."

"You've been through enough."

"This fight is mine as well as yours. More now, I think."

He couldn't argue with her logic, and he didn't try. He heard guerrillas outside banging doors and calling people out into the street. Ramona pulled away from him and moved in the direction of the door.

The villagers were huddled in the street as they had been that morning to listen to Pedilla's soldiers. Jaime was attempting to explain his plan, but Bolan could see he was getting nowhere fast. Ramona moved to stand beside the young man, dredging up a smile as she restrained him with a hand on his shoulder.

Bolan listened, understanding next to nothing, as Ramona spoke to her assembled neighbors. Studying their faces, Bolan picked out apprehension, blatant fear... and something else. It was apparent none of them had seen Ramona's injuries before, although they plainly realized what she'd been through with Pedilla's crew chief. Now the Executioner thought he could recognize traces of guilt on some faces, anger on even more, emotions escalating toward combustion.

The villagers weren't a mob by any means, nor would they ever make a military troop, but they'd suffered long and everybody had a boiling point. Presented with a chance to move against Pedilla, he believed some of them, at least, would grab the opportunity and run with it.

He hoped they would.

In theory the plan could operate without a single villager to help, but they could blow it if they opted to resist. He wouldn't launch a firefight with Pedilla's men if there were innocent civilians in the cross fire. If the men and women of the no-name settlement wouldn't cooperate, the plan would have to be revised.

There were alternatives of course—an ambush on the narrow road outside the village, followed by a thrust against Pedilla's compound. But it would be so much easier if they could seize the trucks undamaged. That way they could drive up to Pedilla's doorstep and deliver a surprise the *narcotraficante* wouldn't soon forget.

Ramona finished speaking, then spent a moment studying her audience. The villagers whispered among themselves. Finally an ad hoc spokesman answered her reluctantly, as if the words stuck in his throat.

Ramona's smile looked painful as she turned to Bolan. "They are frightened," she informed him, "but they will do what they can."

"That's all we ask," Bolan told her. He wondered silently how many of her neighbors would be forced to pay a price because their best was simply not enough.

THEY HAD SECURED extra guns and ammunition from Pedilla's soldiers when they had raided the jungle camp, and Jaime Vargas supervised their distribution now. He dared not let the villagers practice—they couldn't afford the noise or wasted rounds—but he made certain every man knew how to load and fire his weapon as they moved from house to house, preparing their surprise.

If the plan went off without a hitch, there should be a massacre. Pedilla's men—no more than six or seven were expected—would be lured from their vehicles by an apparent show of noncooperation. Jaime's men would do the killing, but he wanted other men prepared to fight in case the confrontation got out of hand and escalated into something larger.

Women and children would leave their homes at dawn to find a sanctuary in the forest. Even if the *pistoleros* came with reinforcements and the battle somehow went against his forces, Jaime thought the enemy wouldn't have time for a concentrated sweep. If any of them managed to survive, they'd be running for their lives and reinforcements.

Running to Pedilla.

There were guns enough to go around among the men and older boys. One man tried to refuse a weapon, finally accepting only when his neighbors started muttering among themselves and glaring at him angrily. His fear was obvious and understandable, but Jaime found his evident reluctance curious in one so young. By rights he should have been a leader for the others, tall and strong as he appeared to be. There was no accounting, however, for differences in personality. A coward might yet prove himself when called upon to function as a member of the team.

The plan was based on swift precision fire with members of Pedilla's team eliminated cleanly and efficiently. Their vehicles were central to the scheme, which Jaime had devised with Bolan, and wouldn't be damaged if the targets stuck to their expected roles. If they attempted to escape on wheels, however, the trucks might have to be sacrificed.

Jaime wouldn't let his hopes be crushed by pessimism. He'd come too far and fought too hard for simple transportation difficulties to betray him now. If necessary, he'd do without the trucks, without assistance from the others—he would track and kill Pedilla on his own.

Justice would be done. Teresa and his friends, his family, would be avenged.

Eight hours before first light. His men would sleep in shifts, with Jaime on the last watch, leading up to dawn. He didn't think Pedilla's soldiers would return to claim their slaves before the scheduled pickup time, but circumstances might be altered if the slaughter in the forest was discovered in the meantime. Anything was possible. Jaime Vargas wasn't leaving anything to chance.

Two men on watch at first. The others would be housed with childless couples while they slept, and he supposed Blanski, the American, would spend the hours of darkness with Ramona.

Jaime scowled, remembering what she'd suffered since that morning. There was pain enough to go around, and all of it would be repaid in kind when finally he laid hands on Pedilla. Years of suffering, oppression, degradation, charged against the soul of the man who was responsible for all of it.

The young man flexed his shoulders, prowling past the darkened houses like a jungle cat in search of prey. He would be honored to collect Pedilla's debt. He only feared the *narcotraficante* might not have sufficient blood to wash away his multitude of sins.

Jaime meant to bleed the bastard dry.

VIRGILIO HERNANDEZ SAT alone inside his house, his elbows on the hand-hewn dining table, staring at the rifle propped in the corner. It intimidated him, like the shadow of a vulture perched on his shoulder.

After initially declining, he had finally agreed to take the weapon. His neighbors expected it of him, and would be suspicious of his stubborn refusal. It was enough, however, for him to have the rifle in his house; he didn't intend to use it. Certainly he didn't intend to use it in some suicidal move against Pedilla's private army. If his neighbors chose to throw their lives away, the choice was theirs, but he wasn't a sheep prepared to follow blindly in their footsteps.

There was an alternative of course. It would require an act of courage greater than resistance in the face of overwhelming odds, and if it was discovered, it would make Virgilio an outcast in the village. He could save them—most of them at any rate—but it was doubtful any of his neighbors would appreciate the gesture. They were angry, spoiling for a fight, and reason had no place in their considerations.

Still, if he could save the village from destruction, was he not obligated to take certain steps on the behalf of people he'd known for years? Could he sit back and watch them be slaughtered when he had the key to their salvation in his hands?

It grieved him to betray Ramona for a second time, but she wasn't herself these days. Her brooding anger over Carlos, coupled with her hurt and fury at the pain she had suffered from Pedilla's crew chief, made her irrational and ultimately self-destructive. He could save her from herself if there was time.

At first Virgilio had thought the knowledge of Ramona's rape might drive him mad. He was surprised to find how swiftly he'd come to terms with the reality, how easy it had been to grant forgiveness. After all, she had deliberately provoked the *pistolero*, taunting him with words that no man—let alone an outlaw—could ignore. To that extent the violence that followed was her fault, and she had endangered every other person in the village, even as she chose to sacrifice herself, her honor.

But Virgilio forgave Ramona, as he had when she'd selected Carlos for her husband, turning a blind eye to the man who truly loved her. If she had been rational in those days, Carlos would still be alive, and she herself wouldn't be nursing bruises to her body and her reputation. When you were hopelessly in love, forgiveness was a simple thing.

Virgilio was proud of his maturity, of the inner strength that let him rise above the petty anger and emotions of his neighbors. He didn't enjoy the visits from Pedilla's people, but he knew enough of life to realize that some things were inevitable. He hadn't been born to wealthy parents, and hadn't earned a fortune in the coca trade. He was a peasant, plain and simple, vulnerable to the whims of bigger, richer men. It was a simple fact of life, but that didn't detract from his intelligence or native cunning. When his back was pressed against the wall, Virgilio could scheme and plot as well as any of his masters.

But he was running out of time. It would be nearly dawn when he reached Pedilla's compound, traveling on foot, and he would run a risk of being shot by sentries when he reached his destination. Still, he saw no alternative. Virgilio couldn't sit back and watch his neighbors bring about their own destruction. More particularly he couldn't allow himself to be a victim of their rash and irresponsible behavior.

At the bottom line Hernandez knew about self-preservation. He wouldn't resist Pedilla, for he knew resistance had its consequences, always painful, often deadly. Neither would he give Pedilla any opportunity to think that he, Virgilio, was part of a conspiracy to frustrate the cartel. If others in his village were determined to destroy themselves for no good reason, he could save himself—and, possibly, Ramona.

In the woman's case it wouldn't be easy. She was already compromised through Carlos and her vocal opposition to Pedilla's people. But Virgilio believed he could pull it off. The dealer would be grateful for his information; there would be rewards. Virgilio would try to name Ramona as a portion of his price.

Trembling, he drew the lantern to him and extinguished it. The darkness seemed to help, obscuring the conflict he felt inside himself. A portion of his mind was diametrically opposed to his selected course of action, but he wouldn't let himself be swayed by anything so trivial as conscience. He had slipped beyond the pale when he had arranged the murder of his brother, and survival was the only thing that mattered now. If he could save Ramona, fine. If not, then he would merely save himself.

It sometimes hurt to think of Carlos even now. His brother had been different, committed to a different set of standards than Virgilio, although their parents and Carlos himself never seemed to recognize the wide disparity between them. Carlos thought of others first, and his altruism had been his downfall. He'd risked himself too often, trusted blindly in the bonds of blood and family. Until the moment of his death—and even then perhaps—he hadn't recognized his difference from Virgilio.

Would Virgilio have spoken to Pedilla, given up his brother's name, if he hadn't been jealous on account of Ramona? Looking back, Virgilio believed the woman had been more excuse than motivation. He was captivated by her beauty, the desire she stirred within him, but he was still a pragmatist. He might simply have watched her from a distance, as he had in fact since Carlos's death, but circumstances had compelled him to take action.

Carlos had been rugged, unafraid of *narcotraficantes* and their guns. He had announced his intention to resist conscription by Pedilla's jobbers, and had encouraged other villagers to do the same. When news of massacres around Caquetá Province reached their village, Carlos had been adamant, refusing to back down.

His death had been an act of mercy for the village, saving untold lives. A general revolt would have provoked Pedilla into swift retaliation, leaving no survivors. Though innocent, Virgilio would have been exterminated with the rest. It was a risk he hadn't been prepared to take.

And so he had betrayed his brother, whispering a name to one of Hector Pedilla's spies. The rest was simple; all he had to do was watch and wait, pretending grief when Carlos fell before the firing squad. No one suspected him of anything. The village had survived because of him, and no one even recognized his secret act of heroism.

It would be the same now, except this time violence on a larger scale seemed guaranteed. With six guerrillas in the village, fighting was inevitable. Several of the villagers had voiced their willingness to stand against Pedilla once the guns were in their hands, and they would likely die, as well. How far the killing spread once it began would be for Pedilla and the people to decide. If few villagers resisted, the reprisals might be limited to forfeiture of food and money. If they fought, the outlook was grim indeed.

Outside, the night was warm and still. Virgilio took great pains to slip silently around the sentries, clinging to the shadows he knew by heart. If the lookouts noticed him, they gave no indication.

Safe inside the trees, Virgilio paused long enough to get his bearings and fortify himself against the long dark walk. He knew the jungle well enough to take his time, make certain he didn't step on snakes or cross the path of jaguars. Caution would retard his progress, but he had no choice. In order to protect himself and his village, he had to reach Pedilla's camp alive.

The forest swallowed him, and he was gone.

STANDING AT her darkened window, shadows at her back preventing any silhouette from being visible outside, Ramona watched Virgilio and cursed him underneath her breath. She knew with certainty where he was going. Worse yet, she thought she understood where he had gone, what he had done two years before.

His cowardice hadn't been a major problem in the past. In daily life their village was a place of tedium where every person did the same job they had done the day before and would undoubtedly do tomorrow. There was no adventure, no major risk beyond the simple fact of living in the middle of a giant, untamed forest. Predators and reptiles crossed your path from time to time, but they were an accepted part of living, treated with respect, not fear.

Virgilio, however, was undoubtedly a coward. She'd seen him flinch when other men or boys disposed of vipers in the fields, and when Pedilla's raiders made their periodic visits to the village, he was always courteous, respectful to a fault. Where others held their tongues and did their best to hide a brooding rage, Virgilio seemed happy—even eager—to comply with any orders from the *pistoleros*.

Given all of that, Ramona still had never considered him a traitor and a murderer.

Until tonight.

His surreptitious exit from the village could mean one thing only: he was running to Pedilla with a warning. Anything to save himself, regardless of the cost to friends and neighbors who had shared his work, his joys and sorrows, through the years.

She might have stopped the spineless bastard with a warning to the sentries. He couldn't have traveled far before they overtook him, ran him down, and then her people could have decided a fitting punishment for his betrayal. There was still time . . . and yet Ramona kept silent.

Her mind was working overtime, examining old clues and bits of information, fitting pieces of a timeless puzzle into place. She felt foolish, having missed the obvious for so long, but now the truth was in her hands. No one else on earth would have the privilege of punishing Virgilio, not while she had strength to do it by herself.

Why had she never recognized his guilt before? Had grief so blinded her that she couldn't pick out the obvious? Ramona knew Virgilio wasn't that clever by himself.

But he'd killed her husband. He'd violated every tenet of the family by murdering his own dear brother. Out of jealousy? Some sibling rivalry of which she had been ignorant? Pure hatred in the blood?

Upon reflection she believed it all came down to cowardice. Virgilio had been afraid Carlos would ignite resistance in the village and that he, Virgilio, would have to make a stand, take risks beyond the normal day-to-day tedium.

And there was jealousy of course. That much had been apparent from the moment she had selected Carlos and agreed to be his wife. Virgilio was angry, sulking, even at their wedding ceremony. He couldn't be honest and confront his brother, clear the air between them, for he would have been compelled to take a stand, reveal himself, and that he couldn't manage. It was easier to bide his time and seek an opportunity to build a snare for Carlos, to cast his lot with enemies and let them do the dirty work.

Too late she saw Virgilio for what he was, and she was sickened by him. The American was asleep, but she would tell him when he woke. By then it would be too late for the rebels to pursue Virgilio. He would be free and clear until the moment when they would meet again, when she would take pleasure in relieving him of all the fears that came with living.

Smiling through the pain of bruised and swollen lips, Ramona was excited by the prospect of at last avenging Carlos. She could do that much, at least, in honor of his memory.

And having done that much, perhaps she could allow herself to live again.

16

The sentries picked up Virgilio Hernandez one hundred yards outside Pedilla's compound. There were two of them, and one had been inclined to shoot Virgilio on sight, but his companion had prevailed, insisting that their master would prefer to have a word with the intruder first. There would be ample time to kill him later.

Prodded with the barrels of their automatic weapons, he was herded into camp, a prisoner. The sentries wouldn't listen to his story, heedless of the fact that he'd come to help them, maybe even save their lives. They laughed at him and drove him faster, forcing him to run.

The compound was ablaze with light from bonfires and strategically positioned torches. Men with tools and surplus parts were on their way to fix the shattered generator, but Pedilla obviously hadn't been content to wait in darkness. Despite the hour several windows of his manor house glowed warmly with lantern light, and Virgilio wondered if the dealer was awake. It might go easier, he thought, if he wasn't disturbing anybody's sleep.

Inside the compound he was viewed with obvious suspicion. Every face was hostile, anxious for an opportunity to classify him as the enemy and act accordingly. By daylight, when he and the rest of the work crew were delivered, they had all been virtually ignored. Tonight, however, he'd come back on his own alone and uninvited. It was almost humorous, he thought, to be regarded as a menace.

On the other hand perceptions could be deadly. He was trapped on hostile ground without a single friend to take his part. Any sudden move might mean his death. Once someone pulled a trigger it would matter little if he later realized his grave mistake. Virgilio drew no comfort from the presence of assorted *federales* in the camp.

His guards delivered him to others with a sketchy explanation, and he told his story for the second time, repeating bits and pieces on command. A runner was dispatched to brief Pedilla's houseman, and Virgilio was left to wait with weapons trained on him while half an hour slipped away.

Had his presentation been forceful enough? Had he been sincere? If he was disbelieved at any point along the chain of command, Virgilio was confident he would be executed on the spot, his body dragged into the forest as a snack for marauding scavengers. Pedilla wouldn't recognize the danger his men were facing in the village and, inevitably, men would die.

There would, of course, be deaths in any case, but if the dealer heard him out, prepared himself for confrontation and secured the advantage of surprise, the village losses might be minimized. Virgilio would be a hero, even if his people scorned him for his efforts.

Now the runner was returning, whispering an order to the taller of the gunmen who were covering Virgilio. The gunner scowled in seeming disappointment, spit into the dust and twitched the muzzle of his AK-47 toward the manor house.

Virgilio could breathe again, his lease on life renewed, if only for a moment. The houseman might agree to hear him out, and then decide to kill him anyway. There were no guarantees, but having come this far Virgilio was stripped of options. He would have to forge ahead.

The front doors of the manor house were boarded over on the inside, plywood covering the bullet holes that scarred the wood in aimless, abstract patterns. He'd been amazed that

morning to discover the house was otherwise undamaged in
the midst of so much devastation. Devil's luck, Virgilio
surmised. Pedilla had escaped the final judgment as he always managed to escape arrest, indictment, prison. Having
bargained for his soul, he was collecting on the deal and
laughing off the efforts of his enemies to bring him down.

The houseman was a hulking brute with two guns on his
hips and murder in his eyes. He listened to Virgilio's report
without a visible reaction, nodded thoughtfully and said,
"This way." Hernandez followed him upstairs, a sallow
youngster with a submachine gun bringing up the rear.

Pedilla's house, while very large, was furnished in an almost Spartan style. It was apparent, even to Virgilio's un-
practiced eye, that furniture and fixtures must have cost a
fortune, but the money hadn't gone for art work, bric-a-
brac or frilly decorations. Every piece of furniture was solid,
masculine, prepared on custom order with an eye toward
function rather than the dictates of a certain style. Some
people in Pedilla's place might have indulged themselves
with sculpture, Persian rugs or doorknobs made of solid
gold, but from appearances the *narcotraficante* was content to build himself a home without the trappings of a palace.

Vaguely disappointed by the dissipation of a fantasy,
Virgilio was frowning when the houseman stopped outside
the third door on their left. He knocked, then disappeared
inside upon command. Long moments passed before he
emerged and motioned for Virgilio to follow him back in.

Another moment would determine everything.

Hernandez offered up a silent prayer and waited for the
door to close behind him.

HE WAS NOTHING but a peasant, filthy and disheveled from
his long hike through the jungle after dark, but Pedilla's
subordinates were all agreed his story might be worth the
master's time. Because the dealer paid them well to make

such judgments, and because his life depended to a large
extent upon the accuracy of their intuition, he decided he
would listen to the peon, drawing any ultimate conclusions
for himself.

At least the man hadn't disturbed his rest. Pedilla had retired some hours earlier, but sleep had stubbornly eluded
him. With nerves on edge, he had lain awake and thought
about the next day when supplies for reconstruction of his
laboratory would begin arriving from Florencia and Medellín. The peasant crews had nearly finished clearing off the
site that afternoon; tomorrow, if fortune smiled upon him,
they could turn their energies to more constructive action.

He wasn't prepared to alter predetermined schedules on
the word of any whining peasant, but his houseman had al-
luded to the possibility of danger, and Pedilla had to satisfy himself that every angle of attack was covered, every
risk foreseen and neutralized.

He let the peasant stand before him like a supplicant before his king. "Your name?"

"Virgilio Hernandez."

It meant nothing to Pedilla. He'd never met this man before, and knew that once their business here was finished,
it was doubtful they'd ever meet again.

"What is it that you wish to tell me?"

"In my village—"

"Where is that?"

"Due south, approximately nine kilometers."

He knew the village—or knew of it—one of countless
settlements throughout the province that were large enough
to earn the designation of a village yet too small to rate a
formal name.

"Go on."

"My people have been privileged to help you with the reconstruction of your damaged buildings."

"So?" He nearly grimaced at the peon's whining tone, his
blatant effort to appear subservient, and therefore worthy

to survive. In Hector Pedilla's eyes Virgilio Hernandez was
of no more consequence or value than a smear of dog shit
on a boot.

"Tonight strange men have come into our village bearing many weapons. They insist the people arm themselves
and greet your men with violence when they come for
workers in the morning."

Pedilla frowned. The specter of rebellion rose before him,
and he slapped it down. A group of peasants, armed or
otherwise, was nothing to be feared.

"How many of these strangers are there?"

"Six, *patrón*. I think one of them is an American."

Pedilla froze behind his desk. "You *think*?"

"He speaks very little Spanish. Everything the others tell
him is translated into English. Also, he has better clothes—
a uniform of sorts—and newer weapons."

"Are you always so observant?"

"*Sí, patrón*. I pay attention when my village and my life
are threatened."

"Very well. How have your neighbors taken to these
strangers?"

"They accept the guns because they have no choice. I
think very few of them will fight."

"Six strangers, then, and possibly a few men from the
village."

"*Sí.*"

"And you?"

Hernandez paled. "Would I be here, *patrón*, if I intended to betray you?"

"Possibly. Your story might be fabricated as a lure to
trick my soldiers and deliver them into an ambush."

"No! I swear upon my mother's life."

"*Your* life. I have no interest in old women."

"How can I persuade you?"

"Very simply. You will lead my men when they return to search your village. If they find an ambush waiting, you will be the first to die."

The man was trembling, but he kept his chin up as he answered. "You will find that I have spoken only truth, as when I helped you last."

Pedilla frowned. "And when was that?"

"Two years ago, when you recruited workers for construction of your camp, I warned your soldiers of a traitor in the village and prevented him from doing any harm."

"Betrayal of your neighbors is a habit, then?" Hernandez wore a pained expression, but Pedilla silenced his response by holding up a hand. "Enough. My men will leave at six o'clock, with you to guide them."

"As you say, *patrón*."

"Exactly as I say."

He called the houseman in and issued rapid orders, tripling the force that he sent to pick up peasant labor under normal circumstances. Every man was to be armed for combat and prepared to deal with stiff resistance, should the villagers be rash enough to make a stand. When the instructions had been acknowledged and repeated back to him in detail, he dismissed his houseman and the peasant, settling back behind his desk to think.

He'd been aware of guerrillas operating in the province for a year or more, attacking caravans and runners on occasion, but up to the present they had provided only minor irritations. An opportunity to catch them in a stand-up fight was welcome, and Pedilla would be pleased when they were disposed of.

The American, however, might be something else again. It was a long shot, but the dealer had no faith in blind coincidence. If there were actually foreign troops or mercenaries in the district, odds were excellent that they'd been involved in the destruction of his laboratory complex. It had been too much to hope that any of his adversaries would be fools enough to linger in the area, and yet . . .

He was concerned about the large patrol he had sent out that afternoon to sweep the jungle in a search for lurking enemies. They had been out of touch for hours, and while they weren't under orders to report unless they made some solid contact, unaccustomed silence from the ranks had set his nerves on edge.

Tomorrow, if there hadn't been some word before his troops were finished dealing with resistance to the south, he would dispatch another search team. And God help the leaders of the raiding party if his searchers found them idling in the forest, wasting time.

Pedilla checked his watch. Three hours yet before his men departed for the nameless village. Suddenly he felt tired enough to sleep. The prospect of contact with the enemy had done the trick, relaxing him and offering the hope that all his problems would be dealt with soon.

Six men.

How could they ever hope to stand against the might of his cartel? Were they so foolish that they didn't recognize their peril? Or was the informer, this Hernandez, lying through his teeth, a minor cog in some machine that had been primed to crush Pedilla when he showed himself?

The rebels would be disappointed if their plans included contact with the master of the Medellín cartel. A canny general stayed behind the lines when he dispatched his troops to battle, and Pedilla was an officer of long experience in the guerrilla war with *federales*, the DEA and narcotics officers in Mexico, the United States, France and Britain. There was nothing to be feared from half a dozen peasants in the jungle, even if they numbered an American among their ranks.

The dealer leaned back in his padded leather chair and let himself relax, still smiling as he drifted off to sleep.

"YOU SHOULD HAVE HELPED us stop him," Bolan said.

Ramona shrugged. "I wasn't sure he was leaving. He might simply have been answering a call of nature. By the time I realized he wasn't coming back..."

She let the statement trail away unfinished. It was obvious that neither Jaime nor the tall American believed her, but it didn't matter now. She had forewarned them of Virgilio's treachery while granting him the rope required to hang himself. There could be no excuses, no forgiveness now.

He was as good as dead.

It chilled Ramona when she realized her responsibility in dealing out the death card to a fellow human being, but Virgilio had forfeited his right to live. A fratricide at best, this time he'd betrayed the entire village, endangering the lives of every man, woman and child in the settlement. Pure chance—or fate—had placed Ramona at her window when the rodent made his move; if she'd slept, or simply huddled in a corner with her shame, they might all be marked for slaughter by Pedilla's troops.

It promised to be desperate even now. They had six men who were proficient with their weapons, some two dozen others who were armed and ready to defend their homes but lacked any sort of martial skill or training. Could they stand against the army Pedilla would undoubtedly dispatch? Was there the slightest chance of victory?

In her preoccupation with the coming battle, there were moments when Ramona forgot the pain and raw humiliation she had lately suffered. Rape was bad enough, without the beating, but the worst of it had been the sidelong glances from her neighbors, coupled with the knowledge they had heard her screams and stayed inside their homes, too frightened to respond.

Of course she had expected nothing more. Pedilla's men would certainly have opened fire on anyone who tried to help her. It would have been suicide, and they hadn't been armed. Not then.

She wondered if their courage would be any greater in the morning when the shock troops rolled into their village, killing as they came. Would any of her lifelong neighbors dare to use the weapons Jaime had distributed among them? Or would they desert their homes in panic, fleeing into the jungle with the gunners on their heels?

It scarcely mattered to Ramona anymore. Pedilla's maggots had already stolen everything a woman stood to lose—except life itself, and they were welcome to the dregs of that, if only she could find the strength to strike a telling blow against them first. She wouldn't have an opportunity to kill Pedilla, but perhaps the pig who had assaulted her, or any of the *narcotraficante*'s gunmen, if it came to that.

Ramona had already tasted loss, humiliation, pain. She thirsted for the taste of blood.

And in the morning, if the Fates were willing, she would have her fill.

The village was awake now, Jaime's soldiers circulating house-to-house. The game plan had been changed by her disclosure of Virgilio's desertion. They could no longer expect a mere half-dozen *pistoleros*; a strike force would be coming to suppress the rebels whom Virgilio had seen and counted in the village. They would come with enough men and guns to do the job.

As Bolan moved away, Ramona stood and watched her neighbors trying to prepare themselves for mortal combat. She knew that in a few more hours many of them might be dead or maimed, their village leveled. She might never see them just this way again.

The knowledge left her feeling empty and impossibly alone.

THE NEWS ABOUT A TRAITOR in the village altered everything. It wouldn't be enough to send the women and their children to the forest now while men with weapons they had never fired before lay back and waited for a handful of Pedilla's gunmen to arrive. They faced the prospect of an all-out firefight with the enemy, and at the moment Bolan wasn't confident they had a chance in hell of victory.

He trusted Jaime Vargas and the others to perform their tasks on cue, but they were only five. The rest of the defenders—twenty-six in all—were lifelong farmers, most of whom had never owned a gun, much less employed one in a desperate life-and-death engagement with professional assassins. It was comical, when you thought about it, but the warrior felt no urge to laugh.

Five hours, more or less, for this Hernandez character to reach Pedilla's compound, if he walked straight through without a break for rest. That put him in the dealer's lap at roughly three o'clock. Bolan wagered that Pedilla wouldn't field his troops before the crack of dawn. That made it nearly six o'clock before they hit the road. While their vehicles would shave a good three hours off return time, it should still be eight or later when the enemy arrived. Assuming, of course, that all of Bolan's calculations were correct, and their adversary rational enough to wait for daylight. If Pedilla jumped the gun and put his men in trucks immediately, they could be in striking range by sunrise.

Either way the little ragtag army had no time to waste. No time at all.

Bolan had suggested—and the others had agreed—that it might now be dangerous to hide their noncombatants in the forest. There was a chance Pedilla might decide to split his forces, ring the village in a pincer movement. If so, the gunners might encounter helpless women and children first before coming in range of armed defenders. That would give them hostages to deal with, and the meager plan of action would collapse before the villagers had any chance to play their hand.

An obvious alternative was flight, but Jaime had no stomach for retreat. And Bolan saw the logic in Jaime's argument that gunners would be likely to pursue them, sniping all the way, while radios were used to throw a lethal ambush in their path. Outside the village, saddled with civilians, they were little more than moving targets. Clapboard houses offered meager sanctuary, but they beat a Chinese fire drill in the open jungle, with enemies on every side.

So they would stand. Bolan set about assigning fire lanes, sectoring the village and its single dusty street, informing each armed man—through Jaime Vargas—of his individual responsibilities. In every home the head of household and his older sons were armed with weapons captured from Pedilla, carefully instructed to control the area they could easily observe through open windows, leaving other sectors to be covered by their neighbors. Overlapping fields of fire fell naturally into place, and Bolan felt a cautious thrill of optimism as he finished pacing off the village square.

They had a chance, no more, no less. If everybody did his part, if there were no surprises from Pedilla, there was still a possibility that they could pull it off.

Yet in combat, Bolan knew, the only thing you could expect with certainty was the unexpected. Twenty-six civilians armed with military weapons were a nasty pack of wild cards, filled with possibilities for lethal error, cowardice, betrayal. Anyone who opened fire too soon could blow the play, and anyone who held his fire too long was offering the enemy an opening to strike with telling force. A war of amateurs was dangerous for all concerned, but mainly for the side compelled to use untrained civilians as its frontline troops.

The enemy would be another unknown quantity, their numbers, armament and angle of attack deciding much of what must follow after their arrival. If Pedilla sent out thirty guns, they would be roughly one-on-one, and Bolan thought his "soldiers" might be capable of handling the odds. Beyond that ratio, if the villagers were heavily outnumbered, you could count on panic and a breaking in the ranks as individuals decided that discretion was the better part of valor. Men with families to guard—the vast majority—would break before the bachelors and widowers, but none of them had been conditioned to resist long odds at any cost.

It had the makings of a massacre. Bolan wondered how much blood his soul could manage to accommodate before the weight alone began to bear him down. How many innocent civilians could he sacrifice before the holy war became unholy, losing its momentum in a mire of doubt?

He checked his watch again. Four-thirty. They had half an hour, at least; four hours, tops. Within that meager span of time some lives would end while others would be irrevocably altered.

Bolan only hoped he could keep the balance on the side where it belonged.

17

Antonio Ybarra didn't mind returning to the no-name village with an army at his back. If truth were told, the prospect of confronting rebel forces was exciting. He was tired of playing shepherd to the peasant cleanup crews Pedilla used for dirty work, although the job admittedly had certain compensations. Antonio had counted on a few more sessions with the dark-eyed widow, but his plans had been revised by circumstance. Unless the reports proved false.

Grinning to himself, Ybarra hoped he wouldn't be disappointed. Armed resistance in the village guaranteed the kind of action that he saw too seldom these days. Besides, there might still be an opportunity to call upon the woman one more time.

He didn't trust their peasant guide. Pedilla had insisted they take the peon with them as a front man. It made sense, but Antonio wasn't about to put his faith in someone who would sell out his neighbors without a second thought. A man who would betray his lifelong friends was capable of any treachery. While Ybarra had this peasant figured for a coward, he'd keep a close watch on the man.

Pedilla was afraid they might be ambushed in the jungle, with the peasant serving in the role of Judas goat to set them up. Ybarra was prepared to kill the bastard instantly if they encountered any opposition, but in his opinion the man was too damned frightened to participate in any tricks just now.

Ybarra had requested twenty men to do the job; instead, he had been given forty. Half of Pedilla's live-in hardforce had been loaded into jeeps and flatbed trucks, every man fitted out with automatic weapons, riot shotguns, itching for the chance to use their toys. They thought it would be nice to deal a blow, since they'd been on the receiving end for too damned long.

Departure had taken place at daybreak, which Ybarra had considered to be a waste of precious time. But now, within a mile of target, he was glad they had waited. Sudden apprehension greased his palms and made him check the undergrowth on either side of the deserted track with mounting frequency.

Suppose it was a trap? Pedilla had been nervous when they'd left, complaining that his jungle strike force had been out of touch too long. He'd huddled with the captain of the *federales*, making ready to defend the compound from attack, as if Ybarra and his men were simply running off to play some childish game.

Pedilla's lack of faith wasn't the issue. Antonio had long been accustomed to the shifting moods of his *patrón* and he'd learned to roll with any mental punch Pedilla threw. Just now he was concerned about the possibility of failure and its implications for his own survival. He wasn't prepared to die just yet, and certainly he had no wish to die while teaching discipline to worthless peasants.

It would have been easier to send the *federales*, he decided, if Pedilla actually thought there were guerrillas in the village. Antonio relaxed a bit, deciding that his master had decided on a show of force to cow the peons, bend them to his will, and wipe out any thoughts of unified resistance. It would be a lesson to the other peasants in Caquetá Province, and if blood was spilled, it would be on the hands of those who dared to rebel against the wishes of the *patrón*.

In simple terms, Ybarra was about to teach another lesson—one that fortunate survivors wouldn't soon forget.

He brought the column to a halt one hundred yards from a curve that hid the village with a screen of trees. Beyond that point they would be riding in the open, easy prey for snipers in the village and surrounding forest. He didn't intend to make it easy for his enemies.

He swiveled in his seat to face their peasant guide. "It's time for you to earn your keep," he said.

The peon looked confused. "What do you mean, *señor*?"

"You will proceed from here on foot and bring back word if it's safe for us to enter."

There was sudden panic in the peasant's eyes. "But . . . what if there are snipers?"

"They should recognize you as a local boy. No problem."

"*Sí*, and they'll realize where I've been all night. They won't think twice before they cut me down."

Ybarra smiled. "In that case, rest assured that you will be avenged, the village leveled. Fair enough?"

"I must protest."

Ybarra drew his pistol, thumbing back the hammer as he thrust it toward the peon's face.

"You must do as you're told, *pendejo*. Otherwise I've no use for you at all."

Reluctantly the man dismounted from the jeep and stood beside Ybarra. He was braced for one more plea, but something in the gunner's eyes dissuaded him. Ybarra's cold gaze followed him until he rounded the curve and disappeared.

"What now?" his driver asked.

"We wait. If someone shoots him, we'll know he spoke the truth."

"And if they don't?"

"I have a plan," Ybarra said, surprised—and then relieved—to realize that it was true.

BEYOND THE CURVE, when he was certain the gunmen couldn't see, Virgilio Hernandez stopped to take a silent reading on the village. Fifty yards of unpaved roadway lay before him, overshadowed by the looming trees so that it took on the appearance of a tunnel, with his village at the other end.

It seemed a thousand miles away.

Virgilio's mind was racing as he started walking toward the village. It was nearly eight o'clock, and yet the street was empty, lacking even dogs to lend a hint of habitation. For a moment he was tempted to believe that everyone had fled, abandoning their foolish plan to fight Pedilla's soldiers, but he quickly realized they were merely following instructions from the strangers. The women and children would be hiding in the woods by now, while men stood watch with weapons most of them had never fired before.

They would have missed him when they woke, or shortly after, when the final preparations had been made. His absence wouldn't have gone unnoticed by his neighbors, and he knew some of them would hate him, curse him for a traitor, even though he had their best interests at heart.

The trick, Virgilio decided, would be slipping in without alerting any of the watchers, getting close enough to speak with them and tell his side before some hothead opened fire. He could explain himself, if only there was time.

Ramona might be helpful, if she hadn't joined the other women in the forest. Somehow he suspected she'd stay behind to watch the action, cheering for the fools who were prepared to throw their lives away. She might despise him for his bumbling efforts to preserve the village, but she was a reasonable woman. She would hear him out, and if he won her over, she'd help him face the others. She wouldn't stand by and see him slaughtered like a mongrel dog.

It would be different, granted, if she knew about his role in killing Carlos. She'd turn against him then, beyond the shadow of a doubt. But he had little fear of her discovering the truth; he had been scrupulous in covering his tracks.

Her house was at the far end of the village. He'd have to circle wide, take cover in the trees, if he intended to escape detection by the others. It would be time-consuming, but at least he had full daylight now, and passage through the forest wouldn't be the same ordeal it had been last night, with every shadow full of menace, every sound the footfall of a hungry predator.

He left the road, took care to make as little noise as possible when he began his circumnavigation of the village. Every step was calculated in advance, precisely executed to avoid the telltale sounds of snapping twigs or rustling undergrowth. He scarcely dared to blink, eyes straining in the artificial twilight of the double canopy to pick out any hint of movement, any snare, before he blundered into danger. If the women and children had been hidden in the jungle, as originally planned, it wouldn't do for him to meet them there.

The village might have been asleep—or dead—for all of its unearthly silence. Creeping through the trees, Virgilio felt like an interloper on the outskirts of a cemetery, checking out the headstones as he passed for any indication that the dead were growing restless. There was danger here; he sensed it, as a forest animal might sometimes feel the presence of a hunter crouching in the shrubbery. He offered up a silent prayer that every eye—and weapon—in the village would be concentrated on the road, from whence their ruthless punishment was bound to come.

Pedilla's soldiers would be growing restless now, but he couldn't afford to rush and thereby give himself away. A few more moments, moving gingerly, with great attention to the placement of his feet, and he was crouching in the shadow of Ramona's one-room house. A stretch of open ground lay between his cover and her doorstep. He could go no farther without emerging, risking everything.

Virgilio swallowed hard, glanced once in each direction, then finally stepped out of cover into glaring sunlight. He was startled by the silence, which was still unbroken, frowning as he realized that someone should have moved to stop him—or to kill him—when he showed himself. Could he be wrong? Had everyone deserted the village after all?

The flesh between his shoulder blades was tingling in expectation of a bullet as he stepped up to Ramona's door, knocked softly, waiting for an answer from within. He was about to try a second time when footsteps sounded on the floorboards and the simple latch was turned. The door inched open to reveal a swollen eye, a slice of bruised and mottled cheek.

A lump was forming in his throat, produced by guilt or gratitude, he couldn't say. He found it difficult to speak. "Ramona..."

"Ssh. Come in." She stepped aside and held the door, then closed and latched it after he was safe inside.

"I was afraid you wouldn't speak to me."

"Virgilio."

He turned to face her, smiling, and was startled when she struck him with her fist, below the collarbone. The impact rocked him on his heels. Ramona backed off with triumph in her eyes, and several heartbeats slipped away before he felt the burning pain.

Virgilio Hernandez had to twist his neck and cross his eyes to see the handle of a kitchen knife protruding from his chest.

RAMONA HAD BEEN WAITING for Virgilio's return. She had no concrete plan in mind, but intuition told her he would try to seek her out, to plead his case before he faced the others with his treachery. It was a flimsy, insubstantial hope, but it was all she had.

And she hadn't been wrong.

As hours passed and daylight made a surreptitious entry to the settlement impossible, Ramona knew Virgilio would have to show himself. He would be wise enough to know he'd been missed, his absence unaccounted for, and he'd have an explanation ready for her. There might even be some elements of truth in what he said, but it would scarcely matter, for Ramona didn't plan on listening.

She meant to kill him, for her husband, for the pain he had caused her, for his betrayal of his neighbors to Pedilla. She wasn't clear yet on the details of Virgilio's involvement in his brother's death, but they were hardly relevant. A simple word to any one of half a dozen *pistoleros* would have done the trick. There had been ample opportunity for whispered words in passing, or a midnight meeting with the enemy.

However he'd managed it, no doubt remained within Ramona's heart or mind. She knew Virgilio was guilty, even as she knew the sun would rise tomorrow, and the next day, and the next day after that.

Of course, she might not be around to see it; there might not be any "next days" in her future. But Ramona didn't care. Avenging Carlos was enough, and having done that, she believed she could rest in peace.

The method would be problematical. If she was right about Virgilio approaching her before he faced the others, there were tools at hand. If he was clever, though, and kept himself beyond her reach, there might be problems. He would certainly be taken into custody for questioning, if he wasn't immediately shot on sight, and as she had no gun, Ramona would be forced to think up some excuse for getting close enough to do her work.

Perhaps, she thought, if she reminded them of Carlos, pleading for an opportunity to face her husband's murderer...

The knock upon her door had been a godsend. She'd known it was Virgilio before she answered—the American warrior and the rest were at their posts, all waiting for the enemy to strike—and she'd palmed a kitchen knife before she cracked the door. Her heart was in her throat as she admitted him, and she could barely speak his name, but it had been enough. She struck him as he turned to face her, smiling, and immediately backed away to watch him die.

And she was horrified, therefore, when, rather than collapsing, he advanced upon her, arms outstretched, as if to clasp her in a fond embrace.

"Ramona." It was like a whisper from the grave.

She dodged aside, the fingers of his right hand pawing at her shoulder in a bid to keep his fragile balance. Blood was seeping from his wound, the long knife damming most of it inside, but as Hernandez lurched around to face her, springs of crimson overflowed his lips, his chin and stained the fabric of his peasant shirt.

The wound was high, she realized—and it had definitely missed his heart—but was it too high? Had she pierced the lung, at least? And if she had, was it a mortal wound? How long could someone with a knife protruding from his chest continue chasing her around the room?

His lurching movements called up childhood memories of dancing bears, a circus her family had attended in Florencia on market day. Ramona felt a sudden urge to laugh out loud, but it was strangled by her growing fear.

If he had the energy to chase her, he might also have the strength to choke her life out, once his hands had closed around her throat. Their jerky dance was getting nowhere, and she longed to end it, finish with the job she'd started.

Edging past the stove, Ramona saw the carving knife and closed her fingers tight around its broken wooden handle. If she'd been thinking clearly earlier, she would have used the longer knife to start with, but Virgilio's knock had startled her and there hadn't been time.

She waited for him now, the knife held tight against her thigh as he came closer, closer. Any moment now his fingertips would scrabble at her throat, and it would be too late.

She took a long step forward, meeting him halfway, the long knife sliding home between his ribs. Virgilio fell against her, grunting at the new intrusion, white teeth clenched against the pain as she began to twist the knife. His arms were heavy on her shoulders, and the handle of the first knife jabbed against her breast. Warm blood had made her fingers slippery; she felt it soaking through her blouse and skirt.

Ramona found the heart, this time, and then his blood was everywhere. It pattered on her feet like rain, soon pooled between them as they stood, embracing, one of her arms wrapped around his torso to prevent his wiggling backward off the blade. She felt his knees begin to fold and let him go, cared nothing when his fingers snagged the neckline of her peasant blouse and tore it open to her waist. Virgilio's blood had painted abstract patterns on her breasts and stomach through the homespun cloth.

In death Virgilio seemed small and shriveled, legs and arms drawn up into a fetal curl around the knives that skewered his torso. It was difficult to read his eyes, but if she had to make the call, Ramona would have said she saw shock there, amplified by mortal terror.

Fair enough.

A coward always died in fear, no matter what the cause of death. For now, it satisfied Ramona that Virgilio had seen his death approaching, felt it like a hot flame in his vitals. He'd known precisely why he had to die, and it was all that she had hoped for.

Conscious of her seminakedness, Ramona shed the tattered remnants of her blouse, the bloody skirt, and took fresh clothing from the cupboard. She'd lost half her wardrobe in the past two days, but she wasn't concerned with fashion at the moment.

She was thinking of survival, and the enemy who was approaching even now.

Virgilio's return could only mean Pedilla's troops were close at hand. They would have sent him forward as a scout—a sacrifice if need be—and they might be waiting for him to report. In any case, when he didn't return, the *pistoleros* would come to discover why... and then, she thought, the killing would begin in earnest.

Moving toward the window, fingers flying at the buttons of her blouse, she scanned the empty street. Her neighbors—some of them at least—had doubtless seen Virgilio as he had approached her house. They had been given certain portions of the street to watch—the American called them "fields of fire"—and three men should be covering her house, the far end of the settlement, from different angles. If they hadn't seen Virgilio, they must be sleeping at their posts, and there was nothing she could do to rouse them now.

Approaching from the north, the sound of engines told Ramona she was out of time.

SEQUESTERED IN a one-room house that had been emptied of its occupants, Mack Bolan had seen Virgilio Hernandez as he'd stepped from cover in the forest, edging toward Ramona's door. The soldier had expected trouble when she'd let him in, but the intervening distance had eliminated any sounds. So he was pretty edgy when Ramona turned up in the open window moments later. He wondered if his mind was playing tricks, or if her blouse, white now, had been pale yellow when he'd seen her last.

If Ramona was in trouble, Bolan couldn't leave his post to help her. Two of Jaime's riflemen were closer, as were several of her neighbors. None of them was rushing to the rescue, and Bolan realized she appeared no worse for wear. Seen from a distance, the bruises on her face looked familiar.

Bolan had the crew chief's face in mind, a mug shot filed for future reference. He was hoping the bastard would be fool enough to lead Pedilla's expeditionary force against the village. Bolan owed him one, and he was itching to repay the debt with interest due.

The growl of engines reached his ears a moment after he glimpsed Ramona in the window. They were closing in from the north. Bolan thought he could pick out at least three or four vehicles.

How many men? If they were riding jeeps, no more than twenty or twenty-five. But several of the engines sounded heavier, like those of trucks. If the troops were riding flatbeds, he would have to double his estimate. The force of guerrillas and village men would be outnumbered, and he wondered, too, if civilians, short of nerve and training, would be equal to the challenge.

Either way his answer was approaching on the narrow unpaved road. He spent a moment double-checking the Colt Commando, ensuring that its magazine was seated properly, a live round in the firing chamber. He flicked the fire-selector switch to automatic and settled into a more comfortable posture, studying the point where trees gave way to road and road widened on the village square.

A jeep came first, followed immediately by two flatbeds, with a second jeep on drag, a third truck bringing up the rear. Two men on point, three in the second jeep, with each truck bearing two more in their cabs. Four gunmen occupied the rear of each truck as they rolled into position. That made twenty-three men.

Bolan recognized the problem at a glance—they had too many vehicles for their abbreviated fire team. Either someone in Pedilla's motor pool had blown it, or there should have been another twenty soldiers. Where were they?

Bolan's mind had barely formed the question when he had his answer, bursting from the trees around Ramona's house, and on the far side of the street directly opposite. The second team was coming in on foot, a circling move designed to hit the settlement from several sides at once, dividing the defenders, scattering their fire.

Bolan and Jaime had allowed for something of the sort in preparation for the fight, but he had hoped the enemy approach would be straightforward, easier to deal with. Now, as Bolan snapped his rifle up and scanned for moving targets, he could only hope the villagers were on their toes.

If not, they would be in their graves.

18

The circling move had been Ybarra's brainchild. When their Judas goat had disappeared without a trace and there had been no gunfire from the settlement, Antonio decided precautions should be taken. Rather than proceed and find himself cut off, he split his force three ways, allowing roughly half his men to enter with the vehicles, while strike teams moved around to take the village from the north and west, as well.

It was a masterstroke, and he was proud. The peasants would be concentrating on a minicaravan of jeeps and trucks, off guard when he attacked them from the flank. They would be sitting targets, ripe for slaughter.

He was ready, in position, when the vehicles appeared, his gunners huddled in the cabs of trucks or crouching on the flatbeds with their weapons poised and ready. Moving in before the enemy could open fire, Antonio had hopes of minimizing friendly casualties, rocking his opponents with a swift, preemptive strike. If he was fast enough, and ruthless, they might pull it off.

And that would leave more time for him to dally with the widow.

Firing as they cleared the trees, his men were peppering the flimsy houses, joined by gunners in the jeeps and trucks, intent on taking full advantage of surprise. For a brief moment he imagined they might sweep the village clean without resistance. Then his hopes were dashed as automatic weapon fire erupted from the doors and windows facing him, and then on either side.

His soldiers were as startled by resistance as they had been by initial silence. Five or six of them were on the ground already, dead or wounded, and Ybarra had no time to count as bullets churned the dust around his feet, propelling him toward cover. Someone clearly had decided to resist, fight fire with fire, and they had drawn first blood.

Ybarra huddled in the narrow runway set between two houses. Through the thin walls he could hear semiautomatic weapons firing out of both, the snipers targeting his soldiers as they scrambled from their jeeps and trucks. He saw another man go down, blood pumping from a ragged leg wound, and knew he must do something quickly while his force still had superior numbers.

Shielded by the trucks from any snipers on the far side of the street, he worked his way around behind the houses, scowling as he saw their only doors were set in front. One of the hovels did have a back window, and a surreptitious glance revealed his enemies inside—a man of middle years, supported by a teenage boy, both armed with military rifles.

Stepping back a pace, Ybarra swung the stubby muzzle of his Uzi submachine gun at the glass, his finger tightening around the trigger as he cleared a field of fire. He dropped the older adversary before the man had a chance to turn and fight, a burst of parabellum manglers slamming him against the window frame and snuffing out his life on impact.

Pivoting, the boy squeezed off a single shot before Ybarra mowed him down, the hasty bullet drilling wood a foot above the window frame. Ybarra didn't waste his time or precious ammunition making sure they were dead. He knew his business, and he always shot to kill.

Along the street a raging firefight was in progress. He could hear the jeeps and trucks absorbing rounds, his soldiers scurrying for cover, fighting back as best they could within the cross fire. Members of his flanking parties were more fortunate. Some were emulating his technique of striking from the rear, where doors or windows were available. Across the village square, his men had seized a house, which they were using for cover now, directing their strategic fire at other dwellings on the street.

The lead jeep detonated like a bomb, its fuel tank punctured, spewing gasoline that spread to form a lake of fire. A human torch erupted from the rolling smoke screen, shrieking as it jittered in the flames, until a well-placed round came out of nowhere, toppling the dancer in his tracks.

Numerical superiority was fading fast, although several shacks had fallen silent, riddled from their thresholds to their eaves by automatic fire. How many dead so far? Ybarra had no way of judging, but he knew something must be done, and soon, if his forces were to prevail.

The answer struck him like a stinging slap across the face. *The women!* So far he'd seen no females in the village, no young children. They couldn't be far away, he reckoned, but he had to find them soon, before they were annihilated accidentally by overzealous gunmen. Hostages were valuable only while they lived. If his new scheme had a prayer of working out, Ybarra would require a different sort of edge, some valuables to bargain with.

Finding the noncombatants would be risky in the midst of battle, but it could be done. He had some thoughts already where to start. He picked up half a dozen men to help him as he scurried off to confront the widow one last time.

MACK BOLAN CHOSE his target as the sounds of automatic fire erupted from the trees. The driver of the jeep wasn't familiar to him—not the man who had attacked Ramona—but he had a weapon in his hands, and Bolan dropped him with a 3-round burst that took his head off at the eyebrows.

Tracking, Bolan nailed a second gunner from the jeep, but missed the third and last when he stumbled on his dying comrade, going down behind the vehicle, obscured from Bolan's line of fire. The street was filling up with gunners, some unloading from the flatbeds, others popping out between the houses on the far side of the street. Unable to determine numbers, Bolan concentrated on reducing them with short, precision bursts.

Around him, Jaime and the other rebels were selecting targets on the run and tagging them with slick, deceptive ease. The villagers, by contrast, seemed to spray the street at random, scoring hits more often by accident than by design. But they *were* scoring hits, despite their fear and inexperience.

Retreating from the window momentarily as stray rounds plunked the wall above him, Bolan worried that the villagers might accidentally inflict more casualties among their neighbors than among their enemies. It was a calculated risk; there was nothing he could do about it now. He could only hope that hostile forces bore the brunt of the shooting.

A jerry can was mounted on the tailgate of the jeep. Bolan sliced it open with a burst of tumblers from his Colt Commando, spilling gasoline into the dust. Another burst secured ignition, but the flames required a moment to take root and spread. He ducked below the windowsill and waited for the secondary blast, emerging just in time to see the jeep touch down, its fat tires melting, thick smoke rolling skyward like a signal to the world outside.

A sizzling dervish tottered through the flames, arms flapping like deformed and useless wings before the soldier dropped their owner with a mercy round. The human torch went down, heels drumming briefly in the dust, and then lay still.

Along the street, on either side, attackers from the forest had secured what cover they could find, exchanging fire with the defenders in their homes. It seemed a fairly even match at first, exposure to the cross fire compensating for numerical advantage. But the soldier knew it wouldn't last.

Already the invaders had eliminated opposition in a couple of the houses, moving in to take advantage of the cover, sniping at their neighbors to the left and right. He calculated that if only one house out of every five or six fell, the village would be lost.

Across the street, obscured by drifting plumes of smoke, a gunner thrust his head and shoulders out the window of a captured house. He shouted something to his comrades in the no-man's land, and several of them broke from cover near the trucks, legs pumping as they sprinted for the sanctuary of the dwelling. Bolan raked them from behind, a long burst tracking left to right and back again before his magazine went empty and a sole survivor slipped inside beyond his reach.

The sniper's nest was close enough for a grenade, but Bolan couldn't make the toss from where he stood, encumbered by the window frame that blocked his windup. He would have to go outside and take his chances if he meant to blast them out before the house became a hostile base of operations.

Heading toward the door, Bolan fed the Colt another magazine and chambered up a live one. It would be chancy, this, but he could see no ready options. If the gunners weren't routed, and soon, the opportunity would slip away forever.

Bolan made his move, erupting from the door and breaking for the trucks, where several of his enemies were still ensconced. One of them saw him coming, rose to a crouch and leveled his submachine gun. But the soldier got there first and stitched him with a burst from belt to larynx, blowing him away before he had a chance to answer fire.

Two others glimpsed the apparition closing on their flank and opted for retreat, both scrambling for safety on the far side of the truck, content to take their chances in the cross fire. Bolan didn't track their progress, concentrating on his destination as he slid beneath the flatbed farthest from the burning jeep.

He plucked a frag grenade from his harness, yanked the safety pin and held the spoon in place. His targets hadn't seen him yet, were unaware of death in waiting, but there was a chance they would spot him when he made his final move. And it could well be his final move if one of them was sharp enough to make him, quick enough to drop him in his tracks.

He moved, and saw the gunner tracking on him almost instantly, his weapon sweeping into target acquisition. Bolan fired the Colt one-handed with his left, already winding up the right and letting fly before the opposition found his aim. The *pistolero* staggered backward, spraying crimson from a shoulder wound, and Bolan's pitch dropped through the window frame, on target, as he scuttled back for cover.

Doomsday overtook the hovel seconds later, thunder rattling the eaves and jagged shrapnel punching through the walls in random, abstract patterns. Bolan waited, recognized the first gray wisps of smoke, flames licking upward as the house began to burn.

One down, the hostile fire was pouring out of two more houses now. He palmed another frag grenade, one of the pineapples he had liberated from Pedilla's men, and started crawling toward the fire.

JAIME VARGAS DUCKED beneath a spray of shrapnel as the house next door to his was rocked by an explosion. He'd been preparing for a run against the enemy himself when he'd seen Bolan coming. Jaime had tried to cover the American as best he could, and he'd braced himself for doomsday as the hand grenade had dropped on target less than twenty feet away.

Now shock waves, like a freight-train gust of wind, set thin walls rattling around him, and the jagged shrapnel ripped straight through like shotgun pellets fired through cardboard. He thought of what it must be like next door and smiled, delighted by the image of his adversaries dead or dying.

Jaime smelled the smoke at once, although initially he passed it off as the residue of the explosion. He was at the window again seeking targets when he realized the house next door was burning. When he risked a glance around the sill, bright tongues of flame were eating at the doorframe, nibbling along the eaves. Dark smoke was pouring skyward, mingling with oily vapors from the burning jeep.

The hand grenade had been a risk; the fire was danger. As the flames devoured plywood and supporting beams, the house would inevitably fall, touching off its neighbor on one side or the other. Jaime had a fifty-fifty chance of being spared, but he preferred to take his chances on evacuation. Between the drifting smoke and shifting lines of battle, he was running short of targets and was eager to inflict more damage on the enemy.

He timed his move between the crackling bursts of fire, dodged left and went to ground between two houses farther down. Another blast drew his glance in time for him to see Bolan firing automatic bursts in the direction of a second house where smoke was pouring out of the two small windows. The American had scorched another sniper's nest.

How many of Pedilla's men were left? Too many, he supposed, but there was no time for the numbers game. He didn't know how many *pistoleros* had comprised the raiding party to begin with; even if he had time to count their dead—which he didn't—the total would have told him nothing.

They were numerous enough to keep on fighting—that, at least, was obvious. Around him the engagement had begun to come apart, the all-out firefight breaking up into pockets of activity, fierce duels between small independent groups. There seemed to be no order, no coordination, but at least the peasants were resisting, fighting back, and some of them were making up in spirit what they lacked in martial skill.

But they were taking losses, too. The houses occupied by members of Pedilla's strike force had been captured, their defenders killed. Inside the hovels torched by Bolan's hand grenades, the flames were eating villagers and *pistoleros* with a fine impartiality.

He scanned the battlefield for targets, checking out the vehicles. Two of the trucks were useless now, with tires and engines shot to hell, their punctured fuel tanks spilling diesel in the dust. Incredibly the third truck and the second jeep seemed relatively free of damage, despite some pockmarks on the bodywork and a spiderweb of cracks where random rounds had pierced the windshield of the jeep.

If Jaime meant to save their only means of rapid transportation, he'd have to act without delay. It was a minor miracle that nothing worse had so far happened to the vehicles, and he couldn't count on continuing reprieves. If he and Bolan managed to survive the present situation, they would need transportation to reach Pedilla with a minimum of wasted time.

Before his common sense could talk him out of it, the young man scrambled to his feet and sprinted toward the jeep, his shoulders hunched, expecting the lethal impact of a bullet every step along the way. Incredibly he made it, slid behind the steering wheel and pressed one foot on the clutch and one on the accelerator as he turned the key.

The engine grumbled instantly to life. He was hauling on the gearshift, looking for reverse, when suddenly the windshield exploded in his face. He heard the bullet whistle past his ear, felt jagged shards of glass dig furrows in his cheeks and forehead. His position, bending forward grappling with the shift, was all that had saved his eyes.

The rifleman was lining up another shot when Jaime thrust his AK-47 through the empty windshield frame and squeezed the trigger. Half a dozen rounds ripped through his human target, dropping the gunner where he stood, the round he meant for Jaime wasted on the clouds instead.

With desperate urgency, Vargas found the gear he needed and powered backward, fat tires spinning for a moment in the dust before they found their grip. The jeep swayed as it rolled over bodies on the way, bones cracking underneath its wheels and hot rounds whispering his name.

So far, so good. Now all he had to do was fetch the truck, and save himself besides.

Without a second thought, Jaime started back in the direction of the killing field.

YBARRA DIDN'T TRY the door before he hit it with a flying kick. The flimsy latch ripped free and shot across the room as he burst through, the soldiers on his heels.

It took a moment for Pedilla's crew chief to interpret what he saw. Their peasant guide, Hernandez, lay curled up against one wall, his clothing and the floor around him drenched in blood. One knife protruded from his upper chest, another from his rib cage, the effect reminding Antonio of something from a bullring. Bloody tracks charted the dead man's movements in the final moments of his life, an aimless, hopeless grappling to keep himself alive.

The woman stood beside her stove, not cowering in fear, but merely waiting. She looked bad, the bruises worse than he'd anticipated, but she stirred him all the same. Her shredded clothing from the night before still lay where he'd dropped it, mingled now with other garments, bloodstains soaking through the lot.

A sudden chill drew fingernails along Ybarra's spine. He could have been the one lying there, he realized, if not for pure, dumb luck. If he had let her reach a knife last night...

The image made him smile perversely, drawing enjoyment from the knowledge of his brush with death. It offered further validation for his handling of women. This Hernandez had approached the widow gently, doubtless begging for her help, her pardon, and his answer had been death. A man couldn't show weakness to a female, or she would emasculate him, turn him inside out and steal his soul.

It pained Ybarra that he couldn't take her there and then. He wanted her among the bloody tracks and clothing, with the dead man looking on. Above all else he wanted her within reach of the knives, a tacit confirmation of his own ability to subjugate her and impose his will on the toughest of her sex.

This was a woman worthy of his talents, but he simply didn't have the time. It would be difficult to break out of the village even now, and he was bent on taking along valuable hostages when he departed.

"You have spared me a tiresome job," he told the woman, nodding toward the body of Hernandez. *"Gracias."*

"I do not want your thanks."

"A little something else perhaps?" He grinned lasciviously. "I would happily accommodate you, but time is short. You will accompany me to find the other women—now!"

She shook her head, retreating to the wall and stopping there, with no place left to go.

"You court disaster if you disobey me, woman. Tell me where the others have been hidden, and I promise that no harm will come to you." It was a lie, of course, but burdening a female with the truth wasn't Ybarra's style.

"I don't know where they are," she answered him.

"Enough." He held his Uzi with its muzzle pointing toward the ceiling. "Are you so determined that your life end like this?"

Ybarra thought she smiled at that, but her swollen lips prevented him from being certain.

"Better death," she said, "than one more moment living in your presence."

"Your tongue is sharper than your wits." Ybarra took a long stride forward, lowering his weapon as he raised his open palm to strike her down.

So sudden was her movement, she nearly caught him by surprise as she lunged for the stove and scooped up the heavy skillet in both hands. Ybarra saw it coming just in time, realized the stove was lit, the skillet's contents simmering, and ducked in time to save his face.

A splash of hissing grease across one shoulder made him grimace, even as the soldier just behind him shrieked in pain. Ybarra held his crouch and kicked out hard at the woman. His heel connected with her ribs and emptied her lungs, propelling her against the wall.

She dropped the smoking skillet and curled in upon herself as he delivered two more kicks for emphasis. He pressed the muzzle of his submachine gun hard against her swollen cheek; the fingers of his free hand tangled in her hair as he commanded her to rise.

A portion of Ybarra's khaki shirt was plastered to his back, and he could feel the blisters forming there. Heedless of the pain, he dragged his captive toward the door, his soldiers falling in behind him. One of them hung back to help his blinded comrade. Ybarra dismissed them from his mind.

"I want the women and children," he informed his prisoner. "You have a choice: direct me to them, or prepare yourself for death. Which do you choose?"

She saw murder in his eyes, and he saw resolution in her own.

She nodded weakly, giving up.

Antonio understood her. He realized she was hoping, once outside, that he might stop a bullet. Fate might free her if she only played the game.

But she was wrong. Surrender meant no more nor less than that. He owned her now, and he would see her dead before he let her go again.

"Outside," he snarled, and pushed her through the open door ahead of him, a human shield to greet his enemies.

If any bullets found them now, Ybarra would be pleased to watch her die before his own life slipped away. And in the meantime there was still a chance he could save the day.

If only he could find the other women.

19

One of Pedilla's men erupted from the burning house, and Bolan dropped him with a 3-round burst. The blackened figure twitched briefly as he lost his grip on life. No others followed. Bolan watched the shack collapse, walls folding inward on themselves, roof settling in a storm of sparks to cap the funeral pyre.

It was the third nest of attackers he had crushed. While he didn't feel a shifting of the tide, he thought Pedilla's men had lost their edge. No less than half of the attacking force were casualties by now, and most of the survivors would be happy just to get the hell away from there with lives and limbs intact.

They wouldn't run, of course. For most of them, Pedilla's wrath was both more certain and more terrifying than the outcome of their present battle. They still had a chance to overcome the villagers, but cowards and deserters would be hounded forever by Pedilla's guns, members of their families subjected to abuse—or worse—until the dealer had his vengeance. Given the choice of dying now or later, Bolan thought most of them would opt for death in combat where they were.

It made his job more difficult, but he wasn't averse to killing each and every one of them. Logistics was the problem. A rapid glance around the village told him the peasants had lost numbers, too. The three huts he had "liberated" would account for six or seven dead, and he was reckoning a minimum so far of twice the body count. If he was right, they had something like a dozen guns against twenty-plus.

He noticed Jaime rescuing the jeep, returning for the one undamaged truck, and gave the young man points for thinking under fire. They would be needing wheels to reach Pedilla's compound when their work was finished here.

Unless they lost.

Unless they died.

It was a possibility, but Bolan didn't linger on the odds. His mind was occupied with angles and trajectories, already seeking targets in the nameless village that had recently become a free-fire zone.

Two gunners broke from cover, running after Jaime as he backed the flatbed clear. They weren't firing at him yet, and Bolan thought they might be looking for a lift, believing their troops were pulling out. No matter. They wouldn't live to discover their mistake.

He snapped the Colt Commando to his shoulder, sighting down the barrel at a range of thirty yards. Despite the running targets, it should have been an easy shot, but the smoke from burning vehicles and houses drew a veil across the killing ground. He took a breath, released a portion of it, held the rest, his finger tightening around the trigger as he locked on target.

Number one went down as if his feet had tangled in a snare no one else could see, his jacket decorated with a chain of brand-new crimson blossoms. Bolan didn't need to check the kill; he was already tracking on.

The dead man's comrade hadn't seen him fall. He charged ahead, oblivious, his arm raised to flag the driver of the truck. Then his stride faltered as he realized something had gone wrong. He grappled with his weapon, bringing it to bear on Jaime. He could scarcely miss, with less than thirty feet between them.

The Executioner hit him with a double punch and watched him fall, a human corkscrew winding down on rubber legs. The gunner's weapon stuttered briefly, but his rounds went wild, and Bolan caught a glimpse of Jaime through the smoke, dismounting from the truck he had saved, returning to the battle.

On the far side of the street, beyond the smoking hulks of jeep and flatbeds, Jaime's men were taking the offensive, mounting an attack against the enemy. Bolan was startled by the sight of several locals joining in the push against Pedilla's crew, ignoring danger to themselves as they stood up to the invaders of their village.

Joining them was something of a problem for Bolan. He had to cross the street, no trick in normal circumstances, but today it meant negotiating burned-out trucks, avoiding sniper fire that came from every side at once. The peasants should know enough to let him pass, but some of them were firing blindly, spraying anything that moved, as if they had an endless reservoir of ammunition.

In fact they would soon be running out of bullets. He couldn't afford to wait for that to happen, though; the time to strike was now while Jaime's men were taking the initiative and doing everything in their power to turn the tide.

He had to make the nearest truck, for cover, on the first leg of his run. From there it would be open ground and hellfire all the way across the square until he joined the tiny rebel force in transit. It was striking toward the east end of the street, where members of the raiding force had gathered in a pocket of resistance.

The fighting would be brisk and bloody then, whichever way the chips fell, and Bolan had to be there in the middle of it, doing anything he could to break the savages.

Beyond that, if he lived, there was Pedilla, waiting at the center of his web. A lethal, bloated spider ready for the kill.

Mack Bolan put the image out of mind and concentrated on the present as he made his move.

AN ACCIDENT HAD SPARED Ramona, finally, from enforced betrayal of her neighbors to Pedilla's men. A small boy, frightened by the gunfire and explosions, had bolted from the house where women and children had been gathered for protection. His stubby legs had covered less than twenty feet before his mother snatched him back, but by then it was too late. Ramona's captors had their target.

Two gunmen held her arms and forced her to match their loping stride as they advanced on the house. Around them gunfire popped and crackled, bullets whispering between them as they ran. Behind Ramona a gunner fell almost on her heels, but she wasn't allowed to stumble. Big hands locked around her biceps, she was scarcely touching ground with every other step when they burst inside the women's sanctuary.

A boy named Pablo had been left on guard. He thrust a rifle toward Pedilla's gunners as they entered, but had no chance to fire. Ramona's rapist dropped him with a short burst from his submachine gun, pumping more rounds at the boy once he had fallen lifeless to the floor.

She knew without counting that there were fifteen women and eleven children in the little house. With half a dozen *pistoleros* and Ramona, it was crowded, but her captors clearly didn't plan to spend much time inside. Their leader was already barking orders, brandishing his weapon in a manner that prevented any questions or dissent. The women listened, shushing children where they could, absorbing every word.

The plan was simple. They would leave the house together, women circling the gunners as a living shield. They would proceed in lockstep to the point where someone— friend or foe, it scarcely mattered—had retrieved one of the trucks and parked it well outside the common line of fire. When all were safe on board, they would drive out of the village, leaving the survivors on both sides to carry on the fight.

No destination had been specified, but it wasn't a mystery. They'd be driven to Pedilla's compound in the jungle, miles away, to serve as hostages in case the village battle went against the dealer's soldiers. Either way Pedilla meant to hold a winning hand.

Outside, the sound of gunfire seemed to come in waves, first faltering and then redoubling to thunderous crescendo. Waiting for a lull, Pedilla's crew chief ordered several of the women out, his gunners crowding close behind them, squeezing through the narrow doorway with their weapons trained behind them to ensure that other hostages would follow. Wedged between her captors, arms pinned at her sides, Ramona had no opportunity to take the lead or lag behind.

New firing had erupted on the far side of the square. She saw one of Jaime's rebels, peasants following behind him in a charge against their enemies. Was that the American running with them? Smoke obscured her view before she could be certain.

Close at hand, familiar voices shouted for a cease-fire as several villagers caught glimpses of their wives and children in captivity. A heartbeat later members of Pedilla's team restrained their firing as well, afraid of picking off their comrades if they shot into the moving crowd.

Ramona started counting footsteps, half expecting someone to forget himself and risk a shot before they reached the truck. Instead, the truce held firm around them. Sounds of battle continued across the square, where Jaime and the others were prevented from observing their retreat.

The group of hostages reached the truck. Ramona was herded toward the cab, squeezed tight between her rapist, on the right, and one of his subordinates who took the wheel. Behind them gunmen clambered into the bed of the truck, their weapons urging hostages to follow, forcing them to organize a ring of flesh against potential sniper fire. Ramona's stomach churned as she realized they were about to pull it off. No one had even tried to stop their exit from the village.

Now their driver had the truck in motion, grinding through the gears until he got it right. The vehicle lurched through a sharp half turn, the passengers in back unsteady on their feet until it leveled out and found the narrow road. Ramona glanced across the driver's seat and watched her village dwindle in the rearview mirror, disappearing as they took the first sharp curve.

Surrendering all hope, she closed her eyes.

YBARRA'S THOUGHTS were spinning as the truck cleared the village, gathering momentum on the unpaved road. His plan had worked without a hitch; they had escaped with hostages whom he would carry to Pedilla as a gift, a weapon to be used against the dealer's enemies if any still survived.

It had been going badly for his soldiers in the village. They'd counted on a token show of armed resistance from the peons. Instead, the crew had suffered heavy casualties and had been unable to secure a solid foothold in the settlement. They'd been losing, damn it, and Ybarra's exit had ensured survival of the fastest on their feet.

There was a chance that those surviving in the village might bounce back and snatch victory from what appeared to be defeat, but Antonio was betting with the odds. His hostage scheme would save the day if matters went from bad to worse. For all their newfound courage, the villagers would quickly fold, with their wives and children on the firing line. He'd already seen them crumble once, and might have pressed home the advantage if he hadn't been intent on putting space between himself and hostile guns. Recovering a bit of his composure now, he concentrated on the problems that were waiting for him at Pedilla's camp.

The dealer would be angry at Ybarra for retreating in the face of hostile fire. Pedilla felt contempt for human weakness, loathing fear above all else. Ybarra would have moments, at the most, to sell his plan for what it was: a scheme to break the peasants and guarantee their ultimate defeat. He must present the plan as something born of wisdom and cunning rather than desperation. If he lost Pedilla's sympathy, the outcome for him personally terrified him.

Ybarra pushed the grisly images away. He needed confidence just now, and he concentrated on the plan unfolding in his mind. With hostages in hand, Pedilla could choose between waiting for the rebels in his camp, or sending out a cleanup team to raze the village. Granted, forty men had already proved inadequate for the job, but neither had they driven in with women tied across the grilles and fenders of their vehicles. Sometimes a little extra touch like that made all the difference in the world.

Once they had finally disarmed the enemy, Ybarra thought, the killing could begin in earnest. No one would be spared. Annihilation of the rebel scum would be a lesson for the other peasants of Caquetá Province. No one stood against the Medellín cartel and lived to boast about it later.

Feeling better by the moment, he reached out and placed his free hand on the widow's thigh. She tried to flinch away, but there was no room for retreat. He laughed aloud and pinched her hard enough to make her yelp.

Perhaps, once he convinced Pedilla that his plan was nothing short of a strategic masterpiece, the dealer might reward him with a gift. The woman would do nicely, he decided—someone he could use until she bored him, then discard like so much rubbish for replacement with a newer model. He would raise the subject with Pedilla when his own position was secure. In the meantime he could think of no good reason why the long drive home shouldn't be entertaining.

Slaves were made to serve, and with the heat of battle coursing through his veins, Ybarra needed service now. It would be cramped and far from private in the cab, but he wasn't a bashful man. If anything, an audience might heighten his enjoyment of the conquest. Still, there was the risk of accidents.

"Slow down a bit," he told the driver, smiling as he spoke. "And keep your damned eyes on the road."

AUDACITY AND SPEED had carried Jaime Vargas past two nests of *pistoleros*, killing as he went. He was gaining on the front line of a moving, shifting battle when his rifle jammed. He tried to clear the chamber, failed and threw the AK-47 down, scooping up an M-16 and bandolier whose fallen owner wouldn't need them now.

Ahead of him his men were locked in mortal combat with the enemy, their weapons hammering at point-blank range. He saw their American ally in the thick of things and wondered where the villagers had dredged up enough nerve to leave their homes and join the charge.

No matter. He was closing in on the action now, with no time left for clear, sequential thought. He moved on instinct, firing when a target separated from the general crush, withholding fire when soldiers of his own side were endangered.

Twenty yards.

Now ten.

Directly in his path a dead man sprang erect, blood streaming down his dusty face, lips curling in a snarl. He swung his rifle like a club and would have flattened Vargas, crushed his skull, if Jaime hadn't flinched and lost his footing. Agile for a corpse, the *pistolero* followed through, his weapon slicing through the air toward Jaime's face, the young man rolling for his life.

The M-16 was set for automatic fire, and Jaime squeezed the trigger blindly, hanging on. At skin-touch range the disemboweling burst had force enough to lift his target bodily and propel it backward out of range. A mist of blood was in Jaime's eyes, dark rivulets like muddy rivers on his cheeks.

He staggered to his feet, glanced once in each direction to regain his bearings and was startled as he saw the only surviving flatbed truck begin to move. To verify his first impression, he raked a sleeve across his eyes to clear the blood.

There were more than a dozen people in the truck. He picked out women, children, huddled under the watchful eyes of riflemen.

Escaping.

Jaime instantly forgot the battle, the American warrior, everything except the truck and its departing cargo. Doubling back, he ran without a thought for the stray rounds whispering around him. The guns had fallen silent at the far end of the village; the defenders wouldn't risk their families. Hostile gunners seized the opportunity to take a breather and double-check their weapons in the sudden, ringing silence.

Jaime knew he could never hope to catch the truck on foot. If he could reach the jeep in time...but then what? Chase the gunners on his own? Confront them on the highway in a duel where only they were free to fire? It would be suicide.

He skidded to a halt, knelt down and thumbed the M-16's selector switch to semiautomatic fire. He sighted quickly down the barrel, knowing he would have one chance and one chance only. If he missed, the price might be too terrible to bear.

Another moment now. His finger tightened on the trigger, squeezing slowly—and a body lunged across his line of fire, the camouflage fatigues obscuring his view. The rifle cracked; his tumbling projectile flattened the gunner who had picked a fatal moment to emerge from cover.

Cursing, Jaime tried to grab a second shot but found himself too late. The truck was disappearing, lost beyond a curve in the highway, screened by trees.

He told himself it was merely dust and drying particles of blood that put the hot tears in his eyes. Disgusted with himself, his failure, Jaime Vargas turned his back on hope and moved to join the mop-up.

20

Pedilla had seen better mornings in his life. Few worse, in fact; none worse since he'd risen through the ranks to wealth and power in the Medellín cartel. He'd been months and years arriving at his present level of achievement, and within a span of days his faceless enemies were threatening to snatch it all away.

A search team had discovered the remains of his patrol an hour after dawn. From all appearances the gunners had been taken by surprise in camp and slaughtered to a man. Several of their guns were missing, doubtless taken by the enemy to supplement their arsenal.

Another hour passed before the ambush team was found, all dead. There had been *federales* in the group, and Captain Munoz wasn't visibly amused. He'd been making noise about withdrawing his forces from the compound, covering himself; and only Hector's promise of a bonus had prevented him from pulling out at once. He would allow Pedilla twelve more hours, as a "favor," but from that point the dealer would be on his own.

Pedilla made a mental note to see the captain crucified as soon as possible. A juicy scandal ought to do the trick: some women—make that children—possibly with drugs involved. By the time Pedilla finished with him, the snotty pup would crawl on hands and knees to beg forgiveness, and his efforts would be wasted.

In his thirty-seven years Pedilla had forgiven nothing, no one.

He remembered every slight and insult from his childhood, every injury sustained in adolescence, every act of treachery that had blocked his rise to power once he had selected a career. He kept a mental list of enemies, deleting names as some were dealt with permanently, keeping track of others as he made them pay installments on their debt.

A case in point: the landlord who had driven Hector and his family from their meager lodgings when the boy was twelve years old. A fat man, greasy and unkempt, the landlord had been angry with Pedilla's mother over her refusal to discharge the monthly rent debt by opening her legs. Out of spite he put them on the street. Hector had remembered him across the years. The landlord had three daughters now, each addicted to cocaine and paying for her pleasure in a Bogotá bordello. Hector's agent there made sure their patrons were the filthiest, most brutal of the brothel's clientele. The fat man had a taste for gambling but was hopelessly inept at picking winners. He'd taken out a loan to cover losses, dealing with a shylock friend of Hector's, but he'd been slow to pay of late. On average he was beaten twice a month by loan collectors for his failure to produce the cash on time.

Poetic justice.

Hector heard the truck before he saw it, frowning as he recognized more trouble on the way. He had suspended renovation on the complex while Ybarra took a fire team to investigate the no-name village and eliminate potential threats to Hector's sovereignty. He was expecting no one else, but Antonio had taken out *five* vehicles, and only one was coming back.

Pedilla watched the flatbed rumble into view, his sentries covering the truck and its human cargo. In the place of *pistoleros*, women and children huddled in the back, three riflemen on guard. In the cab he spied Ybarra, his driver and another woman sandwiched in between them.

After waiting for the dust to settle, he approached the truck. Ybarra dragged the woman after him as he dismounted, shoving her in the direction of the others as they started to unload. Pedilla noticed that her peasant blouse was torn in front, her face discolored by several day-old bruises. There was fresh blood smeared around her nostrils, and Ybarra sported deep, new scratches on his cheek.

"We were attacked, *patrón*," the crew chief said before Pedilla had a chance to ask him anything. "A force of many guns. These men and I were able to escape with hostages. I fear the others may be lost."

"You fear?" Pedilla's frown had deepened to a snarl. "Is there some doubt? Were they alive when you escaped?"

Ybarra shrugged, his eyes downcast. "A few perhaps. In the confusion—"

"You had time to gather up these women, but you couldn't check your men?"

"I knew you could use these hostages against the enemy, *patrón*. To punish them for their resistance."

"It appears that you have used one of the hostages already."

"It was nothing. An amusement."

"Were your men amused?"

"Patrón—"

Pedilla palmed the automatic, thumbing back the hammer as Ybarra bolted, running for his life. The first round struck him high between the shoulder blades and knocked him off his stride. The second drilled his skull behind one ear and pitched him forward on his face.

"Take that trash away," Pedilla said to no one in particular. "And lock these prisoners inside the truck barn."

Besides Pedilla's house, the barn was the only building that hadn't been leveled or severely damaged in the raid two nights before. His soldiers had been sleeping in tents since then, when they had time to sleep at all, but Hector didn't trust his hostages inside a canvas prison.

Antonio had been a coward and a fool who thought with his *cojones*, but he had been right about one thing. With hostages in hand, Pedilla would have leverage against his enemies, whoever they might be. The bastards would think twice before they raided him again.

The news, perhaps, wasn't all bad. If he had lost his soldiers in a fruitless raid against the village, then his enemies would know about the hostages. They would be coming, surely, to attempt a rescue, and Pedilla would be waiting for them when they came.

JAIME VARGAS FOUGHT the steering wheel and brought the liberated jeep back on track. He'd been deep inside himself as they had approached the turn, and had nearly lost it in the trees, but they were stable now and running easily on the narrow unpaved track.

Beside him Bolan made no sound, but Jaime felt the soldier's eyes upon him, studying his profile, wondering if he could cut it in the final confrontation with their enemies. Behind him muffled curses from his two surviving followers told Jaime they were hanging in despite the bumpy ride.

He knew it wasn't good to let his thoughts run out from under him that way. In combat every thought and action had to have a single focus if a soldier meant to walk away intact. A suicidal terrorist could daydream, if he liked, but Jaime Vargas planned on living to pursue his war another day, and he'd have to put his mind in order soon while time remained.

They were an hour from Pedilla's compound now, but he knew they couldn't drive directly to the gates. Sentries would be stationed on the road and in the forest, waiting. In the camp Pedilla held precious hostages who would be sacrificed at once if Jaime and the rest attempted anything as basic as a straight approach. They would be forced to ditch the jeep a mile or more before reaching their destination. Then they would have to hike overland through jungle in a flanking move that would, with luck, take the *narcotraficante* by surprise.

Of course Jaime didn't seriously hope to catch Pedilla napping. There was far too much at stake for the dealer to drop his guard. The camp would be on full alert, perhaps with peasant workers on the scene.

Another twenty minutes before they had to leave the jeep. Then about an hour in the forest to reach their target. It would still be daylight. The tall American had a plan, but it demanded that they wait for darkness, leaving women and children in Pedilla's hands for hours, sitting idle when the bastards were within their reach. The prospect grated on the young man's nerves, yet he recognized the wisdom of the soldier's scheme.

Vargas's lonely war had taught him patience of a sort, but he couldn't deny a certain restlessness within himself, a voice that called for action now. It went against the grain to have Pedilla close, almost within his reach, and still to let the rodent live another hour, another day. Every breath the killer drew was an affront to Jaime's sense of duty, his honor.... But, if necessary, he could wait.

He had been waiting for years already. Hours wouldn't matter in the end.

Unless they failed.

Four men against an army—even one so recently reduced in numbers—was a situation that didn't inspire the utmost confidence. Several of the villagers had offered to accompany them and help in the retrieval of the hostages, but the American had turned them down. Jaime understood his reasoning. Defense of hearth and home had been one thing; bringing off an armed offensive was another game entirely, and the locals had no inkling of where to start. A blunder at the final moment, even well intentioned, could destroy them all before they had a chance to free the hostages.

Ten minutes. Jaime glanced at the odometer and slowed the jeep. They were approaching hostile territory and would soon be forced to move ahead on foot. He glanced at Bolan, found him busy with a survey of the jungle, taking stock and watching out for traps. Behind him Jaime's soldiers had their guns up now, prepared for anything.

They might have gained a few more miles, but here the road began to curve in the direction of Pedilla's compound. Jaime hesitated, then lifted his foot from the accelerator for a moment. Bolan felt the jeep slow and turned to face him.

"Close enough?"

"We might get closer."

"Never mind. I feel it, too."

And he was right. There was a sense of menace in the air around them, molecules and atoms supercharged with danger, trembling on the verge of an explosion that would sweep them all away. Although Jaime didn't yet have a sense of being watched, he knew beyond a shadow of a doubt that there were enemies nearby.

"Pull over there," Bolan suggested, pointing toward a break in the tree line just ahead. The jeep slid easily between two forest giants; in another moment they were covered from the glance of casual observers on the road.

"I could have gotten closer," Jaime said halfheartedly.

"We could have gotten killed. I'd like to save that treat for some other time, if it's all right."

"We have an extra mile to walk this way."

"So, let's get started."

"*Sí.*"

He sensed Bolan's determination and wondered what possessed the man to risk so much for strangers in a foreign land. The soldier didn't bear the missionary zealot's mark; his eyes weren't lit with fever, and he didn't lose himself in fantasies of Armageddon. He was a professional, no more, no less—and he brought grim commitment to his task.

An extra mile, but even so they would make it to their target zone with time to spare. They would have hours to contemplate the killing, to practice every move and nuance of the action in their minds.

And when the time came every man would still be on his own.

THE TRUCK BARN had been built to house two vehicles, with room to spare for tools, mechanics, extra tires. It smelled of grease and diesel fuel and perspiration, stifling with its doors and windows closed up tight. By noon it would become an oven for the hostages penned up inside.

Ramona sat alone, her back against the corrugated wall. Her eyes were closed, her legs drawn up, her forehead resting on her knees. From time to time she heard the others whispering among themselves and recognized the sound when someone spoke her name. She didn't try to catch what they were saying. It wasn't important now.

They blamed her—some of them at least—for what had happened in the village. If she hadn't sheltered the American, made contact with the rebels, spoken harshly to Pedilla's crew chief, they would all be safe at home, their families intact, their men secure. What did it matter if Pedilla called upon them to contribute labor every year or two? Were meager pay and injured pride a reason to destroy the village, to put their very lives at risk?

Ramona understood their feelings and made no effort to explain herself. They understood her loss, her anger; there was nothing more to say. If some of them were widows now, because of her, she would carry that burden to her grave. But she wouldn't forgive Pedilla for his crimes, and she wouldn't abandon her resistance while a spark of life remained.

She'd been startled when Pedilla shot the man who had abused her, but she understood her captor hadn't been punished for the crime of rape. His death was the result of failure to complete his mission by eliminating all resistance in her village. If he'd succeeded, slaughtered every man and woman in the settlement, he would have earned a hero's welcome from Pedilla rather than a bullet.

Understanding only strengthened her resolve to see the dealer dead. She had no inkling of how she could accomplish her desired objective, penned up as she was and under guard, but if there was a way, she would surely find it.

Ramona raised her head, her eyes falling on the rack of tools that lined one wall above a workbench. There were mallets, wrenches, automotive tools she didn't recognize—meager weapons, but she wondered if any would do the job.

Rising from her place against the wall, she moved to stand before the workbench. The sentries couldn't see her, for the truck barn had no windows, and the doors were bolted shut, their guards outside. Apparently it had occurred to no one that a group of women, several trailing children, might be motivated to resist captivity. And, from the general demeanor of her neighbors, Ramona decided Pedilla and his *pistoleros* had been very nearly right.

They hadn't reckoned with Ramona Hernandez, though.

The slaying of Virgilio had canceled any latent doubts she might have had about her ability to kill. Revenge, if not precisely sweet, still brought a certain sense of satisfaction. It scarcely mattered that she couldn't expect assistance from the other women. They weren't a part of her crusade for vengeance. None of them had shared her suffering before today, and even now they had no understanding of her humiliation, of the explosive anger pent up in her breast.

She scanned the tools. Uncomfortable with the hammers, wrenches, tire irons, she finally picked up a screwdriver and brought it close to her face. Its shaft was seven inches long, the flat blade chipped and jagged on one corner. It would do.

Ramona glanced over her shoulder and saw that some of the women were watching her. Hostility was evident in several faces; others held a sorrow she could understand; a few revealed a fear that had no part in her considerations now. With nothing left to lose, Ramona feared only failure, falling short of her intention to revenge herself upon Pedilla.

Almost casually she slipped the makeshift weapon into a pocket of her skirt. It would be ready when she needed it, but she would have to time her move, make sure her target was within striking range. With all the guns around Pedilla, there would be no second chance.

Ramona was prepared to die for one clear opportunity to take Pedilla with her. It startled her to realize that she was truly not afraid.

Soon now. *Madre de Dios,* she prayed, let it please be soon.

THERE SEEMED TO BE no peasant workers in the compound. Bolan spent another moment studying the target from a distance, noting that the piles of blackened wreckage had been moved about and rearranged. The ground was cleared for new construction where the lab and warehouse had been earlier destroyed. In place of Quonset huts, long tents accommodated the surviving members of Pedilla's hardforce. Nothing had been done as yet about the radio and generator shacks.

By night, he thought, they would rely on lamps and torches, bonfires spaced around the compound to provide illumination for the troops on guard.

He recognized the marks of the previous night's bonfires, assumed they would be in the same places for the night to come. At best they would provide the sentries with a certain warmth and sense of false security; they would do almost nothing to defeat the jungle darkness.

Bolan marked the federal troops, deployed around their trucks and stationed at the corners of the compound. He had no wish to engage them, but he couldn't leave them all to his companions, either. Once it was in the fan, each man would have to bear his burden equally, and if the *federales* chose to stand with smugglers of cocaine, they also chose the consequences.

There was a sour taste in Bolan's mouth as he surveyed the camp. A simple hit-and-git had blown up overnight to test his will and his endurance. He was bound to miss Grimaldi's pickup now, and there was nothing he could do about it. He would have to use the alternate evacuation route, assuming he was still in any shape to travel when they finished with the evening's work.

The barracks tents were large, but they wouldn't make a secure prison. He scanned the house, but decided that Pedilla wouldn't take the hostages inside his home if there was any alternative. That left the truck barn. The pair of sentries on the door told Bolan everything he had to know.

On his prior penetration he'd ignored the building, for it played no crucial part in manufacturing and storing drugs. Now it was serving Pedilla as a prison. Bolan's recon had revealed no windows, secondary exits, skylights. He could try to blow the corrugated wall in back or on the side, but there was no way of determining where the captives were inside, and the explosion might prove lethal.

No, he'd be forced to take down the sentries and walk the hostages directly through the killing grounds. It was an ugly prospect, but the placement of the truck barn left him no alternative. Perhaps, with a diversion...

Bolan started counting heads. The *federales* numbered twenty-one in all; Pedilla's gunners added twenty-seven to the count. He allowed for other troops inside the house, the barracks tents, a few on station in the forest or along the road. No less than fifty then, and possibly a couple dozen more.

The odds were lousy, but he recognized them as a standard fixture of the game. He had two options. He could raise, or he could fold.

The Executioner had never folded in his life.

Content to take his chances as they came, the Executioner sat down to wait for dusk.

21

Pedilla lit a thin cigar and blew a cloud of fragrant smoke in the direction of the ceiling fan. The hand-carved blades were stationary, robbed of life by the destruction of the generator, but he had the windows open to prevent the room from getting muggy.

Not that it had helped so far.

The heat and humidity were playing on his nerves. No matter how he tried to calm himself, he still remained on edge, expecting trouble. He was tired of sitting in the semi-darkness with a lantern on his desk, waiting for the enemy to strike.

The hostages would be his hole card, but Pedilla had been looking forward to the confrontation as a way of wiping clean the slate. He didn't wish to bargain with the peasants who had tried to put him out of business. Satisfaction lay in wading through their blood, his bare hands reeking with it, bodies strewn around his feet like cast-off mannequins.

Against the best advice of his subordinates, he had dispatched a four-man team to check the village and collect survivors of the morning's raid. They had returned with grim reports of desolation, *pistoleros* lying dead throughout the settlement, no sign of any rebels or the normal occupants. A gang of men with picks and shovels would be required to perform the burials.

Pedilla waited, anger and frustration growing in him as the hours ticked away toward sundown. Even if they had walked from the village, his opponents should have reached the camp by now. Unless . . . had they simply run away?

He wouldn't let himself believe that. It was preposterous. They wouldn't—couldn't—drop the fight when they were on a winning streak. It ran against the very laws of human nature. Winners stuck, and when their luck began to change, their losses piling up, they still remained in hopes of capturing the magic one more time.

Pedilla had been counting on his enemies to act like normal human beings. They had beaten him—or his men at any rate—on four or five occasions in the past three days. Inherent logic told him they would come to cap their victories with final triumph, and—

The dealer froze, the fresh cigar forgotten in his hand. A sudden chill of panic shriveled his *cojones*, made him flinch involuntarily.

He had assumed the rebels would be coming. What if they had already arrived?

Pedilla burst out of his study with a suddenness that caught his housemen napping. Snarling orders at them, cursing when they hesitated, he was on the stairs before his entourage of bodyguards caught up. Downstairs another team was waiting, already alerted by the noise.

It all made sense. The rebels must have made directly for the compound, but they had kept their wits about them, waiting for darkness to conceal their movements.

It was velvet night outside, the bonfires blazing, and Pedilla wondered if he had delayed too long already. Were the bastards closing in on him even as he reached the front door of his manor house?

He bulled through, heedless of the risk of sniper fire, and shouted for the hostages. Across the compound sentries at the truck barn threw the bolts and disappeared inside, support teams of their fellows standing by to cover them in the event of physical resistance by the women.

Grinning at the darkness like a dog who bares his teeth at unseen enemies, Pedilla waited on the wide veranda, ready to retreat if fired upon, defying any of his adversaries to approach him there. He watched the village women and their straggling children herded from the makeshift prison toward the center of the compound. When they reached a point between two central bonfires, the commander of the Medellín cartel moved out to meet them.

It was dangerous, but he was pumping with adrenaline by now, determined to let action drive away his fear. He scanned the row of harried faces, found the woman whom Ybarra had abused and pulled her out of line. The others were commanded to remain precisely where they stood, on visual display for anyone who might be watching from the darkened forest.

Captain Munoz intercepted him before Pedilla and the battered woman reached the house. The soldier's eyes were moist, his manner nervous.

"I'm not convinced," he said, "that any rebels plan to infiltrate this camp a second time. It will be difficult for me to justify remaining so long after Colonel Rivas...well, you understand."

Pedilla snorted in derision. "*Sí*, I understand you perfectly. You're a coward, and as such, unworthy of the trust I've placed in you. You wish to leave? So be it. By all means, pack up your 'soldiers' and be gone."

The captain wavered, fidgeting. "I didn't mean to leave this moment."

"No? What did you mean?"

"Perhaps the morning..."

"Ah, when it's light. It's the dark that frightens you."

"*Señor—*"

"Enough! You have ten minutes." Turning to his houseman, Pedilla snapped, "If any *federales* are inside the camp at ten-fifteen, I want them shot and skinned. You understand?"

The houseman nodded, smiling like a hungry caiman as Pedilla turned his back on Munoz and retreated toward the inner stairs, his captive trailing.

He imagined the display of hostages would either force his enemies to show their hand or break their will completely. Either way it would precipitate a climax, bring an end to waiting. In the meantime... he had the peasant woman.

He remembered how she'd looked, dismounting from the truck—skirt rumpled, torn blouse offering a glimpse of secret flesh. He didn't mind the bruises on her face. If necessary, he would supplement their number as the night wore on.

The peasants of her no-name village had already caused Pedilla endless aggravation. He could see no reason why a young attractive woman from the settlement shouldn't undo a measure of the damage by supplying him with pleasure.

If he liked her well enough, if she performed on cue, Pedilla thought he might decide to let her live.

CONCEALED IN FOREST SHADOWS near the truck barn, Jaime Vargas had been startled when Pedilla left the house. The sight had been tempting. He believed he could have made the shot, but they weren't prepared as yet. There were the hostages to think of.

When Pedilla's gunmen brought the captives out, it had been obvious to Jaime what the dealer had in mind. Pedilla reasoned that his enemies wouldn't attack with women and children in the line of fire. He hadn't been content to keep them locked inside the truck barn safe and sound. To make an effective tool against his enemies, they needed to be visible.

It was a reasonable plan. Jaime knew they would have to scrap their early strategy, which hinged upon a liberation of the prisoners by means of a diversion, drawing off the lion's share of gunners while the sentries on the barn were silently eliminated. Time had passed them by. Jaime couldn't fetch his men from the perimeter to huddle one more time with the American.

They would have to act on instinct then, responding to the present situation as it stood. Pedilla's gunmen might have orders to eliminate the hostages the moment a shot was fired, but they would have to take that chance. The tall American was scheduled to begin the party, Jaime and the others striking on his signal, and the rebel leadér meant to do his part. He only prayed that both his riflemen were aware of the change, that they would wait and choose their targets carefully, ignoring prior instructions.

Jaime double-checked the safety on his rifle, waiting, taking aim on Pedilla as the *narcotraficante* left his porch and moved to meet the hostages. From his position Jaime couldn't overhear the dealer's words, but he had no difficulty picking out Ramona when the dealer took her wrist and led her off in the direction of the house.

A surge of anger tightened Jaime's finger on the trigger of his weapon, but he fought it down, willpower stifling the urge to kill on impulse. He couldn't risk everything—their plans, the hostages—to help one individual. It galled the rebel leader, but he knew it was true.

A soldier met Pedilla near the house. They argued, voices rising, and Pedilla snapped an angry order to his houseman, then swept on inside the mansion. Jaime watched the shaken *federale* turn away, already barking at his men, collecting them around the canvas-sided military trucks.

Incredibly the troops began to climb aboard, preparing to depart. From all appearances Pedilla had dismissed his honor guard, deciding that a group of hostages would do the job as well.

The young man felt a stab of disappointment as the trucks were loaded, engines started, gears engaged. He would have liked to kill some soldiers. But there was a bright side, too. Removal of the troops would cut the hostile force by roughly half; now they would be facing odds of six or eight to one rather than the previous fifteen to one.

The time to strike had come and gone. The American would be waiting for the federal troops to pull away, get out of earshot, prior to launching his diversion.

They had time.

Ramona, unaware of what was happening, would buy it for them.

BOLAN WAITED SEVEN MINUTES for the sound of engines to diminish, fading in the jungle darkness. He wasn't concerned about the soldiers coming back. Their captain had been nervous, anxious to be gone, and he would manage to convince himself that any sounds of combat were imaginary, tricks of mind and ear.

The seven minutes were enough, he thought, emerging from the shadows like a wraith and creeping toward the nearest barracks tent. Pedilla had his shrunken yard force on alert, no sleep permitted, but the vacant tents were valuable to Bolan as the source of his diversion.

Slipping silently from one tent to the next, allowing canvas walls to screen him from the firelight, he deposited incendiary sticks beneath the flaps of each in turn, their timers running down to doomsday as he broke and drifted toward the heaped-up ruins of the generator shack. The scrap would offer him a bit of cover when the shooting started, and it placed him in position for a short run to Pedilla's manor house.

For Bolan, too, had seen Ramona disappear inside.

The seven minutes had been agony, but there had been no options. Losing half the opposition numbers at a single stroke could mean the difference between survival and annihilation for his four-man team, the women and their children. It meant fewer weapons spraying lead around the compound in a crunch, less chance of someone freaking out and mowing down the hostages in panic.

Never mind that the riflemen on duty with the prisoners might have specific orders to assassinate their captives in cold blood. He trusted Jaime and the others to eliminate that threat, or die in the attempt.

Five seconds. Bolan started counting down the numbers in his mind, his finger tensing on the trigger of his Colt Commando.

Four. A pair of sentries bearing flashlights were approaching, deviating from their rounds and closing in on the pile of ruins where he crouched. Their laid-back attitude told Bolan they hadn't seen him.

Three. He braced himself, prepared to take them out before they had a chance to bring their weapons into play.

Two seconds.

One.

Behind him he could hear incendiaries popping, hungry flames devouring the empty tents. Along the camp's perimeter alarms were being raised.

He came up firing with a hot wind at his back.

RAMONA WAITED on the stairs, impassive, while Pedilla issued orders to his troops inside the house. The dealer was anticipating trouble, making certain his men were on alert and ready in the case of a surprise attack. When he rejoined her, dragging her along beside him, a gloating smile split his face.

Inside the pocket of her skirt, Ramona's fingers curled around the handle of her weapon. She remembered how it had felt to stab Virgilio, imagined that Pedilla would be much the same, although he would be stronger, more inclined to fight.

She had to do it right the first time, for she might not have a second chance.

Inside his bedroom she was ready, waiting, as he latched the door. It should have been an easy move, his back turned, but Pedilla heard her coming somehow and turned to meet her as she lunged. He seized her wrist and twisted, grinding bones together in his fist, and even though she slapped him, tried to kick him, she couldn't break free. Another moment and her weapon clattered to the floor. Pedilla kicked it out of reach and pushed her toward the bed.

Ramona didn't see his fist before it struck her, impact lighting fiery pinwheels in her skull. She sprawled across the king-size bed, unable to resist Pedilla as he ripped her clothes away. A blurred facsimile of consciousness was starting to assert itself as he undressed—and then from somewhere in the compound automatic weapons laced the night with fire.

Pedilla hurried to the window, buckling his belt en route, and cursed at what he saw below. A dull explosion rocked the courtyard, other weapons firing now, and suddenly Ramona felt a surge of panic, terrified that someone had decided to eliminate the hostages. A massacre was under way, and there was nothing she could do to stop it.

The expression on Pedilla's face relieved some of her fear. He might have been disgruntled, even furious, at premature elimination of the prisoners, but what Ramona saw behind his flashing eyes was something more akin to fright.

The rebels!

She was struggling to her feet and having trouble doing so, when Pedilla reached her, hauled her off the bed with steely fingers digging deep into her biceps. He didn't allow her to retrieve her clothing as he dragged her toward the bedroom door, unlatched it and thrust her out into the hall. A pair of guards outside were startled by Ramona's nudity, but echoes of a firefight in the compound stifled any tendency to laugh or leer.

"The jeep!" Pedilla barked. "I want it ready when we get there!"

"*Sí, patrón.*"

The gunners hurried for the stairs, Pedilla trailing, one hand locked around Ramona's arm, the other hauling out an automatic pistol from beneath his jacket. For a heartbeat she believed he was about to kill her, then she realized he had another use for her—alive.

She was to be his shield, a passport to escape.

Ramona matched his stride to keep from falling, nearly stumbled on the stairs, but kept her footing with an effort. There was no point in attempting to escape inside the house. She would require full strength, and all her energy outside when every moment must be made to count.

Ramona was determined that Pedilla not get away because of her. She was prepared to sacrifice herself, if necessary, to prevent him from escaping.

She had nothing left to lose, and everything to gain.

THE GUNNER SAW Mack Bolan coming, turned to meet him, and a burst of tumblers sheared his face away. The guy was dead before he fell. Bolan leaped across his twitching body, breaking for the manor house as bullets snapped around him in the semidarkness.

Jaime Vargas and his men had dropped their marks on schedule, opening a runway to the hostages and startling Pedilla's troopers into firing back at shadows. Moving fast, Bolan had caught a glimpse of women breaking for the tree line, children tucked beneath their arms or dragged along like rag dolls. There was nothing he could do to help them now. His mission and his target lay ahead of him inside the manor house.

Pedilla had escaped him once by hiding there, but he wouldn't find sanctuary in the house a second time. From twenty yards the soldier lobbed a frag grenade through ornate windows, flattening as the detonation filled the air with flying wood and glass. Inside he heard the wounded screaming, but he made his mind a blank to pain and forged ahead.

Three *pistoleros* hit the wide veranda running, spraying automatic fire in all directions aimlessly. A rising figure eight swept one of them away, his partners catching on too late to save themselves. A 3-round burst caught number two flat-footed, blowing him away before he could unjam his Uzi. The sole survivor triggered two quick rounds at Bolan from a carbine, stumbled as return fire cut his legs from under him and went down in a lifeless heap.

Concerted fire was pouring out of doors and windows now, and Bolan rolled away, his Colt Commando answering until the slide locked open on an empty chamber. Feeding in another magazine, he circled left around the house, abandoning the frontal approach in favor of a more circuitous attack. He dropped a pair of yardmen when they tried to intercept him, leaving them writhing in the dust.

The mansion had a large garage in back to accommodate Pedilla's private wheels. As Bolan cleared the corner, one of the dealer's gunmen was standing in the open door, a second cranking the ignition of a jeep parked inside.

The lookout saw him coming, raised a riot shotgun to his shoulder, but tipped over backward in a boneless sprawl as Bolan punched two bullets through his chest. The driver almost missed it, concentrating as he was on the ignition, echoes of the battle ringing in his ears. Too late, he caught a glimpse of the Executioner in the rearview mirror, grim death coming for him in the night.

Ironically the engine caught a second later, grumbled and was flooded as the driver gave it up to grapple with his side arm. Rising from his seat, the guy half turned before a short burst stitched across his torso, tumblers boring through to crack the windshield, daubing it with blood and bits of tissue.

Sudden movement blocked out a spill of light from the connecting doorway. Bolan spun to face Pedilla and found Ramona set between them. She was naked, struggling with the dealer, heedless of an automatic pistol jammed against her side.

Her eyes met Bolan's for a fraction of a second, and he read the message there. She shouted, "Kill him! Do it now!"

Before Pedilla could respond, Ramona twisted in his grasp, ducked forward, free hand thrusting back between her own trim thighs. She found his crotch, her fingers flexed like talons, digging, twisting, even as she sank her teeth into the dealer's hand.

Pedilla wrenched away from her, his pistol rising. The Executioner's Colt was tracking, spitting death in rapid-fire at point-blank range. He heard the sharp report of Pedilla's automatic, saw the dealer's shirt and jacket ripple with the impact of a dozen tumblers. Blood exploded from him as he jittered like a puppet on a string.

It was over in a heartbeat.

Bolan crouched by Ramona on the ground. His eyes and hands sought gingerly for wounds, afraid of finding hurts they couldn't heal. He knew Pedilla's single round had missed her when the lady raised her battered face to his and smiled.

The moment lingered, broke, Bolan's mind recaptured by the sounds of battle emanating from the compound. He stripped the jacket from Pedilla's fallen lookout, helped Ramona put it on and steered her toward the darkened trees.

"Come with me!" she urged.

"I'm not finished here."

She took his hand and squeezed it. *"Vaya con Dios,"* she offered.

He went with fire instead and took it to the scattered remnants of the enemy. Ramona watched him go, then turned and started for the trees.

EPILOGUE

"You've missed your plane."

"There'll be another," Bolan answered, smiling. "You should be getting back."

"We have a little time," said Jaime Vargas. He was favoring a wounded arm, fresh dressings visible below his rolled-up shirtsleeve. It had been a clean shot, in and out.

"There should be words to tell you what I feel," Ramona said. The morning light accentuated bruises on her cheek and jawline, but her beauty was unspoiled in Bolan's eyes.

"Not necessary."

"You have given me my life."

"I have a feeling it was right here all the time."

"My vengeance, then."

"Okay. Just bear in mind it's not the same."

"The *federales* will be waiting," Jaime told her softly, hesitant to break the moment.

"*Sí*. What shall I tell them?"

"Anything you like," Bolan replied. "Pedilla won't be contradicting you."

"They won't believe we killed so many men ourselves."

"Let rebels take the credit," Jaime offered. "There's work for us to do yet in Caquetá Province."

"Julio Navarro?"

"He's one of many who must pay."

"Good hunting," Bolan said, and shook the young man's hand. They most likely wouldn't meet again, but there was nothing more to say.

Jaime moved away to let Ramona and Bolan have some privacy. The Colombian woman rose on tiptoe and kissed the warrior softly. "I will not forget," she told him.

"No."

"Will you be back?"

He thought about it, knew how easy it would be to lie, and shook his head. She nodded simply, kissed him one more time with feeling and then turned away.

The soldier watched them disappear, the jungle swallowing them whole. He had a long hike north to Bogotá and the connection with his contact there. Grimaldi would be sweating, but with luck they should be talking in a day or two.

At home within the forest, Bolan started north.

Alone.

TAKE 'EM NOW

FOLDING SUNGLASSES FROM GOLD EAGLE

Mean up your act with these tough, street-smart shades. Practical, too, because they fold 3 times into a handy, zip-up polyurethane pouch that fits neatly into your pocket. Rugged metal frame. Scratch-resistant acrylic lenses. Best of all, they can be yours for only $6.99.

MAIL YOUR ORDER TODAY.

Send your name, address, and zip code, along with a check or money order for just $6.99 + .75¢ for postage and handling (for a total of $7.74) payable to Gold Eagle Reader Service. (New York and Iowa residents please add applicable sales tax.)

Remove from pouch...

unfold once...

GOLD EAGLE

Gold Eagle Reader Service
901 Fuhrmann Blvd.
P.O. Box 1396
Buffalo, N.Y. 14240-1396

unfold twice...

and they're ready to wear.

GES-1A

Offer not available in Canada.